Sarah Jasmon lives on a canal boat in Lancashire, which is also the setting for her two novels – *The Summer of Secrets* and *You Never Told Me*. She has written short stories for a wide selection of publications, and in 2018 was shortlisted for the *Harper's Bazaar* Short Story Competition. She is an Associate Tutor in Creative Writing at Manchester Metropolitan University, and is currently studying for a PhD in Creative Geography.

www.penguin.co.uk

D0281810

Also by Sarah Jasmon

THE SUMMER OF SECRETS

and published by Black Swan

YOU NEVER TOLD ME

Sarah Jasmon

BLACK SWAN

TRANSWORLD PUBLISHERS
61–63 Uxbridge Road, London W5 5SA
www.penguin.co.uk

Transworld is part of the Penguin Random House group of companies
whose addresses can be found at global.penguinrandomhouse.com

First published in Great Britain in 2020 by Black Swan
an imprint of Transworld Publishers

Copyright © Sarah Jasmon 2020

Sarah Jasmon has asserted her right under the Copyright,
Designs and Patents Act 1988 to be identified as the author of this work.

A CIP catalogue record for this book
is available from the British Library.

ISBN 9780552774048

Typeset in 11/14pt ITC Giovanni by Jouve (UK), Milton Keynes
Printed and bound in Great Britain by Clays Ltd, Elcograf S.p.A.

Penguin Random House is committed to a sustainable
future f
is mad

LANCASHIRE COUNTY LIBRARY	
3011814003793 2	
Askews & Holts	24-Mar-2020
AF	£8.99
HGR	

For Jo, and for Katy

(In an ideal world you'd have had a book each for your fabulousness, but I didn't want to count on how long that would take . . . Bird in the hand and all that. Love you both xx)

One

The bar on the ferry was packed. Charlie hitched her bag more firmly onto her shoulder and began to push her way through the crowd. She'd got enough cash for a drink, but food would have to wait until she was back in Bangkok. If she ever wanted to eat anything ever again. An overweight tourist pressed against her, the sour waft of his BO making her gag. She wasn't going to be sick, not here, not now. She just needed to get to the bar, get a cold Coke. A Thai man banged into her as she paused to take a deep breath. The impact sent her sideways, her bag falling to the floor. Automatically she apologized, even as she heard him calling out some comment that made his friends laugh. Sometimes there were plus sides to not knowing the language, even after a year of living here.

There was the breath of a breeze at the bar, though it was hard to tell where it was coming from. Charlie turned towards it, landing her arm in a puddle of beer. No beer towels, of course, or serviettes or anything useful. She lifted a hand, trying to catch the bartender's attention. He took no notice, ignoring the shouts of other customers as well to tend to the blonde girl on the

1

far side. She was leaning towards him, one hand pointing at a particular type of beer. Charlie couldn't see her face behind the shining sweep of her hair, but she knew she hated her. She hated everyone just at that moment: the bartender, flirting away as if he had a chance, the crowd shoving behind her, the sweaty tourist. But she especially hated little blonde backpacker girls, floating around with their smiles and their entitlement and how they didn't even know how lucky they were.

The girl looked around as if she could hear Charlie's thoughts, and flashed a sudden beaming smile. A perfectly nice kid probably, full of notions about how her gap year was going to change the world. It wasn't her fault the people around her were old and cynical and disillusioned. Charlie picked up a cardboard beer-mat, flapping it in front of her face. Behind her, someone opened the door to the toilets, and Charlie waved the mat faster, as if the small action was enough to keep the stink away. Another surge of nausea began to build. When she finally got a drink, she'd have to see if she could find somewhere to sit on the outside deck. If she ever got out of here.

'Yes, what you want?'

The barman's voice startled her. She turned, reaching for both her purse and her few Thai phrases. The swell of impatient voices behind and around pushed at her, and she fought to get her order heard.

The deck was as packed as she'd expected, every corner jammed with backpackers, locals, traders. What did the Thai passengers think about the noisy crowds of Westerners? Did they resent having to share their space with

2

them, wherever they went? Charlie paused at the top of the open metal stairway, picturing a parallel scene back home. A commuter train at the end of the day, with the last few people trying to squeeze into an overcrowded carriage. Jammed bodies ignoring the unwelcome contact of others, the odd rolled eye sharing frustration at the general discomfort. Charlie could almost taste the condensation, the heated fug, and the memory brought sudden tears. Not for the rush-hour squeeze, but for the familiarity. She wanted, with a sudden and physical need, to be cold. She wanted the edge of frost on her bare fingers, the need for layers and wool. The heat here was heavy, hallucinatory, leading her into bad decisions. What had happened over the weekend was just the finishing touch. She was the wrong person in the wrong place at the wrong time, and she didn't know what to do about it. Go home? But to what?

From the corner of her eye, she spotted a boy edging his way out. Trying not to stumble over the lines of outstretched feet, she reached his vacated spot just before the crowd shifted enough to fill in the gap. The island was disappearing behind them, its tree-lined slopes blurring into a solid, green mass. Only two days since she'd seen the process happen in reverse. Two days and another world, a different timescale, an alternative future. She squeezed herself down into the tiny space on the metal deck. It wasn't much, but it was better than staying inside. By the time she looked up again, the ferry had shifted course and the island was out of sight. Koh Chang, sold to them on the booking website as an island of dreams. The irony.

3

The others would all still be in bed. Briefly, she let herself picture the scene. Was Dan even a bit sorry that she'd left? Or was he lying back in relief, laughing as everyone agreed that everything would be a lot more fun now? She didn't want to think about it, any of it, but the memories kept playing. The arrival at the beach and the first day of giddiness. Swimming in the miniature pool, lounging, drinking. All the time the anticipation that something would happen with Dan. His eyes catching hers at every turn, his hand brushing against her thigh. Her smiling back at him, complicit in the game. Then Kelly turning up, with her long, shining hair and her entitlement. Throwing herself into the middle of the group, throwing herself on Dan. *You'll let me stay, won't you? I'm literally here with a sarong and a lipstick.* Dan looking round with that little shrug as if to say, *What can I do?* And all she, Charlie, had been able to manage was a fake smile, pretending that it was all fine. Such a long way from that night in Bangkok.

* * *

They're all sitting in a bar, flopping over their drinks in an exaggerated response to the day they've had at the language school. A normal day, in reality, despite a higher than average number of timetable clashes making the shortage of classrooms even more of a problem. The language school pays them a pittance, someone moans, even though the owners must be raking the money in. Someone else suggests they go on strike, but everyone knows there are dozens, if not hundreds, of other backpackers just waiting to step in. It's Heather

4

who starts off the idea of a team-building weekend away. 'We need to do this,' she says, tipping her head back to drain her beer in one long swallow before slamming the bottle down on the table. It's one of the things Charlie likes the most, being part of the gang, the only worry who's going to buy the next drink. Never mind that she's a decade older than the rest. This is something she missed out on when she was the 'right' age. Her eyes meet Dan's, and they share a hidden smile. She's almost certain that something's happening between them, and she's as giddy as she was with her first ever crush. She feels reckless and young, and in a permanent state of fizzing desire. 'Never mind a hostel,' she says, cutting in over Jack's rambling description of some place on the Laos border. 'We should go for luxury. Room service and a pool.'

* * *

She should have just gone along with the basic plan. They'd have been cramped and sweaty, yes, but it would have been a joint effort. And the attraction of joining them would have been less. Though Kelly had always had Dan in her sights; it was always going to be when and not if. Charlie squeezed her eyes shut, the sun burning a red light through eyelids that weren't thick enough to get rid of the pictures. The windows would be open in the bungalow, muslin drapes shifting in the soft breeze from the sea. It was about time for the girl to bring in the huge platter of fruit that started every day. Dan would be sprawled across the main bed, indistinct through the floating draperies. Was Kelly there with him?

5

'Excuse me, would you mind if I joined you?' A voice broke into her thoughts, English and with a Home Counties tone. It was the girl from the bar, already sinking down next to her, even though there was no space there at all. She was still talking. 'I've been all round and there's just nowhere! But I'd die rather than stay inside.'

Charlie's head was thumping – from the heat, from her hangover, from everything falling apart. It was easier to give in than argue. Without a word, she shifted across as far as she could, ignoring the sharp comment from the Thai woman seated next to her. The girl leaned forward to make an apologetic-sounding remark, and the woman nodded, waving her hand in acceptance, smiling. Charlie had to hand it to her; not many gap year kids bothered to learn any Thai, let alone with that fluency. She hadn't learned any to speak of herself. The girl was still burbling away.

'I won't talk if you don't want to, I promise. I know what it's like to get stuck with someone when all you want to do is think.' She flopped back against the bulkhead with a sigh, pushing her sunglasses up to rub at her face. 'I'm always so conflicted when I leave the islands. I mean, they're so beautiful, but real life doesn't actually happen there, does it?' She gave Charlie another radiant smile. 'Isn't there a little bit of you that's glad to be going back to the city?'

'I don't know about that.' Charlie shifted, trying to find a different way to distribute the pressure of her weight against the hard deck. What was she going back to, after all? She didn't think she could bear the language

6

school on Monday. Already she could hear the whispers spreading round the staff who hadn't been there, the ones who were already sore from missing out on the fun. *She tried to get Dan into bed, you know. Yes, I know! And then, when Kelly turned up, she just flipped out, was so unreasonable! Kelly, you know, that cute little blonde girl? There was plenty of space, none of the rest of us minded. And she'd only brought weed with her, nobody minds weed. You'd have thought she was dealing smack, the way Charlie went on. It's her age, she just doesn't fit in.* And they all still owed her money for the bungalow. Fat chance she'd ever see that again, which would mean problems until the language school decided to pay up for this month's wages. A throb of pain sliced into her temple. 'I might've had enough of Thailand altogether for now.'

'Really?' The girl's bright-eyed optimism was so loud. Charlie took a moment to swallow a mouthful of Coke, trying to convince herself that it was settling her queasiness. It went down the wrong way, making her cough, but not enough to interrupt the girl's flow. 'I don't think I'll ever get tired of it. Freya, by the way.' She stuck out a hand.

'Charlie.' She gave Freya's hand a quick clasp. 'My mum's from Norway,' she carried on. Why on earth was she sharing that? The last thing she wanted was a conversation. It was the heat making her babble. 'But she went full English with me and my sister. Charlotte and Eleanor.'

'Your mum?' Freya looked confused. 'Oh, you mean my name! We've got no connection to Norway, sorry. Mummy just wanted something unusual.' She rolled

7

her eyes. 'My sister's called India. At least Mummy had been there.'

Mummy. India. That confident tone and easy assumption of her place in the world. Had she ever had to question her path through life? Charlie felt a burn of jealousy starting to compete with the acid in her stomach. When had she got so judgemental? It was as if her father's voice was being channelled through her head, and she wasn't going to be like him, ever. 'Have you been here long?' she asked, forcing herself to smile. 'Your Thai is impressive.'

'Do you think?' Freya giggled. 'I wouldn't rate it as much more than adequate, really.' She rummaged in her bag, pulling out a reusable bottle full of still-cold water. Charlie could see the condensation as she flipped the lid and took a tiny sip. 'I spent a year working in an orphanage up in Chiang Mai. It was so much fun with the children, it honestly didn't feel like I was having to learn it at all.'

She couldn't be more than twenty and she'd already done a year at an orphanage. That had been one of the things she'd planned to do, Charlie thought. Volunteer for something worthwhile, use her time for making things better. She remembered telling people about it, making it sound as if the trip wasn't for her but for the greater good of the world. That had worked out well.

A runnel made its way down her back. She'd be sitting in a puddle soon. The ferry was moving at a steady pace now, the air a too-warm hand pushing against her face. The high chatter of the women along the deck mingled with the churn of water metres below. Beside her,

Freya was rubbing sun cream onto her arms with slow, deliberate sweeps. Being totally mindful, presumably. Maybe that was the answer, to take the emotion out of decisions, do things for the right reasons. What *were* the right reasons, though? She had been so convinced of hers in those months leading up to her departure. Now she wasn't sure about anything.

'How long were you on the island for?' she asked, not because she wanted to know, but because she didn't want to be alone in her head any more.

'Just the weekend.' Freya moved on to her legs and gestured at the bottle next to her. 'Do you want some?' Charlie shook her head as the girl chattered on. 'I was there to meet someone, friend of a friend of the family, you know?' Charlie didn't know. She couldn't imagine having the sort of background that included contacts all over SouthEast Asia. She half listened to how India's godfather had been at school with this lovely guy who was really into ancient Thai manuscripts, remembering her own family's reaction to her plans. She'd driven up to say goodbye, the boot of the hire car loaded with possessions she'd hoped to leave at the house. There was plenty of room, after all, with the empty garage space if they didn't want it inside. Bella had been with her, their last weekend together. Charlie had had some ridiculous idea that she could rest, take Bella for walks in the hills, recover a little from the emotional wringing of leaving her home. It hadn't turned out anything like that, of course. From her father's refusing to agree to any kind of storage arrangement to his banning of Bella from the house, they'd fallen into an argument

9

uncovering every slight and disappointment of the past thirty years. Her mother hadn't reacted to any of it, had just sat there, looking out into the wet garden. There had been something about her expression, though, a quick glance that had made Charlie think she was about to say something. And then Eleanor had paused from her constant state of wiping mouths and clearing away toys to add her contribution. What was it she'd said? *No one's saying you can't do these things, Charlie. But why go to the ends of the earth?*

To get away from you lot, was her first thought about that. And then Jon, her sister's husband, had caught her with that little glance of knowledge, as if he knew exactly what was on her mind. 'Anyway, he might have a lead for me, some work across the border in Cambodia.' Charlie struggled to reconnect to what Freya was talking about. 'Can you imagine? I'm so happy! What about you?'

'Me?' Charlie's mind was a blank. For a brief second, she imagined spilling it all out. How her future had been so unnervingly fixed: the house, the dog, the safe long-term boyfriend, the wedding date chosen. The suffocating assumption that Charlie would change her mind about not wanting children once she and Max were married, even though she knew she'd been slowly falling out of love with him, that the only part of her life she truly wanted was Bella, the little, shaggy rescue terrier who liked to snuffle her way under the quilt in the night. That since she'd left she'd worked so hard on not feeling guilty that she couldn't remember the last time she'd been in contact with anyone at home. That

10

the freedom had gone to her head and left her with nothing but . . . No, just nothing. She had nothing. But she had to say something. Freya's head was tilted, almost as if she was genuinely interested. 'I don't know, to be honest. I had this idea when I set out, of what I was going to do, then I fell into this teaching job and, well, you know . . .' She ran to a halt. How did you say that the one thing you couldn't forget was the way your dog had looked as you'd left, head on one side with a question in her eyes you couldn't answer? And then, suddenly, it all came together. Of course she knew what she wanted to do next. 'Actually, I'm wondering if it's time to go home.'

At that moment, the sound of shouting made them both look round. A man's head came into view at the top of the metal stairs. He was holding a beer in one hand and using the other to pull himself upright. Swaying, he bent forwards to bellow again at someone below before making a grab for the upper handrail. Charlie held her breath as he swung backwards, surely on the verge of plunging down. He got his balance just in time and took an uncertain step forwards, tripping over some raucous Aussies. There was a chorus of good-natured jeering and Freya let out an exclamation.

'Ethan!' She was already on her feet, sweeping her possessions back into her bag. 'Ethan, over here!'

Charlie watched as she fluttered up to the man, throwing her arms around him. He gave a shout of approval and dragged her with him on his progress to the other side of the boat. She'd left her sun cream on the deck. Charlie picked the bottle up and turned to

11

call after her, but she'd already gone. After a moment, Charlie flipped open the lid and squeezed a bit out. It was light, smelling of oranges, and it absorbed into her skin with expensive speed. She'd keep hold of it in case she saw Freya again as they disembarked. She already felt this to be unlikely. Travellers came and went, leaving just a surface impression. The scent of the sun cream would last longer than most relationships out here. It wasn't a negative any more. The weight had lifted, and even the heat seemed to be less oppressive. She would go back, take Bella, make a new start. A new life, without the disapproving voices always in her head.

Two

Charlie stayed in her place as the boat docked. The calm sense of a clear decision made speed unnecessary, and she watched with detachment as the first wave of passengers disembarked below, crowding in a noisy flood along the concrete jetty. They all had somewhere to get to. She was the last to pass through the car deck, though the space still seemed to reverberate from the revving of truck engines and scooters, and the smell of diesel and packed bodies lingered. A couple of crew members were pulling at ropes. The heat was solid in the dim, stinking space, and the men were both shirtless, dripping with perspiration. They ignored Charlie as she made her way past.

The minibus ride was hot and cramped, and brought her nausea rolling back. As she lurched against her neighbour at every turn, trying to block out the wailing child and the smell of somebody's bad stomach, she lost track of her new resolutions. It was mid-afternoon by the time they reached the city, and the heat seemed to have doubled down. In a daze, she walked as far as the nearest train station and stood there, hair and clothing both plastered down in the humidity, with the

13

realization that she had no cash left, no way to buy a ticket. Stupid, stupid, stupid. *Always have enough money to get back from wherever you're going.* The words, slipping into her head in her mother's voice, made her pause. When had they been said? As she began to walk again, she sifted through memories, trying to pin the moment down. She could hear them so clearly, whispered in a furious undertone, but for the life of her she couldn't think what had caused them to be said. She and Eleanor had been biddable children, well-behaved adolescents. Before she left for university, Charlie had pushed the odd boundary: a party in the village, or the illicit glamour of smoking behind the bus shelter after dark. A stone thrown at her sister's window was always enough to get in, though, and Eleanor had always covered for her, tight with disapproval but knowing that not doing it would make it worse for everyone. Had her mother known about those nights? Charlie had never asked.

Her sandals slapped on the pavement, matching the beating of her head, and suddenly the moment came to her in excruciating technicolour detail, the damp chill of a Derbyshire afternoon taking over from the crowded noise of the Bangkok street. There had been some disagreement, an arbitrary line crossed, and her father had forbidden her and Eleanor to leave the house. As usual her mother had stayed in the background, a pale and insubstantial presence as their father's shouting had wound itself down, until the house was silent, tingling slightly with the tension that only her father could bring. And Eleanor had chosen to defy him, one of the few times she ever had. Charlie had watched her slip

14

out from the back of the house as she'd sat in her room, shaking with that mix of anger and fear and shame at being afraid.

Eleanor hadn't been back in time for tea, nor well into the evening. The atmosphere as they'd waited to hear something had been thick, nauseating. At what point would they have called the police? She was pretty sure no steps had been taken by the time Eleanor had finally stumbled in, wet and exhausted. Now Charlie could imagine the thoughts that must surely have been building in her parents' minds, but back then the worst thing she'd imagined was that Eleanor had run away. She'd felt a fleeting sense of envy, even, dimmed by her sister's reappearance but remaining as a fragment of possibility. There had been explanations, of a missed bus or not enough money for the bus leading to a long walk home, Charlie couldn't remember which now. Then there had been a prolonged lecture about obedience and thoughtlessness, and causing your parents to worry, and through it all Eleanor had somehow remained impervious, sliding away from saying why she'd gone in the first place.

It was this that Charlie had been thinking about, in the aftermath of the recriminations and the weight of spent anger. She could remember it so clearly, lying in her bed unable to sleep and wondering what had happened to her sister to give her that sense of distance. She didn't think she'd imagined that it was a boy, though over the following summer Jon would become part of the household in such minimal stages that he was a fixture before anyone really noticed. And she'd pictured

15

herself running away, the first in a progression of fantasy enactments which would last until she left home for university. In the middle of it, way after midnight, her mother had come in, without explanation, to whisper those words. *Always have enough money to get back from wherever you're going.* She hadn't responded, hadn't paused to wonder why her mother had felt the need to share that piece of wisdom at that time. And it was an interesting choice of words. Why not enough money to get home, Charlie thought now, coming back to the noise of people and traffic, the hot grease of the street food stalls and the fumes of the scooters and tuk tuks. Had she seen what Charlie was thinking, known how little she wanted to be where she was? Maybe she, Charlie, should have listened more carefully.

Mrs Yee was sitting by the door as usual, either asleep or feigning it, Charlie could never be quite sure. Her plastic chair had been positioned an hour or so before to be in the shade, but the sun was far enough around now to be catching her face. Soon she would give up and go inside to bang things around in the tiny kitchen. Charlie paused a couple of metres short, trying to judge her chances of getting past without being noticed. She couldn't face awkward questions just now, and she especially didn't want to get into a conversation about rent. With extreme caution, she edged her way past. She was nearly inside when the tiny head snapped round.

'Hey, you!' Charlie stopped, waiting for one of her two standard phrases: *You eat now? Where money?* Instead, the little figure struggled up and limped over. 'You phone

16

home, OK? You phone quick.' She carried on past, muttering to herself, before stopping again, darting another quick look around. 'This not answering service. You tell!'

Charlie followed her inside, feeling a faint stirring of worry in the pit of her stomach, like an early twinge of period pain. Maybe that was all it was. Automatically she began to calculate dates, her mind using the action to distract itself from the issue at hand. She knew, of course, that a call couldn't be for anything less than a genuine emergency. Her own mobile was dead, its screen smashed from a pavement drop some weeks ago. She'd never given anyone the number to the boarding house, had not, in fact, even known there was a number to call. Which meant that whoever wanted her would have had to go through the language school for her address, and then convince them to look up the number. That amount of effort wouldn't be for good news. The kitchen door was about to swing shut, and nobody had ever been able to get Mrs Yee to come out once she was in there. 'Mrs Yee, can I use the phone here?' Her voice was a croak.

The closing door paused. Then, 'You pay rent, I give phone.'

She went to an internet café in the end. She had a voucher, something that had been sitting in her bag for days, offering a free twenty minutes of computer time with a complimentary drink. Her sister – and it had to be Eleanor – was practical and would have tried every way possible to contact her. There would be an email, with

17

a rebuke about keeping in touch. A reminder about a birthday, or the passing on of something that she thought might be important. That inbuilt habit of keeping her little sister out of trouble, however annoying she might be. As she stood in the crowded café, waiting to catch the attendant's eye, Charlie tried to remember the last time she'd checked her emails. She realized with a pang of guilt that it had been a couple of weeks. She could feel her justifications crowding in for space. There'd been nothing to talk about, no news to pass on. And they could go for weeks not being in contact back in normal life, in England. She'd had no reason to suppose there was anything going on. It would be nothing, a false alarm. Underneath, her thoughts were of Bella. Run away, run over, lost, dying. *Please, not that.*

The computer was slow, the keys still slightly slippery from the previous user's touch. Charlie fidgeted as it churned through its process, almost spilling the over-brewed coffee that came with the booking. She was thirsty, probably dehydrated, but drinking that would make things worse, not better. There was no air-con, the stuffiness increased by the throng of users. Around her, the noise of a dozen languages swelled, the sound an almost physical mass. It was hard to tell if any of the seemingly intimate groupings had been friends for years, or if they'd only just met. In a swirl of good-humoured activity, they drank their coffee, updated their blogs, booked their next flights. The information-swapping, bragging and planning was relentless. Charlie remembered, as if from a great distance, how it had seemed so invigorating at the start of everything. Now

18

she wanted to yell at them all to shut up, to give her some space. Then the email site finished loading, and she forgot that they were there at all.

The message, when she opened it, was short and to the point. *Tried to call, Mum in hospital. You need to get back.*

Her first reaction was irritation. The email made it sound as if Charlie was just down the road, that she could get on a bus and be there in no time, that she was being unreasonable not being there already. Charlie felt the din around her recede, as if she was somehow in a bubble. Her hands, way down in front of her, one set of fingers still wrapped around the mouse, seemed to belong to someone else entirely. She wasn't being fair, she knew that. Eleanor would never leave a message so lacking in detail unless something was really wrong. She was scrupulous about information, about accuracy. And this message needed to be acknowledged.

Charlie tried to concentrate on breathing, taking a minute for long, slow inhales and exhales. *What exactly is wrong?* she typed. Maybe whatever had happened had resolved itself. And if it was serious, she needed to hold out here for a couple more days, put her pride aside to go and find Dan, make him pay her back. That would just about cover a flight. If she didn't pay her rent before she left.

Eleanor must have been waiting, because her answer came almost immediately. *They're doing tests, but it doesn't look good. You really should get back.*

A voice came from behind. 'You OK, mate?'

The sound made her jump, her arm catching again at

19

the coffee cup, this time spilling the whole lot over her leg. She concentrated for a moment on mopping it up, trying to remember the man's name. She knew him by sight, in the background at parties, but he wasn't someone she'd ever particularly spoken to. Like her, he was older than the average traveller, maybe even late thirties. It was why she'd kind of avoided him. She hadn't wanted to be stuck in some kind of age ghetto. She remembered being at a party soon after she'd arrived, overhearing an argument about who was in a band from the eighties. Someone, Kelly now she came to think of it, had giggled that they should ask *that new one, you know, the oldie. Or Kitsch. It's their time, after all.* The name had stuck in her mind because of its unlikeliness. Why Kitsch? Something to do with his tattoos? Whatever, she really didn't want to be dealing with anyone else right now. She spoke in a hurry, not quite looking far enough back to actually make eye contact. 'No, I'm good.' The computer screen had dropped into its screensaver mode, and she jabbed at the keyboard to keep it open but was too late. She'd have to put the password in again. Where had it gone? Her hands were shaking and she couldn't think where to look. What was wrong with her?

Kitsch's hand came over her shoulder, reaching for the puddle where the coffee had spilled. 'Are you looking for this?'

She could make out the last few numbers, written in felt-tip in the counter girl's round handwriting. The first couple were almost illegible, the ink spreading through the brown stain. Was that an H or an A? She tried them

20

both. Nothing happened, and she banged at the table in frustration. Kitsch put a hand on her shoulder. She knew what would come next. *Calm down. Not the end of the world.* The air in the café was suffocating, the voices even more shrill than before. She pushed her chair back with a shove and ran for the door.

Three

It wasn't until she was down the street and stumbling past the first umbrella-shaded stalls of the market that she realized her bag was still in the café. Not that there was much in it: her empty purse, her room key. There wasn't anything in her room that she'd miss anyway. The thought hit her, a depressing summary of her big adventure. All that money and time, and what did she have to show for it? She couldn't really skip without paying, though as things stood, she couldn't afford to either settle up or pay for a flight. She'd have to message Eleanor back, ask her for a loan. That would go down well. Though how was she going to do that, now that her free twenty minutes had run out? Damn Dan, damn Kelly, damn her stupid dream of a luxury beach resort. She pushed away the little voice that wished she was still there, ignorant of anything but the sun and the waves and lying around with no idea of dramas happening elsewhere. And then she remembered something worse. Her passport. In her bag. With a sob, she turned to go back, only for the street to swim in front of her as the route slipped and wobbled in her mind. It wouldn't still be there anyway. Someone would have it, would probably be selling it on already. She felt a hand on her arm and twisted round, ready to belt whoever it was touching her up, or trying to steal whatever they thought she had. But it was Kitsch, holding her bag out with a grin.

He took her down a side street, leading her with enviable knowledge to a tiny square, sheltered from the sun and almost giving the impression of a cool breeze. There were spindly chairs lined up outside a small bar, and the space was filled with the sound of birdsong. He left her in a chair, her recovered bag held tightly on her knees, to return with two beers. Condensation ran down the sides of the bottle in front of her, hypnotic and unreal.

'We've not been properly introduced. It's Charlie, isn't it?' Kitsch held a hand out. 'Kitch, short for Kitchener.' Charlie shook the hand, trying to work out what he meant, and he clearly picked up on her expression. 'Like the recruitment guy, you know, pointing finger, big moustache?' He pointed at her, a stern look on his face. 'Your country needs you!'

'I did know your name.' Charlie gave a slightly manic laugh. 'I just thought it was because you were kitschy.' She heard herself at the same time as he chuckled.

'Cheers!' He lifted his bottle in salute. 'I'll have to remember my plastic palm trees next time.'

'I'm sorry, I didn't mean . . .' She gave a wobbly laugh, feeling the tension leave her, if only for a moment. Her hand felt lightweight and insubstantial as she picked up the beer. 'Thank you so much.' She gave her bag a shake. 'Losing this would have been a disaster.' The other

23

impossibilities in between her and home were still there, of course. She tried to put them in some sort of order, but they refused to settle down. One thought kept poking through. *Phone Eleanor, ask for the money.* She heard her father's voice this time. *Don't go expecting us to bail you out.* She was thirty, a responsible adult. How had she managed to get into this mess?

Kitch was taking a swallow of his own beer. 'And so, Charlie,' he said, the bottle back on the table, both of his hands loosely clasped around it. 'What was bothering you in the café?'

He took over everything, leaving her in the square whilst he somehow managed to contact Dan and get him to talk a friend at the school into paying back what she was owed for the bungalow. And not just his share, but everyone's, including Kelly's. Then he went with her to Mrs Yee's, keeping the landlady occupied as Charlie went up to shove her belongings into her rucksack. The expression on the old lady's face was positively playful as she gave Kitch an admonitory tap on the arm before taking Charlie's payment with almost a smile. And then they'd gone to a hole-in-the-wall ticket shop where somehow she'd had almost the exact amount needed for the flight home, with enough cash left for food on the way. The last thing she saw of Bangkok was Kitch waving as the doors to the airport slid shut.

She managed to phone Eleanor during the stopover in Abu Dhabi. The flight reps were sympathetic, clucking around her in a flock of sympathy. None of it felt real.

24

The news wasn't too bad, though: the tests had been inconclusive but their mother was stable for now. The relief in Eleanor's voice when she heard that Charlie was on her way shook Charlie more than she would have liked. This was different, serious. She was to go straight to Sheffield, to the hospital. Anything could happen.

The final hours of the flight went no faster even though she was sitting forwards, willing the plane to speed up. She couldn't relax. Instead of sleeping, she stared out of the window at the dark sky, at the collage of countries, continents, below, their borders blurring into one vague mass. She tried to recall the journey out, the places she'd stopped at on the way, the people she'd met. Then, it had all been gilded with newness, with the sense of adventure. Now, she was finding it hard to picture one specific face, any one setting. Instead, her mind threw up random scenes: summer holiday boredom in her shared room with Eleanor, a school trip to some museum, a rained-out Guide camp. This was how it must be to get old, she thought. Too many memories to hold on to, the brain rationing out its available space to allow for only what was important. But that was the wrong way round. Age remembered the negligible. Would her mother last until memory became muddled, her youth appearing in perfect clarity whilst she forgot who Charlie was? If only there was a way of choosing what went, and what was retained.

Daylight came with the green of Europe, the air clean and unspent above the cloud layer. Charlie eased past knees to wait in the fug of stale night breath for the toilet to be free. A child was sprawled across his mother's

25

lap on a seat opposite, and Charlie watched him, counted his regular breaths. She could almost feel the heat of his sweat-flattened hair. It was only when she was about to go into the cubicle that she realized the mother was watching her as well, with indifferent eyes. When she was done, the tepid water from the taps making no difference to the thick tiredness of her head, she went back to her seat without looking. She saw them again in Manchester, the child now running in circles as they all waited for the carousel to deliver its promises. The boy's voice, demanding attention, followed her as she pushed her way out towards passport control.

And then there was the run for the train, the steady pull over the Pennines. The carriage filled with walkers, all cheerfully indifferent to the outside drizzle, the lack of available seats. Charlie allowed their hum of conversation to fill her head, drifting into half-sleep as stops were made. The station announcements ticked off the distance for her: Belle Vue, Brinnington, Romiley, Hope. The names clicked through her brain with the rhythm of the wheels, calming her thoughts. She was fully asleep by the time they pulled in to Sheffield, and she surfaced to the sound of an elderly lady wondering if she should wake her, the feel of a hand on her shoulder.

'We're here, love.' The woman's voice was soft. 'Last stop.'

She didn't have enough money left for a taxi, but was glad of the chance to walk. She felt strangely calm, the one part of the journey when she could physically change the speed of transit leading her instead to a slow, almost dreamlike, movement. She accepted it all, the

26

cool greyness of the air, the pavement reeling away from her feet, the presence of the houses, the surrounding hills. It wrapped her in a sense of familiar unreality which clung to her as she approached the hospital. She tugged it behind as she followed signs for the ward that Eleanor had told her to find. It was with her as she took in the aura of disinfectant and efficiency until, finally, accompanying her to the curtained side of her mother's bed.

She didn't need to be told. Her father and Eleanor were standing together on one side of the cubicle. The machines, filling so much of the space, were quiet. Charlie came to a stop herself, her eyes fixed on the space that the something that wasn't quite her mother was occupying. Hair spread out on the pillow, still thick, still the ash ghost of blonde. Charlie couldn't speak. Her mouth moved, her throat worked, but nothing came out. She just stood there at the end of the bed, barely noticing the clatter as the hanging notes fell to the ground.

Before anyone could speak, a nurse put her head round the edge of the curtains, catching Eleanor's attention. Eleanor gave her an acknowledging nod before lifting a hand towards the silent figure next to her.

'Dad, I think we need to go and sort a few things out.' Her voice sounded too loud in the hushed atmosphere, yet he didn't seem to hear her. Charlie wasn't sure he'd noticed her own arrival. His face was blank, his stance rigid and fixed. He was looking not at the figure on the bed, but at a point just a little to one side, as if disassociating himself from the scene. Charlie watched Eleanor put a hand on his sleeve. 'Dad? Are you OK to do it? I can manage, if you like.'

27

At this, he gave a start and seemed to realize where he was. 'No, no, I'm fine.' As he came past, Charlie took a step back, uncertain of her place. Was he ignoring her deliberately, or was it that he hadn't quite realized she was here? At the last minute, she made to move towards him, but Eleanor intercepted her with a small shake of her head.

'Wait here,' she murmured, glancing round to check where the nurse was taking them. 'I'll be right back.'

A different nurse came around the edge of the curtain. Seeing Charlie, she made as if to back away. Then she stopped.

'Everything all right, my love?' she asked.

Charlie made an effort to concentrate. Maybe it was jet lag starting to kick in, but she felt as if her head had no connection with her body, or with her surroundings. 'Yes, sorry,' she said, and found herself smiling to reassure the nurse. She was only young, probably the age of most of the backpackers Charlie had spent the last few months with. 'I'm just—' She gestured back to the bed. What was she doing? What was she supposed to be doing?

'Just ask if you need anything,' the girl said, and hurried off in her squishy white shoes.

Charlie dropped into the single chair that was squeezed between the bed and the curtain. Just ask if there was anything she needed. What she needed was for this not to be happening, for someone to tell her she could wake up now. She wasn't ready, she didn't know what to do. Should she hold her mother's hand, tell her how sorry she was that this had happened? Apologize for not being in touch, for moving away, for always

28

wanting her to be a different sort of mother? Nothing felt right. Max would know. She imagined him being next to her, a bulwark against the strangeness. He would hold her and reassure her that what she was feeling was normal, that she didn't need to worry about some imagined standard of behaviour she was failing to meet. For a moment it seemed possible, that she could call him and he'd drop everything. He might do that: he was a kind man and he had loved her. But it didn't seem to be playing fair to call on him just because she was in need. The words from one of their final conversations kept popping up in her head. *You know if you leave, that's going to be it? I'll go with you anywhere, try anything, but if you go, you go.* His voice had broken at that point, tears running down his cheeks. *You can't leave me and still have me, you know that?*

'What do you really think about it all?' Charlie spoke without thinking in the end, the words surprising her. Somehow, her hand had reached out, resting itself lightly on her mother's arm. It lay still and straight, resting on the laundry stamp of the hospital sheet, warmer than Charlie expected her to be. It really was as if she was lying there, listening to her speak. A moment of intimacy, the last chance to talk. Except they'd never sat together like this, not really. Charlie tried to remember the last time they'd talked, just the two of them, and her grip tightened. She'd left it too late. Numbly, she sat on in silence, with every minute taking her mother further away. Gravity pulled at skin and muscle, leaving her mouth slack and lop-sided. There was nothing Charlie could do.

*

29

They drove home in silence, Eleanor at the wheel of their father's Rover. He had stayed at the hospital to *sort things out, please, leave me to do this,* but Eleanor had been insistent that Charlie should go back. There hadn't been any point in arguing, so here she was, in the passenger seat, letting the passing views roll by. Her body knew every stone of the route. It counted off the junctions and bends in the road so that at any given moment she'd have been able to say where she was, even with her eyes closed. She forced them to stay open, couldn't risk giving in to the almost overwhelming desire to sleep yet. This road had been her way in and out of the village for her whole life. She'd had years of school bus mornings and evenings, packed in with the same crowd, day in, day out. Then there were the giddy escapes during long summer holidays, and tired returns on the last bus back, her head on someone's shoulder, blanking out the recriminations ahead. *Where have you been? Do you know what time it is? Why can't you think?* She'd last taken it just before she'd left for Thailand, fuming as she drove away from the village. Bella had been with her then, watching anxiously from her cushion on the back seat.

Now Eleanor made the final turn into the drive and switched the engine off. They sat there in the silence, listening to the tick of metal as heat ebbed away. The sky had taken one of its spring turns, dark clouds whipping the air. On the far side of the valley, Charlie could see where the rocks pushed through the thin grass in their familiar patterns. They had names for them all: the sewing machine, the bonky man. Secret names to be counted off like charms on a bracelet, from a time when she still held her mother's hand and they told stories as they walked, the three of them together. The memory made her uneasy. That was a part of her life she'd chosen to forget. Chosen, or been given no choice? Somewhere a sheep bleated, and was answered by a discordant volley of sound from the rest of the scattered flock.

In front of them, the house was unchanged, stark on the side of the hill. Its angular seventies lines were unsoftened by the years of moorland wind, though she could see signs of age. She hated it, she realized. Not just the sense of it. She was used to that, to low-level apprehension building from her stomach as she walked up to the door. The not-knowing of what mood would be there to greet her, silence or a brittle pretence at normality. Now she noticed streaks down the white walls where the rain left green trails, and cracks in the render. Had they always been there? The house would disintegrate now her mother had gone. Which didn't make sense: her mother's disregard for any issues with the fabric of the place had been one of her small rebellions. And now she'd slipped away from it for good.

'Come on, it's going to rain any sec.' Eleanor spoke but didn't move, though she had one hand on the door handle. Her body was angled away, her face turned towards the hills. Charlie wondered if she was noticing the rocks as well, what her memories were bringing back. She was right about the rain. Charlie could see black clouds massing behind the house. A spot landed on the windscreen in front of them. Eleanor spoke again, more to herself than Charlie. 'Right, let's get on.'

Charlie followed her up the path, her feet crunching on the gravel as if they belonged to somebody else entirely. Once inside, she let her rucksack fall with a tired thump. There it was, the smell of home. It made her want to run away.

'Will you be OK?' Eleanor had gone straight through to the back of the house, looking for something in the drawers and cupboards of the utility room by the sound of it, but now reappeared. Her voice had a snappy edge, as if this was all Charlie's fault. Charlie vaguely wondered if they should be hugging, sharing what they felt. Surely that would be the normal reaction? It would be hard, mind; at that moment, she couldn't begin to work out how she felt, and maybe her sister felt the same. And maybe she should also be apologizing, for not being there, for leaving when she had, but Eleanor interrupted the slowly forming thought. 'I'm going to have to run home for a bit. The girls are with Jon's mum, but Poppy won't eat unless I'm there. I'll just have time to feed them before Jon gets back, then I'll go and get Dad.'

Charlie almost asked why Jon couldn't sort all that out, but bit the words back. It wasn't her role to interfere. And anyway, her sleepiness was reaching an unbearable pitch, a monstrous weight pushing all other considerations out of its way. Wrapped in its haze, she watched Eleanor leave before stumbling up the wide, floating boards of the stairs and collapsing onto her old bed.

32

Four

The room was dark when she woke. Charlie lay still, her mind grappling to make sense of the quiet. There should be lights, departure boards, the reassuring chatter of a surrounding crowd. With a surge of adrenaline, she sat up, trying to find her bag. If that was stolen, how would she get back? Then the shadowy contours of the room began to settle, and she remembered that she'd already arrived. She slumped down again, piecing herself together. Her mouth was dry, her body stale and acrid, and her stomach empty. Maybe if she closed her eyes and went back to sleep, everything would go away.

In the end, she had to get up. Out on the landing she paused, trying to work out what time it was. Eleanor had talked about coming back, but would she have been and gone again? Charlie didn't think she could face talking to her father by herself. From downstairs she caught the chink of movements, a tap running, then the low murmur of voices. Both of them, but did that make things easier or not? She could stay where she was and pretend to be asleep, put off everything until the morning, but that would double the awkwardness of the next day. Plus, she really needed the toilet. Maybe a shower would wake her up enough to be coherent.

The water was a stinging heat, scouring off the last of Thailand. Strange that it was less than a day since she'd left. It felt as if she'd never been there. She stood under the spray for minutes longer than necessary, unable to move. Then the water made the decision for her, changing to the sudden blast of cold that signalled the boiler's limit. Back in her room, she emptied her rucksack and looked at what she'd brought back. Not much. The bundle of thin cotton trousers and embroidered tops were creased and dirty, and not up to the chill of an English spring. It was a pathetic pile. She should have made sure she had something wearable. And anyone else would have brought gifts, mementoes from away, offerings to those left behind. No one would be expecting it under the circumstances, but Charlie felt a dull guilt that it hadn't even crossed her mind, for Eleanor's girls at least. She turned to the chest of drawers where there were still the odd bits of clothing that had accumulated over the years. Leggings, and a T-shirt she must have brought once as a nightshirt. It was one of Max's, oversized on her and with a daft slogan, and she was afraid for a moment that it would smell of him. There was nothing but the floral waft of washing powder, but she put it back in the drawer anyway. It wasn't hers to borrow any more. In the end, she settled on a saggy vest top, crumpled and feeling slightly damp. She was cold now, goosebumps covering her arms, the chill made worse by the water dripping down her neck. Giving her hair a final rub, she went back out onto the landing.

34

After a moment's hesitation, she crossed over to her mother's door and pushed it open.

The covers on the bed were thrown back. Charlie stood at the threshold, taking in the clothes folded neatly on the back of the chair, the half-full mug of tea on the bedside table. It had been years since her parents had shared a room and, for the first time, Charlie wondered why her mother stayed in this room after she and Eleanor had left. It was by far the smallest of the bedrooms, with just one small window looking out over the driveway. There was a sense of warmth, clutter even, not to be found in the rest of the house. Feeling like an intruder, she went further in, sitting down on the bed and looking about. A book lay face down on the floor, the pages splayed, and she picked it up, smoothed it shut. *Offshore*. She'd never come across it before. The pages were soft at the edges, the spine broken. This had been a well-loved copy. Charlie studied the cover before putting it down next to her. Maybe it was the last thing her mother had done. Eleanor had said something about her heart. Charlie pictured her sitting up in bed reading, and suddenly feeling that something was wrong. Did paramedics tramp through the house, or had she gone to the doctor's surgery in the next village? There was no sign of anything here being disturbed. The room felt peaceful, untouched by drama and tragedy. It was almost as if any moment her mother could reappear. Would they sit down together in this little room, and talk? Probably not. And would that be because she was avoiding it, or her mother was?

She jammed her hands between her knees, again

trying to remember the last time they'd had a proper conversation. It felt important, to be able to pin down a moment, a time when they'd connected. What sort of a daughter sat on her mother's bed on the night of her death and couldn't come up with a single occasion when they'd shared more than the essentials. *How was your day? OK. Good, I'll let you get on then.* And it hadn't even bothered her, not really. Yes, she was aware that it wasn't normal, but then she was used to keeping things from other people. There had been tricky moments, Max's parents wanting *to get to know your family, darling,* but they'd listened with sympathy to her explanation of agoraphobia. Who made up psychological diagnoses for their parents? She squeezed her eyes shut, blocking out the thought. If she could think of one moment, she would go downstairs and get the meeting over with. But she needed to think of it before anyone came upstairs and found her sitting there.

And there it was. She and Eleanor squashed into the same bed whilst their mother told stories to them. There was a princess, Charlie thought, maybe more than one princess, and snow. A soldier, and a troll. They had to be good to hear the stories and go to sleep quickly. It was worth it, though, because no one else's mummy could tell them fairy tales from another country. Their mummy was the only one who came from somewhere that wasn't Derbyshire. Another echo came through: someone at school shouting that there wasn't anywhere called Norway. She blocked that voice out, trying to keep the story alive instead. It was almost as if she was hearing it again, the whole tale present in her head for a split-second, her mother's words quiet in her ear. Then the focus began to slip and, when she pressed the memory, it was harder to be sure it was there at all. A noise, the closing of a door downstairs, shook her out of her thoughts. Leaping up as if she'd done something wrong, she grabbed a jumper, the soft grey wool as warm in her hands as if it had only just been discarded. It was wide, falling in loose folds from her shoulders, and reaching almost to her knees. As she was about to leave the room, she caught a glimpse of herself in the wardrobe mirror. Her, or a brief visitation of her mother? She didn't wait for a longer look.

Eleanor was in the kitchen, clearing plates and cutlery to one side to make room for a litter of paperwork. Charlie hesitated before going in, watching Eleanor's movements, her father's closed face as he sat waiting for her to finish. It all looked so ordinary, a normal evening with no one missing. But none of them was normal, she thought with a sense of revelation. They were all just pretending to do what normal people did. Briefly, her sister's and her father's faces settled at the same angle, and Charlie was struck by how similar they were. It must have been something about their expression, because they didn't look alike at all in person. Eleanor had her mother's blondeness, her hair still naturally pale in a way that strangers never accepted. Charlie had heard it her whole life, first about her mother and then her sister, the disbelief that no chemicals were involved. She'd used it as a pass, the sort of offering that got people's attention, made them notice her, even if it was at one remove. Her own colouring was from her father,

37

though in photos she could sometimes see an odd resemblance to her mother. Eleanor glanced up to see Charlie standing there. She stopped what she was doing, sending a quick, undecipherable look at their father before moving towards her.

Her hug was unexpected, and Charlie stiffened slightly before returning the gesture. As they stood in the unfamiliar closeness, she felt Eleanor registering the jumper, where it was from. Her pause was followed by a brief stroke before she returned to the sink, asking if Charlie wanted something to eat as she went.

'Ah, Charlotte, good of you to join us.' Her father turned to regard her, and she felt herself stiffen again, but this time with anger. It was the most he'd said to her since that final, disastrous visit before she'd left. If he hadn't been so pedantic about the importance of her standing on her own two feet if she was going to do *ridiculous things*, so inflexible about dogs belonging outside, she would have been there at the house for more time, maybe even enough to create that moment with her mother so she'd have something to remember now. What might they have said if they'd had some time alone, just sitting there together? And now she'd lost the chance of ever talking to her again.

Charlie took a deep breath, stepping towards the far side of the table without reacting. He seemed crumpled, his head poking forwards from the collar of his soft checked shirt, the skin loose on the front of his neck. Was he this old when she left for Thailand? For some reason, she thought back to when Poppy, Eleanor's younger daughter, was born. Martha had been about five and

38

seemed a tiny girl until it was as if she'd swelled overnight in comparison to the baby. Perhaps death did the same sort of thing, but marking the changes with the passage of time instead of size? She looked up to find Eleanor looking at her and her father giving his displeased grunt of impatience. Had they said something to her?

Before she could respond, her father was standing, taking time to manoeuvre around his chair as if his legs weren't as reliable as they should be.

'We'll finish this off tomorrow,' he said, gesturing towards the paperwork.

'Don't let me stop you,' Charlie replied, aiming for a neutral tone which even so sounded passive aggressive to her ears. The kitchen seemed to be in double-sharp focus, throbbing slightly under the bright overhead light. She felt that she'd collapse if she didn't eat something soon, at the same time uncertain that she could stay awake for long enough to manage anything.

'That's very kind.' Her father's voice was brittle with sarcasm. 'But the thought was far from my mind. It has been a long day.'

And then he was walking out of the room, and Eleanor was putting a plate of some kind of stew in front of her. She looked down at it, unable to work out what her next move should be.

'Can you not leave it, just for one evening?' Eleanor dropped into the chair vacated by their father, leaning her head into one hand. She looked exhausted as well.

'What, me?' Charlie stared, then shook her head. 'You honestly thought that was me?'

'No, not really.' Eleanor pushed cutlery across the table.

39

'Go on, eat. I'm sorry, I spend too much time with squabbling children.'

Charlie picked up the fork automatically, chewing a mouthful of stew as she processed her sister's words. Everything was taking a long time, and she'd swallowed two lots before realizing how hungry she was. She began to eat more quickly, taking a moment to acknowledge it. 'This is delicious. Thank you.'

'It's nothing.' Eleanor sat there, watching her shovel it down. Finally, she spoke again. 'I'm worried about him, actually. He won't admit it, but his memory . . . He's starting to forget things, get confused.'

'He seemed to be remembering plenty just then.' Charlie caught sight of her sister's expression. 'I'm sorry. It's just so hard to take it all in.' She put her fork down, suddenly not hungry any more.

'It's not just because of Mum.' Eleanor was fiddling with a pencil, bouncing it on its rubber tip before lining it back up with the edge of a sheet of paper. 'Maybe it's made me notice more, but he's been like this for a while. Not enough to put your finger on anything in particular . . .' Her voice trailed off. 'It's like he's not always there.'

Charlie didn't answer straight away, instead picking at the piece of bread Eleanor had put on her plate. The soft white doughiness compressed to a solid lump between her fingers. 'What actually happened, El? I mean, do they know the cause of death?' It felt odd saying it out loud like that and she sounded unreal, as if she was a character in a bad TV programme.

Eleanor sighed. 'There'll have to be a post-mortem,'

40

she said. 'With her not being under a doctor for anything, you know. She'd been feeling ill for a few days, apparently, but didn't tell anyone.'

'So she might have been OK, if she'd been to see someone sooner?' Charlie squashed more bread pellets, lining them up in order of size.

'I don't know. Maybe.' Eleanor's face screwed up, a little girl about to cry. 'We were here last week, she was fine. Seemed fine.'

Charlie reached over, grasping for her sister's hand. There was so much to say, and it was so hard to imagine actually saying it. Eleanor gave her fingers a squeeze, then stood up.

'I'd really better be getting home.' She was turning around, not meeting Charlie's eyes. Maybe she was just looking for her bag, or maybe she was trying to avoid talking any further. 'Have you got everything you need?'

'Yes. I mean, nothing that matters.' Charlie paused, wondering how much to say. 'It is, I mean—' She came to a stop and gave a helpless gesture, taking in the kitchen, the rooms beyond. 'Is it all right for me to stay here? After, well, you know . . .' Her voice trailed off again and she had to force herself to continue. 'It's just with flying back and not planning it, I haven't got much spare money.'

'No, it's fine.' Eleanor's reply, brisk and practical, came quickly back. There was a pause, as if she was deciding whether to say something. Charlie glanced at her, catching an odd expression passing over her face. When she spoke again, it didn't seem to connect to the look. 'Dad will be pleased to have you here.'

Charlie doubted that, but she wasn't going to argue. That was new, hearing Eleanor call him 'Dad'. He'd never been a dad figure, still less a 'daddy'. Charlie had avoided using any variation since she was, what, thirteen? It had felt significant, refusing the intimacy of any of the choices. As an adult, if pushed, she used his name, Hugo. It didn't suit him, was too jolly. A Hugo should be someone with a deep laugh who pulled chocolate coins out of his ears for children and gathered people to him with warm bonhomie. That was what she thought, every time it came up. *You don't deserve that name. It's not yours.* Max and his siblings had so many expressions for their father: Pops, Papa, Old Guy. Mingus, from a distant family joke no one could ever explain. He was everything she would have chosen, a quiet, warm man with a dry sense of fun. She missed him more than she could say. Pushing that thought down deep, she followed Eleanor to the front door, both of them stopping for a moment of decision before jointly, and silently, making the decision not to hug again.

She couldn't sleep, of course. The house hung around her in its silent whiteness, the wind picking up across the hilltops outside. Her thoughts fell in with the cadence, gusting in swoops around her mother and her father and a lifetime of things not said. In the end she gave up. There was no sidelight in here any more, and the shade had been taken off the central bulb. She propped herself up, reading the book she'd taken from her mother's room under its harsh, surreal light. A woman on a boat, daughters playing in the mud of the Thames. Disagreements,

42

hardship. The sense of tragedy about to descend. The pages took on an almost hallucinatory significance as she carried on, page after page, and dawn was lightening the curtains before she finally dropped off. She dreamed of the story: boats and mud, absent parents and struggle.

Five

Over the following days, they entered a time of limbo, an equilibrium reached and maintained by the fewest possible words. Charlie kept out of her father's way, partly through design and partly because he was clearly keeping out of hers. They used the kitchen at different times, waited for the landing to be clear before crossing over to the bathroom. He disappeared into his study for long periods; she went out for walks across the damp fields, where she managed not to think too much, concentrating on the movement of her feet, the ticking off of footpaths and turnings, the accumulation of miles travelled. Sometimes, she wondered about calling Max. He'd need to be told, about her mother, maybe even about the funeral. It was hard to be sure of the etiquette, easier not to do anything. It wasn't as if she could have Bella with her. And there were bigger questions lurking out there, things that had been easy to put to one side when the thought of coming home had been shadows beyond a brave new life. The house, her share of it, all of the things they'd managed to ignore before. At the back of her head, she'd kind of expected not to come back. Her future would happen overseas, somewhere

44

exotic and different, where house prices and solicitor's fees didn't exist. She thought that Max might have been hoping, despite his words, that she'd come back and they could pick things up with whatever was bothering her finally out of her system. At times now, it was a solution which sang to her. But what if he said no? But what if he said yes?

So she stayed where she was and did things when Eleanor asked her to, sorting out cupboards or snipping at things in the garden. It was clear they were activities aimed at keeping her out of the way, straightforward tasks requiring little or no decision-making. Eleanor kept that for herself and Charlie couldn't summon up the energy to question her right to do so. Their initial rapprochement had retreated from the first couple of days, and Charlie could sense what her sister's response would be. *You took off and left the responsibility to me. I'm just following through. And I'm not talking about your delayed gap year, I'm talking about before that, when you waltzed off to university and left me to be the one who sorted things out.* Was that Eleanor's voice or her own conscience, though? Because she couldn't help but recognize that her sister was taking the same approach with their father. They were two more children, in effect, to be ordered and occupied. No wonder Jon kept out of the way. Charlie packed boxes and cleaned windows, trying to keep her mind empty. Only once did she go back to her mother's room, to find the bed stripped, the surfaces cleared.

Then, on a day when numerous decisions had to be made, with a string of appointments with undertakers and banks and solicitors and other things she hadn't

45

really listened to, they hit upon a plan which helped everyone to sit a little easier together. Eleanor had arrived with her whole family, trailing a slip-stream of discord. The girls spilled into the house in a noisy bundle, Poppy still in her pyjamas and Martha with tear-stained cheeks. Jon followed behind, taking no notice of the effect his daughters were having. Eleanor took Poppy off to be sorted, and Charlie followed Jon into the living room. Martha was already in there, crouched in a corner with her back showing just how much she was hating the day.

'Did something happen?' Charlie asked, remembering what it was like to be nearly eleven and never quite sure how you wanted to behave.

Jon was slumped in an armchair, scrolling through something on his phone. He cast a casual glance at his daughter and shrugged. 'Nothing more than the normal,' he said, and went back to the screen.

It was almost the first time she'd seen Jon since she'd arrived back. She wandered over to the fireplace, leaning on the mantel to surreptitiously study him. Mid-height and dark haired, he had the sort of face that didn't give much away. She'd always found it hard to tell if he was genuinely grumpy, or just bored. Or maybe she'd never tried. He was just there, wallpaper in her sister's life, though Max had always said he was trapped in a place he hadn't seen coming, and there was an interesting guy under there somewhere.

'So, what are you doing next, then?' His words caught her off balance, his awareness of her scrutiny making her blush. 'Going back out to the sun?'

46

Charlie glanced down at her arms, at the fading tan she'd sometimes found herself staring at, as if wondering where it had come from. 'Not sure yet. Everything's a bit up in the air.' As if her life was like confetti, to be thrown around for the wind to take where it would. 'Eleanor says you've got a new job?' If only she'd thought to check what it was in. All she could remember was Eleanor saying it was taking up a lot of his time. The extra hours seemed to be agreeing with him. He'd shaved his hair short, which made him look younger, and lost weight. His T-shirt was new as well, the logo on it familiar and expensive.

'Yep, all going well.' He sat back, lifting his arms to stretch out, with something satisfied in his demeanour, as if he'd discovered a secret to life. 'Nothing like a change, eh?'

There was something off in his tone. She realized he wasn't looking at her, not really. His mind was elsewhere, occupied with whatever was on his phone. Poppy's voice came down the stairs, shrieking in fury. Clearly dressing wasn't going to plan. Charlie was glad of the distraction. 'I don't know how Eleanor does it,' she said. 'She's always so calm.'

'You'd think so.' Jon had picked his phone up again. 'But you haven't seen her when—' Whatever he was about to say was interrupted by Eleanor herself, coming into the room with Poppy in tow.

'Right, she's ready.' There was something about Eleanor's voice that made Charlie feel uncomfortable. It was stretched, a little wobbly. Poppy was dressed for a dance class, though she didn't seem thrilled at the idea. She was letting her legs buckle under the blue net skirt, using her weight to try and escape from her mother's grip. 'Jon, are you going to take her?' The tension in her tone went up a notch, and she gave Poppy's arm a shake. 'Stand up. You're being very silly.' She spoke a little more loudly, towards where Martha was still hunched on the floor. 'Come on, Mar, time to go!'

The forced cheerfulness of her tone didn't seem to make Martha any more enthusiastic, but she got to her feet with an exaggerated effort.

'I still don't see why I have to go,' she muttered. 'I could walk to the library. Or I could stay here. *Anything* would be better than watching Poppy's stupid class.'

'No, you couldn't, it's too far and there's not time.' They'd clearly had it out before. 'I said I'd make sure you went next week. Jon, Poppy's going to be late, and you know how they are!'

'What's the problem?' Charlie couldn't help wondering why everyone was going to something nobody wanted to do.

Eleanor gave an exasperated sigh. 'They have things on at different ends of the town,' she explained, 'which is usually fine, but I have to do these things with Dad today. Martha's just being silly.'

'I'm not!' Martha's eyes filled with tears. 'But it's not fair that you're doing Poppy's thing, not mine. She doesn't even like ballet!'

'Could I go with her?' They all turned to look at Charlie with differing expressions. Eleanor was surprised, Jon sardonic, Martha hopeful. Poppy managed to slide away, landing on the floor where she started to take her shoes off. 'Really, I don't mind. We can go to the library thing or go for a walk here. Whatever.' *Anything to get out of this house*, she added in her head.

By the day of the funeral, everyone seemed to accept that Martha would sit with her aunt. Charlie was gratified to feel the small frame leaning into her as they waited at the front of the chapel, though it did make the moment more surreal than it already was. Charlie was wearing a dress of Eleanor's, a suitably understated outfit which made her feel as if she was having an out of body experience. This wasn't her, tucked down at the end of the single filled pew. On the other side of Martha was Jon, then a squirming Poppy, Eleanor, and finally her father. Hugo had discouraged the idea of other people being invited. There was no one, he'd said, who was close enough to his wife to make it a necessity. Charlie couldn't think of anyone to counter this statement with, but it still felt wrong, as if they'd not tried enough.

'We are gathered here today to remember Britta, a much-loved wife, mother and grandmother.' The minister's voice caught Charlie by surprise. She was young, with a fresh, shining face tilted towards them in sympathy. Her tone felt theatrical in the setting, perhaps more practised in a church, or with a larger number of mourners. The words went on. 'Britta was a quiet woman, happy to stay within her close family circle.' She was doing her best with what she'd been given. Charlie bit down on her lips, tuning out as much as she could whilst she looked towards the coffin. It was so small. She hadn't gone with Eleanor and Hugo to the

49

chapel of rest, volunteering instead to stay behind with the children. She hadn't been able to bear the thought of standing there with them, feeling the pressure of all the things you were supposed to say, the ways you were expected to behave. She still wasn't sure what she actually felt.

Now she looked at the small brown box with its neat brass handles and wondered what her mother would have wanted, given the choice. Surely not this sad remnant of a family, sitting in a fake chapel and going through the form of a service she'd never sought out in life. She'd been an only child with no living parents, had spent her lifetime away from her homeland; maybe that explained the lack of family. But surely there were people who had known her, who would want to remember? And why no friends, no evidence of any social circle? Had she really been so satisfied with this small, inadequate group? If she hadn't been, then Charlie was too late to ask her; to do anything about it.

A faint rustle from behind made her turn. It was a latecomer, sliding cautiously into a seat right at the back. Charlie had never seen her before, but gained the impression of a solid, older woman, her face shaded by the brim of her best hat. There was something comforting about her presence. Then the minister was asking them to read something from the service sheet, and Charlie felt Eleanor give her a reproving look. By the time she looked round again, the woman had gone.

50

Six

Eleanor passed on the news that the house was to be sold a week to the day after the funeral. They were in a café (*My treat, we could both do with some time out*), sitting in silence, watching the rain batter down on the windows. Charlie was wrapped up in what on earth she was going to do next. Travel again? She wasn't at all sure she wanted to jump back into that. Anyway, she'd need to save, unless she waited until she and Max sorted out what was happening to their house. And she'd need somewhere to live in the meantime. She stirred at the froth of her coffee, wondering what Eleanor was about to say. Maybe she'd be expecting her to volunteer to care for Hugo. In the general weirdness of the past month it had become almost normal to share the space with him. Though 'share' was the wrong word. With that unspoken pact, they still inhabited it at different times. At least, she assumed they had the same intention.

'How are things with you and Max?'

Charlie put down her spoon. That wasn't the opening she'd expected. Eleanor's tone was casual, which usually meant she was hiding something. 'He knows I'm here.' She'd had to call him in the end, to tell him about

Britta. 'I told him not to come.' The words sounded unnecessarily defiant. He'd offered to drive up, of course he had. He was well brought up, after all, knew how you were supposed to behave. He'd sounded reluctant, though, and Charlie had been quick to say the funeral was just for close family. She didn't want to think he was feeling sorry for her.

'Did he say I spoke to him?' Eleanor fiddled with the sugar, lining the little paper sachets up in alternate colours. 'I wanted him to know he'd be welcome at the funeral.'

'Oh.' Charlie wasn't sure how she felt, about Eleanor talking to him, about Max not mentioning the offer. 'At least he knows we're all on the same page then.'

'I'm sorry.' Eleanor changed her pattern to a zigzag, then scooped them all up and tipped them back into the bowl. 'I should have checked with you. I always liked Max, you know.'

Charlie said nothing. This clearly wasn't what they were here for.

'Do you know what's happening between you two yet?' She glanced up. Charlie could feel her face closing in, becoming defensive, blocked. 'Sorry, none of my business. Look, what exactly are you planning next?'

The question didn't come as a surprise. It was what Charlie had been trying to work out for weeks. 'I don't know.' Charlie let her head fall back. 'I have absolutely no idea.'

Eleanor drank the last of her coffee and pushed the cup to one side. 'We've had an offer for the house. I had a call today. Someone wants to buy, cash. Had his eye

52

on it for years, apparently.' She twiddled with the handle, turning the cup from side to side.

'Oh. Right.' *Don't make it all about you*, Charlie was telling herself. She needed to see it as a positive, a nudge from the universe telling her it was time to jump. 'A good offer?'

'Pretty good. The estate agents keep saying we could hold out for more, but to be honest, I don't think anyone's got the energy to play games.' Estate agents. Everyone else knowing. How had she missed this going on? Eleanor was still talking. 'The thing is, it could happen within a couple of weeks. The buyer's very keen, and without a mortgage of course . . .' She waited, presumably to give Charlie the chance to nod wisely at this piece of luck. 'Dad'll come and stay with us, the girls can share for a bit.'

'That'll be tight.' Eleanor's house was a small stone terrace, bought before they had children. *Don't be upset. You have no right to be upset. You don't even like the place.* Except she should have been asked what she felt. That was fair to think. She bit down on her mouth, lips drawn in between her teeth. After a moment, she was able to carry on. 'Is there even enough space for two beds in Martha's room?'

'Well, the thing is—' The change in Eleanor's tone made Charlie look up. There were spots of colour in her cheeks that hadn't been there before. 'It'll only be for a few weeks. We've put an offer in on a house, a bigger one, with an annexe for Dad.'

'So much going on.' She felt the urge to get out, to walk away from it all. But that didn't work, did it? Look where it had got her last time. 'It's a great idea,' she said

53

instead, trying to inject enough enthusiasm into her voice. It sounded like a terrible idea. Was it her job to point this out? 'Are you sure? It's, well . . .' She shook her head. 'It's a surprise, that's all.'

'I would have said something before, but we thought we should wait until it all went through.' Eleanor spoke quickly. There was an edge to her words, as if she'd been expecting more of a fight. 'We really don't have enough room at the moment. The girls will be needing more space, a garden. It'll solve all sorts of problems. And we'll make sure it's reflected in Dad's will. You won't lose out.'

Charlie waved that away. She really didn't want to think about money. The obligation, the responsibility. And there was something else nudging at the edges of her mind: that not benefitting from the house, from anything Hugo had to offer, would give her a sense of freedom. 'I'd better get a move on with finding some-where to live. Job hunting as well.' She caught sight of Eleanor's face. 'It's OK, I need to do it.'

'It's not that.' Eleanor sounded impatient. 'There's something I should—' Her phone began to buzz, leap-ing along the tabletop in little sideways hops. 'Oh, for goodness' sake, what now?' She turned away as she answered, her words clipped. 'Yes, it's me. What is it?' There was a pause, and Charlie saw her sister's eyes squeeze shut. Annoyance or tears? 'Are you sure? Why? It's just that I'm here with . . . Oh, never mind.' She stopped to listen to whatever was being said at the other end. Her voice became tighter still. 'I said never mind. But why can't you—?' More words, unsatisfactory ones

54

if the tautness of her mouth was anything to go by. After a minute more, she ended the call and stuffed the phone into her bag. 'Look, I'm sorry, we'll have to go. Jon was supposed to collect the girls today, but something's come up at work.'

The house sale was agreed, and Eleanor descended into a frenzy of planning and sorting. And it was all right. Charlie found that she could pack and sort and nod at ideas without it meaning very much. She had no connection, not to here, not to anywhere. Whenever Eleanor asked her how she was getting on, she made some reference to looking for vacancies – in jobs and housing – but in actual fact she couldn't make herself do anything about it. Mostly it felt as if she was pushing against a wall of lethargy. How did you make a decision like that, of where you wanted to go and what you wanted to do? And if there was no need to go anywhere in particular, the choice of everywhere made the decision impossible. If she thought about it too hard, the impossibility of ever finding anything was too much. It was easier to shut off, to refuse to accept delivery. Then there came moments of absolute calm, when she could feel with certainty that something would turn up. It wasn't something she could explain, so she kept on nodding at Eleanor's enquiries. Yes, there were some possibilities. Yes, she was sure she'd find something by the time they had to leave.

They were into the beginning of April, and Charlie had been back home for a month, the longest month of her life. A timeless month, outside the bounds of any

55

calendar. Charlie had taken a carload of bags to the charity shop a couple of villages along. There was a surprising amount to get rid of, considering the deliberate minimalism of the house, and they were trying to spread it over a number of destinations. It was her first visit to this particular shop, anyway, and a string of bells chimed as she pushed open the door. A woman came out from a back room. She seemed slightly familiar, though that happened to Charlie a lot, half recognizing a face without being able to put a name or connection to it. She hadn't wanted to get involved with any catching up or recollections, though, and generally found a blank response made most people decide they didn't know her after all.

'I've got some donations,' she said now, holding up the two binbags she'd brought from the car. 'There are some more outside as well.'

'Lovely, thank you so much.' The words came out pat, a well-rehearsed response. 'I'll take them to the back.' She took one in each hand, dropping them inside the open doorway of the stock-room and coming back for the next load almost before Charlie was inside.

There was a rack of reduced items at the rear of the shop, and Charlie changed direction just as she was about to leave. The big woollen jumper she'd found on the first night was still her only warm layer, and a month or so of continuous wear was leaving its mark. She began to browse through the hangers of assorted knitwear, aware of the woman's eyes on her. What did she think, that Charlie was going to sneak something under her top? Without thinking too hard, Charlie unhooked an oversized sweatshirt and a long, chunky cardigan and took them to the till. The woman took some time to examine the labels for errors before entering the information in the ledger open before her. The figures were typed into the till with heavy presses of her forefinger. Charlie idly noted the heavy brown colouring of the woman's coarse, bobbed hair, the powder thickening the lines of her skin. She had reading glasses with gold-flecked plastic frames hanging from a beaded cord, lifting them in front of her face to check the till display before letting them drop. She put on a professional smile. 'Seven pounds ninety-eight, please.'

Charlie felt in her pocket for her purse. It was made from faded black cotton faced with the bright geometrics of Thai embroidery. As Charlie unfolded it, fiddling with the zip, which was inclined to jam, the woman spoke.

'Aren't you Britta's daughter?'

The zip came open with a jerk and a handful of coins rolled out onto the counter. 'Yes.' Charlie let the money settle. It wasn't the first time someone had asked about her mother, of course. There'd been the woman at the Post Office, one or two awkward neighbours who'd clearly felt under obligation to say something.

'It was such a shock,' the woman said, helping to collect the coins together. 'She was such a great help in setting up the shop. She talked of you often.'

'Sorry, she worked here?' Charlie was too startled to cover up her surprise.

'Oh yes, every Wednesday afternoon.' The woman stopped, looking over to the door as if expecting to see

57

Britta walk through. 'I know it was difficult for her, getting away, but she never missed a Wednesday. Until the end of last year, that is. She stopped coming then.' Her voice dropped so that her next question was more of a whisper. 'I did wonder if that was when she started feeling poorly?'

'I don't know. I was away.' Charlie didn't even know that her mother had been helping in the shop, let alone how she'd been feeling. Because she didn't know anything, had never tried to know anything. A surge of guilt made the words come out sounding clipped and offended.

'Of course you were.' The woman reached across and touched Charlie's hand. 'It's a shock, losing your mother, whatever your age,' she said. 'And so suddenly. It must be very difficult for you.'

Charlie felt her own fingers tighten on the woman's hand, aware of the smooth slip of rose-scented cream, the pressure of crowded rings. For a moment, it was like holding on to a rescuer, and she suddenly wanted to blurt it out, how she couldn't cry, how none of it seemed real. And had her mother really talked about her?

'I hear the house has been sold?' The woman dipped her head, inviting confidence. 'To a man from London, they were saying.'

For a second, Charlie felt almost hypnotized into answering. Then the shop's bells gave their tremble of ringing as someone else entered, and she slipped her hand away. 'I'm not sure where he's from, to be honest. I've not met him.' That was probably still too much information. The story would be going around that the

58

younger girl didn't want the house to go, that there was something fishy about the buyer. Gathering up the jumpers, she gave a quick smile, nodding also at the newly arrived customer. Was that really true about her mother coming to help in the shop, or had it been a ploy to get information? As she left, she glanced back to see the two of them watching her go, their heads nodding. Would it be odd for them, going through the donations? Maybe they'd take keepsakes for themselves, or put together a memorial rack, hung with the softly neutral layers and textured scarves. Charlie almost wished they'd had a bonfire, with its sense of a cleansing ritual. It was only as she got into the car that she realized where she'd seen the woman before. At the back of the chapel, wearing a hat.

The weather since the funeral had been unpredictable, with savage episodes of rain sweeping through without warning. One caught her as she got out of the car, and she came in shaking herself like a wet dog. Martha and Poppy were sitting at the kitchen table in unusual harmony, surrounded by a litter of paper and felt-tips. Martha gave her a small wave. Poppy didn't look up. In here, things looked much as they always had. In the rest of the house, gaps were spreading, meeting up, taking over.

'Where is everyone?' Charlie asked, crossing the room to make an exploratory scan for any sounds in the house. She stopped behind Martha's chair. 'This is good. Is it the pony you were riding last week?'

'They're in there.' Martha answered her first question with a roll of her eyes as she tilted her head towards the living room. She was still in her school uniform, her plaits in their end-of-the-day state of disarray. Charlie tucked some of the loose strands back in as she listened. 'Talking and talking. Mummy says there's still a lot to sort out.' Martha paused for a moment, adding a ribbon to the pony's tail before looking up with a conspiratorial grin. 'Stay with us? We've got chocolate fingers to keep us quiet.'

Charlie gave her a hug. 'I might take you up on that in a minute, but I'd better see what's going on.' She reached for one of the biscuits. 'Make sure Poppy isn't eating them all.' Poppy, her face smeared with chocolate, continued to ignore them.

Eleanor was sitting by the coffee table, a handful of pictures fanned out on the surface in front of her. There was a shoebox on the floor as well, holding more loose photographs. Jon slouched on the sofa next to her. He was in his work clothes, a crumpled suit jacket draped over the back of the sofa and his tie loosened around his open shirt collar. As Charlie came in, she caught him looking at Eleanor, something very close to contempt in his expression. He shifted his gaze to her as she moved towards them, the look replaced by an ironic smirk. It made her feel oddly complicit.

'Where did you find these?' she asked, avoiding Jon's eyes. She squatted down next to Eleanor, picking a photograph out of the box. It was from Eleanor and Jon's wedding, a snap rather than a formal picture, taken just as the family group was breaking apart. Charlie's main memory of the day was being constantly nagged by Jon's mother. Catherine – was that her name? – had done most of the planning, clearly appalled by the lack of

60

interest from Eleanor's parents. Charlie had been sixteen, torn between disdain for anything as stupid as a wedding and a hidden, guilty pleasure in how she looked. Her bridesmaid's dress had been deep raspberry, its chiffon pleats clingy and sophisticated, or so she'd thought then. The photo had caught her scowling at something Jon's mother was saying in her ear. Behind them, Eleanor was trying to herd everyone into position and Jon was checking his watch. Hugo stood to one side, gazing into the distance as if he had nothing to do with any of it. There was no sign of Britta. Charlie, in a deliberate response to everyone's strictures, had drunk too much champagne and ended the day snogging a tall, gangly boy, some cousin of Jon's.

She reached for another print. The colours seemed overly faded, the hairstyles faintly ridiculous, as if the wedding had taken place decades before. It was almost half of her lifetime ago, she realized with a jolt, the thought followed by another even more unsettling realization. If she hadn't left last year, there would have been more wedding photos here. Her and Max, posing on the rustic bridge next to the lake. A hundred guests consuming wittily themed cocktails and canapes, crowding into the photo booth and leaving cheerful wishes in the happiness jar. Maybe that had been the problem, thinking that she could get away with such an ostentatious display.

'Mum had them under the bed in the spare room. I've no idea who took them.' Eleanor bent down to look at the picture in Charlie's hand. It was of her in her wedding dress, her stomach a barely discernible bulge. That

61

was why the wedding had happened so fast. Such a short time ago, yet from another world. Eleanor had lost the baby anyway. Charlie put the photo aside. They'd never talked about it, a weird hangover from a time when those sorts of things hadn't been discussed. Though that was more of an excuse than a reason. Now, Charlie wondered, questions flitting through her mind. Had Eleanor regretted the domino effect of events? Presumably not, because she and Jon had stuck in there, and three years later Martha had come along. She picked up another shot, this one of their parents, standing stiffly side by side.

'My God, did anyone enjoy that day?' The words came out unbidden, and she screwed her eyes shut in mortification. It was her sister's wedding she was talking about.

'Jon's mum did.' Eleanor didn't seem to mind. She took the photo with a shake of her head. 'What are we going to do with them?'

'Martha and Poppy'll love them one day. Can you stick them in your loft for the time being?'

'Oh no, not the loft.' Jon's voice was unexpected. Charlie turned in response, half registering how Eleanor took no notice. 'Lofts should be visited on a regular basis, so that dead wood can be pruned to leave space for new growth. Isn't that right?' He addressed his final remark at Eleanor, in a tone that wasn't at all amused.

She responded by placing the lid back onto the shoebox, resting her hands flat on its top. 'Maybe it would be a good time to take the girls home.' It wasn't a question, or even a suggestion. 'Dinner's ready, it just needs microwaving. Don't wait for me.'

There was a charged silence before he levered himself up and went out to the kitchen. Martha appeared some moments later to give her mother and Charlie fierce hugs. From the other room, they could hear Poppy protesting at the proposed move.

'She wants to finish her picture,' Martha explained. 'Will you be back before bedtime, Mummy?'

'I don't know.' Eleanor gave her a kiss and another hug before pushing her away. 'Go on, before Poppy brings the walls down.' She grimaced as Martha rolled her eyes and they both giggled at a private joke. 'Don't forget your teeth. And twenty minutes reading, not twenty hours!' She sat and watched as they left, listening to the sound of Jon's car starting, pulling away. It was only when the engine noise had gone completely that she sank down into the sofa.

'It's lovely, seeing you with Martha,' Charlie remarked, as much to fill the silence as anything. 'She's such a beautiful kid.'

'I know.' Eleanor was rubbing her eyes. She looked exhausted, and old. Not in a bad way, just older than Charlie thought of her. Grown up. 'She's very fond of you.'

'How do you do it?' The words came out in a burst, a question to an answer she hadn't realized she needed.

'What, have a daughter?' Eleanor gave her a half-smile. 'I think you know the answer to that one.'

Charlie ignored the joke. 'No, the hugs, the chatter.' She waved a hand in the air, stirring up what she wanted to know. 'How do you know how to be a mum? A proper one?'

Eleanor didn't reply straight away, instead leaning

63

forward to take the lid back off the box of photos. Her hand stopped before she'd touched any of the prints inside. 'What do you remember about Mum?' she asked, tilting her head round.

'Mum?' Charlie felt her head lean to one side, like Bella's did when she was working out the right answer to a command. Was this how dogs felt when tasked with something, a complete blank where action should be? 'I don't know. Came to the country in her twenties, got married, had kids.'

'Yes, all that. But little stuff. What's the picture you have in your head?'

'Uh, blonde? Quiet.' She wrinkled her brow, trying to think. 'Didn't like going out much.'

Eleanor pulled out the photo they'd been looking at before, the one that didn't have Britta in it. 'Do you ever wonder if she was trying to disappear?' She looked at their own past selves, standing in a room, caught in a moment. 'She's not left much behind, you know.'

Charlie thought of the book she'd found that first night, and the jumper she'd picked up at the same time. She thought of the women in the charity shop, separating Britta's clothes onto hangers, keeping back the things they wanted. 'There were some things,' she said, picking her words carefully. 'But they were all things we didn't want to keep.'

'I don't mean clothes.' Eleanor stood up, dropping the photograph down onto the open box. 'We'd better have something to eat as well. And some wine.'

Charlie followed her sister into the kitchen, watching as Eleanor opened the fridge, rummaged inside. It was

64

as if her sister was signalling that she was a mum, just a mum. Her jeans were shapeless, her top half hidden under a tunic printed with random foliage. No make-up, hair pulled back into what was clearly one of the girls' hairbands.

'Is pasta OK? I'm not sure I can be bothered with any-thing else.' Eleanor turned, came back to the table with a bottle of wine in her hand.

'Sure, anything.' Charlie went to get some glasses. This was the first time since the café trip when they'd been together, without the girls or visitors or Eleanor rushing off to take someone somewhere. A creaking floorboard reminded Charlie of Hugo, up there in his study.

She stopped, mid-kitchen, her face turned to the ceil-ing. 'Is he still writing that book?' Hugo's book had dominated their childhood. They'd tiptoed around so as not to disturb him, accepted that they didn't go on holidays because he needed the time to spend on what he referred to as research. Charlie had gone through a phase of being interested, more for the attention it brought than from any real passion for stargazing. It had earned her freezing hours of standing on the flat roof, pretending to understand his complicated theories about star movements. 'You'd think anything he had would be outdated by now. If he ever had anything.'

Eleanor was filling the glasses. 'He still goes off every Wednesday to argue about it with his buddies.'

The mention of Wednesdays reminded Charlie of the woman in the charity shop. Eleanor listened to the story, not saying anything after Charlie stopped talking. The silence stretched out.

65

'What is it?' Charlie asked in the end. In response, Eleanor dug in her bag, bringing out a padded envelope, the sides distended by whatever was inside.

'I've been meaning to talk to you about this for ages,' she started, then broke off to drink some of the wine. Charlie watched her, apprehension building in her stomach. Finally, her sister carried on. 'It was in the hospital. I was waiting with her while Dad went off to do something, get a coffee, I don't know. You know how she always looked at him before she said anything?'

Charlie nodded. It had been a tic, so familiar as to be unnoticeable until you were looking out for it.

'Well, this time, she opened her eyes as if something had woken her up. I thought she was disorientated, from the medication. She tried to sit up and kept asking if he was there. I was telling her he'd be back, but that made her more agitated.' She broke off, went to pick up her glass but seemed to forget halfway. 'Then she wanted her handbag, that leather rucksack? And she couldn't open it, kept looking at the door. Her heart rate thing was going up and I thought I'd have to get the nurses back in. But she managed to get in there and gave me this.' She pushed the envelope along the table, and Charlie put her hand out.

The glue was sticky enough to still be holding the flap shut. Charlie fumbled at the edge, unnerved by the story. She seemed to hear the beep of the machines, sense the brightness of the overhead lights. The contents fell out, some folded papers, and a set of keys attached to a round cork ball. 'What's this?'

'I'll get to that in a minute.'

66

Charlie straightened the papers out. The top sheet was a statement for a savings account, the figure at the bottom making her look twice to be sure she'd read it right. 'What the—'

'I know.' Eleanor moved her chair in closer, pointing at the top. The account was in her name. 'She asked me to sign something a couple of months ago, said it was a savings account for the girls. She was pretty odd about it, actually. And I thought she meant pocket money amounts.'

'But where did it come from?' It was like some elaborate practical joke. Her mother hadn't worked, had relied entirely on her husband for what she still called housekeeping money. There was no way she could have saved this much. Charlie looked again.

'I didn't ask.' Eleanor lifted her hands in a gesture of helplessness. 'There was no time. She was almost, well, frantic. She just kept saying it was for us, and that we weren't to tell him. We had to live our lives with it, not settle for second best.' She drank some more wine, then topped up both their glasses. 'And she was grabbing my hand, making me promise. And then he came back in and we didn't have any more time.'

'So this is all for us?' Charlie checked the amount again. 'Is it legal? Does it not have to be declared or anything?'

'For tax, but that's down to us. I ran it past one of the other mums from school, she's a solicitor. It's in our names, so doesn't get counted for probate.' Eleanor corrected herself. '*My* name, but I'm sure that's just because you weren't here. Mum was really clear it was for both of us.'

67

Charlie sat back, shaking her head. This was too much to take in. 'That doesn't do much to explain where it came from. Do you think she won the lottery?'

'Who knows?' Eleanor separated the paperwork. 'The point is, this is basically the only official thing she's left behind. I mean, I guess there are certificates, birth, marriage – I don't know where, Dad's got all that – but no other signs of who she became, what she wanted to do. Where she came from.'

'And what about these?' Charlie picked up the keys, sliding the ring over her finger and letting the cork ball swing beneath her hand.

'Oh, those? Those are for her boat.'

68

Seven

'Mum bought a boat?' Charlie could hear the words, even see them rolling out in front of her, but they made no sense. They were surreal, a story one person had started before turning down the top of the paper and passing it on for the next player to continue blind. 'She—' Charlie could think of nothing to say, but sat there, staring at her sister, her mouth hanging open.

'I know. Me neither.' Eleanor drank some of her wine. 'A narrowboat, to be precise. Bought and paid for outright in cash, currently moored at a marina near Macclesfield.'

'Macclesfield?' Charlie tried to picture where that was. Over to the west, on the other side of the Peak District. 'I didn't know there was a canal there.'

'Apparently there is. To be honest, I'm struggling more to imagine Mum getting over there by herself, never mind buying a boat there. When was the last time she went any further than Sheffield? And that was always with Dad taking her.' They both fell silent.

'It can't be more than an hour on the train,' Charlie said at last. She thought of the woman in the charity shop saying she'd never missed a Wednesday, until the

69

end of the year. 'She always had Wednesdays, right? When did she open the bank account?'

'Start of January.'

Charlie fiddled with a crayon left behind by the girls. She was picturing her mother waiting for the sound of the car leaving for the day before slipping out of the house herself. Hugo's Wednesday science day had been a weekly event since the day he retired, sacrosanct and unchangeable. He would leave at ten thirty in the morning, never returning before seven because of the rush-hour traffic. After listening to a particularly protracted complaint about the number of cars on the road and the inadequacy of the motorways, Charlie remembered Eleanor suggesting he waited until later, to avoid the traffic. He could, she said, spend the time with his friends. His reply had been irritable. They were colleagues, not friends. *It's not some knitting circle.* Britta didn't do social activities either. *We don't have time for that sort of stuff.* Hugo again. It was a line Charlie hadn't really questioned before. But the woman with the unmentioned windfall, the secret boat? That didn't make any sense.

'We'd better have that pasta.' Eleanor's voice broke into her thoughts, and Charlie watched her fill a pan with water, turn the gas on under it.

'Why didn't you tell me about it before?' she asked.

'What?' Eleanor glanced over her shoulder then back to the cooker.

'The money, the boat. You've known about it for weeks. Why not tell me before?'

Eleanor didn't answer at first. Charlie followed her movements as she opened a bag of pasta, poured the

70

hard, dry spirals into the pan. She should have waited for the water to come to the boil. Now the pasta would be too soft on the outside, the centre too crunchy. *Al dentist*, Max had always called it. Finally, she set the lid to balance on top, adjusting the flame before she came back to her chair. 'I was trying to find the right time at first. You know, in the middle of everything.'

'Nice try.' Charlie found her hands had balled up on her lap. She made herself spread them out, flattened them along the top of her legs. 'There were loads of times. Were you thinking of not telling me?'

'No, of course not!' To Charlie's surprise, tears welled up in her sister's eyes. 'I'd never do that. It was just . . .' She paused, wiping the edge of her sleeve across her face. 'It was about the timing, I'm not making that up. And it was really hard. The whole thing was so . . . so ridiculous that I kept thinking I'd made it up.' She took a deep breath in through her nose. 'And then, it was partly because of how you are.' She immediately held up a hand. 'No, that came out wrong. How *we* are, as sisters. You'd just got back, we'd not talked for the whole time you were away . . .'

She didn't really have to say any more. Charlie reached her own hand out and, after a moment's pause, Eleanor met it with her own. 'I get it.' Her fingers tightened, and she felt her sister squeeze in return. 'Anyone else, it would have been, hey, here's a weird thing.'

They sat in silence until the water reared up in the pan, knocking the lid sideways. It was Charlie who went over this time, turning the heat down, giving the clumped-up pasta a stir.

71

'You know what you said before, about being a mother?'

'Yes.' Charlie kept her back turned, concentrating on breaking every last spiral free from the pack. This whole sharing thing was all very well, but she wasn't ready for her sister to ask her when she was thinking of having kids. Eleanor continued to surprise her, though.

'The thing is, I don't know. Nobody does. But I have to keep trying, and keep getting it wrong, and then work out why and keep trying again. And that was another reason, if I'm honest. Why I couldn't tell you.' She picked up her glass, drained it, then reached across for the bottle to top it up. 'I've been going for help this year, and one of the things my therapist has made me realize is that I'm really angry with you for running away all the time. Not just this time, but every time. Whenever things get hard. No, not done yet.' She stalled Charlie's exclamation, instead pouring her more wine. 'And then she made me realize that what you do is up to you, not me. And most of the time I can let you be an adult and make your own decisions. But you were here, right in front of me, and it just felt that if I told you about the money you'd be gone again, and I wasn't ready for that.'

The pasta was left untouched in the pan whilst they worked their way through the rest of the bottle of wine, opened a second.

'What I want to know,' Charlie said, trying to rest her head against her hand but finding it hard to balance, 'is what you, of all people, were doing with a therapist in the first place.'

72

'I'd have thought you, of all people, would know the answer to that.' Eleanor went to stand, getting halfway before giving up. She raised her empty glass and angled it towards Charlie. 'How else was I supposed to deal with a dysfunctional upbringing?'

'How many syllables does dysfunctional have again?' Charlie asked. They both giggled, more than the joke was worth. 'We should have been getting drunk together for years.'

Eleanor nodded. 'And if you get me a glass of water,' she said, 'I might even share with you what the therapist had to say. Though that's not how it works, really. You have to do the hard work to get the benefit, you know.'

Charlie hauled herself up and filled an empty mug from the tap. It slopped over her hand as she brought it back. 'There you go. Now spill.'

'You've already done that.' Eleanor sat up very straight and took a deep swallow, like a rugby boy drinking beer. 'But I will let you off. So the therapist said I was very angry with you,' she pointed at Charlie, 'for disappearing. She also said I had to make up my mind what I really wanted, and then make sure I was doing it.'

'And what did you really want? To have your dysfunctional father living with you?' Charlie made a grab for the mug, but there were only a few drops left.

'No, but I'll come to that. What I realized was that I wanted, more than anything, to make a good childhood for Martha and Poppy. And I'm doing that.' She ran a finger through the puddle on the tabletop. 'But I also had to realize that I couldn't do that for everyone. Not you, not Mum. Just Martha and Poppy.'

73

'So I've got to do it for myself?' Charlie said, tipping the second bottle of wine and finding it empty.

'Yep. Though I can help you.' Eleanor managed to stand up this time, and took the bottle away. 'The obvious thing would be for you to take the boat. It'll give you a place to start from, and you can work out what the hell Mum was doing at the same time, OK?'

They were all there on the final morning, a rare moment of April sunshine at the end of a month of rain. It was a curiously formal gathering, not unlike the day of the funeral. In that curious stasis of waiting, they stretched out along the path, nobody saying very much. The new owner had been due three quarters of an hour earlier, and Charlie had already missed one bus. It felt wrong to leave, though. There was already too much unfinished business. Martha appeared to have taken on her grandfather as a project and was asking him questions about the garden. They made a slow progress along the lines of collapsed daffodil leaves and bedraggled bluebells. Hugo seemed to be making an effort in return, pointing up at the waxy flowers of the old magnolia tree with his newly acquired stick. The stick looked like a prop, a way of signalling that he was now old. Charlie couldn't work out how deliberate the ploy was. Beyond them, Poppy sat on the ground, scraping gravel into peaks and rivers. Jon stood next to her, but without any indication of noticing what she was doing. Eleanor was at the gate, her phone pressed to her ear.

Finally, a vintage Jag rolled up to the gate, the short and well-groomed man who'd bought the house making apologies about traffic and mishaps and unavoidable detours. He shook their hands in turn, talking enthusiastically about the design of the house, how he'd fallen in love with it on visits to the area. He was eager to tell them how carefully he'd look after it, standing with his head to one side to listen to Hugo's explanation of the suitability of the property for watching the stars with every appearance of fascination. It was impossible to tell if his enthusiasm was genuine or he just wanted to garner as much good karma as possible. He deserved some at least.

The next bus bumped past, and Charlie made her excuses. She didn't want to wait for another hour or get into complications about lifts in the car. And it was better to leave without things dragging out. She ran for the stop, Martha panting along beside her. The last thing she saw was her niece waving madly, reminding her of her promise that she could come and stay.

As the bus once more took its familiar turns, it occurred to Charlie that this might be her last journey down the road. She tried to picture herself in the future, coming back to show her children where she grew up. They would stand in a cluster as she pointed out landmarks and features: *There's the Post Office where I used to go and buy sweets. That's the corner where I fell off my bike and skinned my elbow, look, here's the scar.* For a moment, the image was close enough to touch. She was bending down with an arm around each small person's shoulder whilst, to one side, a man stood, his features indistinct. Was that how Max had imagined things? She couldn't blame him for that; it was how most people seemed to think, after all. As the musty velour of the seat filled her

75

nose, she allowed the passing landscape to blur. She didn't want to be a mother, that decision hadn't changed. For a brief moment she felt an equilibrium.

The marina wasn't that easy to find. She had a sketch map, passed over by Eleanor along with the keys, but it seemed to be fooling her, leading her up a hill when surely canals were downhill, in valleys. The street went on for as far as she could see, lined with nondescript houses opening straight onto the pavement. They had an air of disappointment, as if this was as good as it was ever going to get. Then, just when she was about to turn back towards the town centre for better directions, she was on a bridge and there, below her, was the canal.

She stared down, taking in the opaque brown water moving in sluggish ripples. The ripples began to rock a little faster, spreading out in suddenly organized lines towards the bank on either side. Seconds later, the nose of a boat appeared from under the bridge. Charlie watched the long, thin roof emerge, one flowerpot at a time. There was a rope coiled halfway along, and a figure was balanced on the side of the boat just next to it. A shout came from the back of the boat, still just hidden by the road. The man on the side lifted an arm in acknowledgement of whatever had been said, before reaching out and catching the rope up. With slow precision, the boat moved towards the bank, its whole length coming to the edge as the man watched the ground approach. Charlie studied him as he jumped off, walking along beside the boat as it slowed, and then digging in his heels and leaning back into the stretch of the rope.

76

The boat pivoted, moving inwards and coming to rest with a bump that Charlie couldn't hear, but seemed to feel from her viewpoint. She carried on watching as another man came into view. The sound of his mallet knocking a metal pin into the earth rang in her ears. She would be there soon, on a boat like that. She would be there, knowing nothing, able to do nothing. She wondered how her mother, quiet and withdrawn as she was with outsiders, had managed to come here by herself, to buy a boat, spend time on it. By the time she moved, the two men from the boat below had long gone, their voices disappearing towards the nearby pub.

The marina was on the side of the canal without a towpath, reached by an anonymous side road. Charlie was pointed in the right direction by the second passerby she stopped, and to begin with, she thought she'd been sent to the wrong place. Inside the gates, all she could see was the bulky red brick of an old mill, the chimney reaching high above. To one side were a small, prefabricated office and a couple of caravans. There was no one around. She walked towards the corner of the mill, where she knew the water was. There they were, boats filling a wide basin in serried ranks. The lines were separated by wide gangplanks, bobbing and shifting on their anchoring chains. Charlie took a couple of steps towards them. She didn't even know what colour her mother's boat was, all she had was a name. The weight of her ignorance transferred to the water as the walkway swayed under her weight.

A head appeared out of a hatch in the side of the nearest boat.

'Bob?' It was a woman, around her mother's age, though her hair was turbaned in an old towel which made it harder to judge. Her solid torso was half wrapped in a dressing gown.

'Oh, sorry, love.' She didn't seem surprised at the sight of a stranger or embarrassed about her undressed state. 'Thought you were the old man, can't have a cup of tea until he gets back with the milk.' She chuckled. 'And I can't start my day without a cuppa.'

Charlie smiled back automatically as the woman continued to talk.

'You might ask why my day's starting this late in the afternoon.' The woman gave another throaty laugh. 'You don't want to know, I tell you. Are you looking for young Danny-boy? I keep telling him, he's not supposed to hand out the key like that.'

'The gate wasn't locked.' Charlie lifted her hand to show her own key ring, complete with the cork ball to keep the keys afloat if she dropped them. That would be a great start. 'I'm here for a boat.' She came to a stop. Were canal boats supposed to be female, like the ones at sea? Her ignorance washed over her in a wave of embarrassment. 'It, she . . .' Neither sounded right, now. She went for the name instead, the word feeling clumsy in her mouth. 'It's a Norwegian name, Ski—?'

The woman interrupted her. 'You mean Britta's,' she said, leaning out to gesture towards the other boats. 'No one ever knows how to say it. Fourth along. She's not selling, is she?'

'No, but . . .' Charlie took a deep breath. She'd been picturing her here alone, her boat moored away from

78

the world, not in the centre of a kind of watery housing estate. Was that something else to find out, that on the water her mother had been some kind of chatty extrovert? 'It's my mum's boat, *was* my mum's boat.' She paused, deciding what to say. 'Mum died last month. I'm moving onto the boat for a while.'

'What, Britta?' The woman tilted her head to one side, eyes wide and one hand clapped to her chest. 'That's terrible, love, what happened?' Without waiting for an answer, she carried straight on. 'She did have that funny turn, but the last time I saw her she looked proper sparky. And she'd only just had the name painted!' She stopped herself with a visible effort, holding a hand out. 'I'm sorry, love, I do go on, but it brings it home, doesn't it? I'm Libby Rae, by the way. Libby Rae Jones.'

Charlie bent to give the hand an awkward shake. The day, the place, it was all building up around her, and she wanted to get to the end, the boat. She would ask more, later on. See how much Britta had shared about her sudden decision to buy the boat. Just now, all she wanted was a cup of tea. Which, she realized, she'd forgotten to bring milk for. Or teabags. Too late, she remembered thinking she'd have to find a shop of some sort on her way. Would there even be water on board? The noise of the gate sounded again, and they both looked round to see who was coming. It was a thin man with a neatly trimmed goatee. His face was lined and brown beneath the brim of his hat, which he wore unselfconsciously, as if it was part of him.

'Gate's not locked,' he said, giving Charlie a brief nod in passing. He had a glass bottle of milk in one hand

79

and a cork-float key ring like Charlie's in the other. Charlie felt for her own keys, saw herself coming in, leaving the gate as she'd found it. Not her fault, really.

'Oh, Bob, you'll never guess.' Libby Rae stood back from the hatch, tightening her dressing gown around her. 'This is Britta's girl, you know, from that boat with the difficult name.' She turned to Charlie with a confiding look. 'I've never been able to say it. Britta told me what it meant, but I've no head for foreign words.'

The man regarded her with a patient, resigned look. 'Did you want some tea or not?' he asked, holding the bottle out. Libby Rae shook her head, eyes wide.

'Bob, listen to me! Britta's dead!' she said, her tone admonishing him for talking about tea at a time like this. 'And this is her daughter, who's moving onto the boat. What did you say your name was, lovey?'

'Charlie,' Charlie said, automatically waiting for the standard response, the nod of the head, the pinched mouth of sympathy. Nothing came, though. The man stood there, his face oddly blank. It was just for a moment, and then Libby was talking again, saying something about how Bob and Britta had always been talking, how upset he was. She didn't seem to find anything wrong, and Charlie couldn't think and listen to her at the same time. Maybe it had just been a case of two silent people making a bond in the face of unending conversation. It did suggest that Britta had spent time here, though, making relationships, becoming part of society, hard as that was to imagine. She needed to get to the boat, find out what was there. And she was beginning to realize it wouldn't work to wait for a pause.

80

'I'd better get going,' she said at last, gesturing along the line of boats.

'Yes, of course.' Libby Rae was practically clucking. 'If there's anything to do with the boat, just ask my Bob. I remember when I first got here, didn't know my arse from my elbow, did I, love?' Bob's expression gave nothing away. 'Left the taps running, drained the power with my straighteners.' She gave a throaty laugh. 'It helps being here with hook-up for leccy and water handy. And for work, of course. We don't get out as much as Bob'd like, but it's a balance, isn't it?' Charlie took advantage of a pause for breath to move away. Libby Rae's exclamations were still audible when she finally reached the boat.

Skíðblaðnir, the boat of the gods. It had been written on the documents that had been with the bank statement. Charlie had Googled how to pronounce it, though the sound still felt strange to say. *Skithblathnir*. Her mother hadn't spoken Norwegian to them, had never used casual terms from her native language, so the choice of name must be significant. Charlie remembered what she'd read, about the boat that had been a gift to the god Freyr. It would always receive a fair wind and could be folded like a handkerchief when not needed. Which of these attributes was her mother hoping for? They both sounded like escape. The name was painted in yellow on the glossy blue of the boat, the letters curving above a porthole. Charlie stroked a finger along the curling lines, feeling the lumps and contours of whatever name had been painted over. What had it been? Someone, somewhere, had owned the boat before. She could track them down, find out the details of the sale. Did it matter, though? The boat felt secretive, sealed. Much like its owner.

There was a kind of cover over the front deck, the way in complicated by a reluctant zip. It would be so stupid to slip before she'd even got a foot on board. Finally, it gave way and she clambered over to the shrouded space. Under her feet, the boat rocked in greeting. Greeting or irritation. There was a squat door, the lock stiff. As she wrestled, it felt as if the boat was waiting, judging.

The inside was dim, the curtains drawn but thin enough to let some light through. Taking in a breath of air that was both cool and stuffy, Charlie went slowly down the two steps from the front deck and the boat shifted under her feet. It was as if it was feeling her weight, considering its response, and then rising to meet her. She had the odd sense that she'd experienced it before, that someone had even said those words to describe the sensation. But when? Déjà vu or a line from a book. She tucked the thought away and looked around her.

She was standing in a living area, with wood-panelled walls painted a soft blue. As her eyes adjusted, she could tell that the curtains were made from a cheerful flower-patterned fabric. A small wood-burning stove stood four-square beside an armchair covered in worn cretonne. Charlie crossed the floor, sinking down into the sagging cushions. She didn't recognize it. It had the feel of being inherited, a loved item passed down when houses were downsized, or lives wound up. Charlie thought of the house in Derbyshire, with its stretches of polished wooden floors, each room defined by rigidly clean lines and a lack of clutter. Here, the spaces on the walls were filled with oddments: prints, a quotation, a chain of small hearts. She tried to picture her mother here, sitting in the chair and looking around her. Had she bought the boat with everything in place, drawn in by an atmosphere missing in her own life? Or had she put it together, piece by careful piece? Impossible to tell. Impossible to imagine her doing any of it, in secret and with so little time to use.

On the far side of the wood-burner was a low bookcase, the shelves crammed with colourful spines. Charlie went over to it, bending to read the titles. Poetry. Novels, by writers whose names she couldn't place. She slid one out. *Winner of the 2003 Man Booker Prize*. Were these normal choices for her mother to have read? If she was honest, she couldn't remember seeing her mother read anything in particular. Was that something else she'd hidden, or a part of her new, secret life? Slowly, Charlie ran a finger along the shelf until she came to a little stack of worn paperbacks which brought her up short.

The narrow spines were worn, much more so than the other books, some peeling off in curled strips. *Mrs Pepperpot*, *Pippi Longstocking*, *Finn Family Moomintroll*. Charlie sank to the floor, easing out a faded volume and turning it to see the cover. Six blonde-headed children climbed out of a window into the branches of a tree. The background was a creased burnt orange, the little puffin standing on guard in the top left corner. *All About the Bullerby Children*. All Scandinavian authors. Her mother's childhood books, preserved until she had

83

a place of her own? But why weren't they in Norwegian if that was the case? She turned back to the book. The title was familiar for some reason, though she couldn't remember having seen the book before, not any of them in fact. She opened it to the first page carefully, aware of the cracking sound of dried glue.

My name is Lisa, she read. *I'm a girl. Well, you can tell that from the name, of course.* An image popped up in Charlie's mind. She is in bed, tucked up next to Eleanor. It's not their bedroom at home, but a small, square room with busy wallpaper. She is trying to work out what everything is, but it's getting quite dark so she keeps losing count of the trellises and leaves and flowers and birds. It's cold as well, but that's all right because they're wrapped in a sort of quilt which is shiny and smells funny, like when her jumper fell down the back of the washing machine when it was wet. The quilt was cold to start with too, but now it feels like a snuggly caterpillar. Mummy says it's an eye-der-down. Charlie says the word out loud, and Eleanor pokes her and tells her to shut up, because she wants to hear the story. The picture was there one minute, as immediate as if it had happened yesterday, and then it was gone. Charlie turned another page, reading on. *Britta is nine and Anna is the same age as me. I like them both just the same. Well, perhaps I like Anna a tiny, tiny bit more.* Already the details of the moment were fading. She was sure she'd never seen the book before, and she would have remembered, wouldn't she, with one of the characters having her mother's name? Maybe she was making it up. She had no memory, after all, of when this had taken place, where

84

they might have been. And there was just something . . . odd about it. She screwed her eyes up, trying to pin it down, and a tiny voice in her head spoke. *It wasn't Mummy reading, stupid.*

The sound of the words stayed with her as she explored the rest of the boat. Immediately beyond the living room, with a space between them rather than a door, she found the kitchen. Or was it called a galley, if it was on a boat? Charlie made a mental note to check with her neighbours at some point. A gas cooker and small microwave oven sat on one side, the sink opposite. There was a window over the sink, presently looking out onto the side of another moored boat, and across from that two doors which clearly opened out to a side hatch, like the one Libby had been looking out from. Directly on from this was a narrow corridor, and the rest of the dividing wall was made to look like a dresser, with waist-high cupboards and painted shelves above. Hooks held mugs swinging in a row, all smooth, creamy white with phrases stamped in blue and pink lettering. The one nearest said *blithering idiot*. She remembered her mother finding amusement in odd English phrases, so maybe these had been her own purchases. Charlie read the others: *fine specimen*, *rare breed*, *secret agent*. *Bluestocking* sat next to the washing-up bowl, a ring of dried tea in its base. One mug. So could she assume that Britta had been here by herself? It hadn't occurred to her or Eleanor that the boat might involve a third party, somehow.

One of the cupboard doors was painted with blackboard paint, the remains of the last words to be chalked

85

on it smeared and unreadable. Charlie squatted down, trying to make them out. Was it Britta's writing, or something left by the previous owners? It was impossible to tell. The marks were shadows, smeared curves. She couldn't even see what language the words were in, or if they were in fact letters at all.

Beyond the kitchen was a bedroom space. It couldn't be called a bedroom, she thought, because it didn't have a fourth wall. The bed comprised a wide platform built against the wall and a cupboard underneath fronted with mellow, salvaged wooden doors. The mattress was soft and covered with a delicate patchwork quilt, the pillow smooth. It didn't look as if it had ever been slept in. Charlie touched the quilt, stroking one finger around a square made up of pinwheeling flowers. There was nothing here, no personal possessions, no nightwear. Of course, if Britta was just coming over for the odd afternoon, she wouldn't have needed much. Charlie eased open the cupboard doors. Nothing, a wide empty space. She felt reluctant to leave it, though. Was that because she could feel her mother here? More than in the living room, even with the books.

Next came a bathroom, this time with a door blocking the corridor to make the little room the whole width of the boat. There was a short bath, a little sink which looked as if it had come from salvage, along with its old-fashioned upright taps. The porcelain was cobwebbed with hairline cracks. On the surround was a pump bottle of soap and some matching hand cream. Charlie squeezed a little onto her palm. Lavender. It wasn't a smell she associated with Britta.

Another door opened into a back bedroom, this one with the air of uninhabited space. Nothing had been added, no decorative touches to soften the edges. The floor-space narrowed as it reached the back of the boat, and the bed had been built to take the shape, with one side straight, the other tucking into the slope of the wall. It gave it the look of a coffin. Charlie shivered and retreated to the friendliness of the patchwork quilt.

This time, she kicked off her shoes and hoisted herself up onto the bed. The pillow rested alongside a small porthole, its glass shrouded by a square of cloth patterned with small, flying birds. The blind was held on by a ring at each corner, and Charlie unhooked the top one nearest to her so that she could look outside. And there, tucked into the porthole's wooden surround, was a photograph.

Charlie eased it out, her heart thumping. A black and white square with a thick white border, the figures on it small enough that she had to hold it up to the light to see them properly. Two women sat on the front of a boat. The older of the two was wearing work dungarees, and her hair was cropped closely to her head. Even in this tiny print, Charlie could tell that she had grease worn into the creases of her hands, that the dark shade of her skin was as much oil as sunburn. The other was really just a girl, wearing wide-legged shorts and a hand-knitted jumper. She had her face held at the same angle as her companion, both of them tilted towards whoever was taking the picture, both of them squinting against the sun. Britta.

Charlie knew it straight away. It was the way she was

87

sitting, the curve of her hair where it sprang away from her forehead. She was happy here, though, radiating an unreserved delight in her surroundings, in her company. Charlie held the photograph closer, staring at that small, happy face. How old would she have been? Hard to tell, and not just because of the size of the photo. It reminded Charlie of seeing other post-war images, with girls who stayed as children for a long time, before suddenly taking on the stiff perms and middle-aged clothes of adults. The Britta here couldn't be more than sixteen. That couldn't be right, though. Britta hadn't been in England when she was that age. Little as she knew about her mother's background, one or two facts had made it through. Britta had arrived in England well into the sixties, when she was already out of her teens. *I didn't have the swinging time,* she'd said once, when Charlie was doing a history project at school. *It wasn't there in my part of London. I had a job, I became married, and then I had your sister. There was no time for other things.* Maybe this had been taken in Norway, then? Could the other woman be a sibling, perhaps, or an aunt?

There was something about the background, though, that made Charlie feel sure this was England. She tilted it further towards the light, trying to make out the details of the boat. There was the beginning of the name just visible, at least she thought that was what it was. Not painted on the side like her boat, or most of the others she'd seen, but on its own little plate, in raised metal letters. Only the end of it was showing, but Charlie could work out 'EMOT'. That wasn't much use. It was an old boat, she could see that, with a boatman's cabin

88

behind the two women and side doors open to show the corner of a proper old engine. She could see a similar boat here, just across from her porthole. The engine was central, with a room to itself rather than being tucked away under the back deck like the others. It was running, and she could feel the throbs of sound almost more than she could hear them. A figure crossed in front of it and disappeared, and moments later the throbbing stopped. Charlie went back to the photograph.

Further away, down the portion of towpath just visible to the left of the scene, was a waymarker, the distances painted in black letters on a white background. Charlie screwed up her eyes, trying to bring the letters of the place names into focus. If she could work out where the photo had been taken, maybe she could find out what the boat was called. There must be people who'd know, enthusiasts who could recognize an old working boat from this sort of visible portion. The canal equivalent of a trainspotter. The marker was too small, though, the letters too far away. Perhaps with a magnifying glass ... Then she had another thought and turned the picture over. There was something in the corner, a tiny mark. *With M on boat, 1964.* No clue as to the place. But still, 'M'. It might narrow things down a bit, if she could identify the boat.

89

Eight

Charlie could hear the birds singing from the trees on the far side of the canal. She had to be early to catch it, not the dawn chorus but a secondary burst of joy after sunrise was established but before the day got going properly. Charlie could appreciate the sentiment. As she had every morning since she'd arrived, she'd let the hatch doors fall out, one to each side, so that she could drink her morning tea looking out at the canal and enjoy the sense that her legs were underwater. There she was, standing in her dry space, whilst outside the water swayed at about thigh level. As he did every morning, the resident swan glided up to take a piece of bread from her fingers. If she was late, he'd taken to knocking on the side of the boat, his beak imperious, demanding. Sometimes she could hear voices coming from the other boats, the sound of engines starting up, though she couldn't see anything of them from where she stood. This morning, a yellow and green boat was going along the main channel of the canal. The name was painted halfway down, *Dolly Hockeysticks*, though the elderly couple on the back deck didn't look as if they played much competitive sport. Charlie lifted a hand to acknowledge them, at the same time feeling the disturbed water reach her, sending *Skíðblaðnir* into a slow jiggle of response.

The first days had gone by as if she was actually underwater rather than sitting on top of it. She'd never have managed if it hadn't been for Libby Rae. There were so many things to learn. Finding out about water and how the toilet worked. Remembering to run the engine when the power got too low. Where to get fuel. When the bus went past to get into the town. Libby Rae stopped to talk at any opportunity, unleashing an endless stream of information as she stood at her side hatch, or on the jetty on her way back from work. A lot of it was the minutiae of her day: how long the bus took getting to work, the comments made by the marina manager when she went to empty her rubbish into the communal bin. There was no need for Charlie to dig for details about Britta, either. Libby brought her up constantly, the expressions of shock still threaded through the words but mixed with hints of the everyday. A woman who was friendly but not one to chat. Who knew her way around a boat without any help, though she'd only been for a couple of short trips down the canal.

'I wondered if she'd been out,' Charlie said. They were sitting on the back deck of Libby's boat, making the most of some late afternoon sun. May had arrived with blue skies and temperatures high enough to trigger headlines, though rain was forecast for the week ahead. Libby had caught her as she trudged back from the bus stop, weighed down with the first really substantial shop she'd done since arriving. Their back deck was big enough for a couple of deck-chairs, and it was

91

nice to sit there with a cold beer, feeling the water sway beneath. It was good timing as well. Charlie had decided to ask her neighbour about the photograph, see if she could throw any light on the location, or even the boat.

'Oh yes.' Libby had her eyes closed and her skirt pulled up, the skin on her legs already slightly red. 'She said she hadn't been on a boat for a bit, but you could see she knew what she was doing. And of course, she'd been there from the start, really.'

'From the start?' For a moment, Charlie thought she meant from a baby, that her mother had grown up on a boat. How would she not have mentioned that?

'The revival, love, when they were fighting to keep the water open. She had a hand in all that.' Libby held her beer bottle against her cheek. 'Sweltering, isn't it? Not that I'm complaining. We'll have enough of the other before we're done.' She caught sight of Charlie's expression. 'Did she never mention it?'

'Not really.' Charlie was imagining her mother as an activist. 'I was going to ask you something, actually. I found a photo of her on an old boat, when she was young. I was wondering if I could find out where it might have been taken.'

'You can try, love, but I don't know if I'll be much help.' Libby closed her eyes. 'I'm an incomer like you, my love. It's Bob you want.' She turned her head. 'You pop your shopping on board and bring it along. I'm expecting him any minute.'

Bob took the little picture and held it in close. 'Hard to tell, that.'

92

'You need your glasses,' Libby told him, coming up to his shoulder to have another look herself. 'Here, use mine.' She'd not been able to help, beyond an exclamation over the young Britta, confirming Charlie's identification, but she was already invested in tracking down the boat, and the identity of the other woman. 'Well, what do you think?'

Bob settled Libby's sparkly frames on his nose, tilting his head to get the right spot. Charlie watched his face, holding her breath with the suspense. His expression gave nothing away, and he said nothing, even as he took the glasses off and held the photo back out to Charlie.

'Well?' Libby grabbed Charlie's hand so that she could look at the picture again. 'I can't get over how young she is. Does the other one look familiar, love?' She turned back to Charlie. 'Bob knew a lot of the old ones. His dad had a boat back in the sixties, went on all those festivals and what have you. The photos he had – should have been in the museum.'

'Could be Margareta, that.' Bob spoke quietly, but he had their attention straight away.

Charlie waited for him to say more, but he just stood there, his eyes fixed on the figures. Libby wasn't so patient.

'And who's Margareta?' She gave Charlie a nudge. 'Old girlfriend?'

Bob didn't react to Libby's joking tone. He rarely did, and Charlie had thought before that he must tune out most of Libby's chatter. 'She was one of the volunteers, down Sneasham way. That's the boat she lived on, old working one. *Guillemot.*'

Charlie looked again at the picture, the letters visible

on the side of the boat now part of a whole name. 'I don't suppose she'd still be there?'

Bob gave a slow shake of his head. 'I've not seen *Guillemot* since, I dunno, sometime in the eighties. And I think it was already sold on then. Lost track of Margareta a long time ago.'

'And she'd be a fair age now.' Libby was back at Charlie's shoulder. 'You should head down that way and ask around.'

'What, take the boat?' Charlie blinked. The thought of going anywhere on the canal hadn't occurred to her before. Other people might move about, her mother even, but she could never learn how to do it. She glanced up, half expecting to see them both doubled up at the joke, but neither of them seemed to find the thought of her moving sixty feet of steel down a waterway no wider than a single-track lane funny. Instead, Libby was nodding.

'Bob'll come along tomorrow and get you started,' she said. 'If he can teach me how to do it, you'll have no problem. And maybe he'll let on more about this,' she tapped the photo, 'whilst he's at it.'

Nine

Bob turned up early the next morning, before she'd even got dressed.

'Best to get on,' he said, when she looked out from the side hatch in answer to his knock. No preamble but also no sense of impatience. He nodded towards the back of the boat, indicating he'd wait there for her to open up. As she tugged on some clothes, not bothering to wash her face, she wondered if she should ask him more about Margareta. She had a feeling he might have more to say without Libby there. But, as they stood in the dark oiliness of the engine room, she couldn't think where to start. If he wanted to say anything, he'd start the conversation himself.

They went through oil checks, coolant, tightening something called a stern gland so that the canal wouldn't leak in along the propshaft. The words buzzed in Charlie's head, unfamiliar, important. The fuel tank was more than half full but she was running low on water. Bob didn't stop to explain what she needed to do about this, instead rummaging in a side locker, pulling out a metal winch arm 'for the locks' and a straight handle, which he eased onto the truncated curve of the tiller. Charlie trotted after him, trying to keep a list in her head of what she needed to do, wishing she'd thought of having pen and paper to hand.

'Don't worry,' Bob said, catching the expression on her face. 'You'll get it all. Second nature after a couple of times.' He scanned the space, looking for something else. 'There should be something for holding the tiller arm in,' he said, holding his hands apart to give an idea of the size. 'Brass, probably, spike to go through the holes.'

Charlie remembered seeing something on a shelf inside and ducked back through to find it. There it was, next to the box of teabags, a little figure in the shape of a troll. He was squatting on top of an eight-inch spike and looking up with a grimace, the fingers of one tiny hand spread across his mouth and chin. Bob got her to line up the holes of the tiller arm, sliding the spike in to join the two parts together. The face leered up at her, daring her to put a foot wrong. When Bob turned away, she swivelled the troll round so it was facing out, looking back down the canal. She didn't want it watching her make a fool of herself.

Following his quiet instructions, she started the engine. To her slight horror, Bob left her standing at the tiller whilst he went back onto the jetty and pushed off. The breeze was freshening and blew into her face as she stood on the small back deck, tiller arm grasped in her hand. Bob was too far away, more than halfway down the boat. He'd left it too late to jump back on board, would leave her floating helpless midstream. At the last minute he shifted, timing the move perfectly to step onto the gunnel. With relaxed ease, he cross-stepped

96

along, one hand on the rail, until he was back by the deck. Not on the deck, not coming to take over. *Skíðblaðnir* was at an angle across the canal, her nose heading for the far bank.

'OK, ease the tiller across,' he said at last, leaning on the side with every appearance of trust in her ability. Charlie had a moment of blankness. They'd been through this. Which way was she supposed to go? Bob waited, giving her time to work it out. What was it he'd said? Push the tiller in the opposite direction to the way you wanted the nose to point. She made a tentative move to the right. 'Bit more throttle.' Bob's voice was calm, unconcerned. He took it for granted she could do this, and the thought gave her some confidence. 'And you can go a bit further, that's right. Now bring it back to centre.' The boat seemed to swivel, smoothly shifting so that she was pointing back down the middle of the cut.

Charlie let her breath out, but still kept the tiller in a tight, sweaty clutch. They had a straight section ahead, which was a relief, but within moments *Skíðblaðnir* was heading again towards the bank.

'Little bit the other way,' came Bob's voice. 'Touch of throttle, not too much.' She heaved over, pushing at the throttle to speed up, and watched in dismay as they swung right over to the other side. Bob stepped up and took hold of the tiller, easing at the arm, manipulating the speed. Within seconds, they were back on a straight course.

'Sorry,' Charlie said, staying back to let Bob carry on. 'What did I do wrong?'

He gave her a grin, gesturing for her to take back

control. 'Everyone does it to start off,' he said, stepping out to the edge and leaning on the roof while he rolled a cigarette. 'Steers too much, sends the boat off. You want to push over to start the move then draw her back in. It's not like a car.' He lit a match, pausing for thought. 'Helps if you don't drive.'

'Why's that?' Charlie kept her gaze fixed ahead, trying out tiny moves with the steering for practice, watching intently as the boat's nose wiggled. She was starting to feel what he meant.

'Car drivers, they want to steer in the direction they want to go. And they think they can control it, keep a smooth curve. And you've got brakes. Boating's different, you have to work with the boat, work with the water. You're picking it up quicker than most.' And with that, he settled into a contemplative silence, his eyes also turned to the front of the boat but, she felt, taking in more than the almost imperceptible movement of the passing trees. He had to put out an arm occasionally, helping her make a turn as the canal curved in a wide swoop, but Charlie felt him most as a reassuring presence, unflappable and relaxed. It made the process of learning almost easy.

The decision to take control of the boat tipped other decisions into being. That night, she called Max. They were awkward, two voices in mid-air, not quite able to meet. Though that was what they needed to do, to meet.

'What is there to say, Charlie?' He sounded different somehow. Almost impatient, maybe a little resigned. There were things that hadn't been decided before, about the house, about Bella. He'd been adamant it was the best course; *keep things neutral*, his words had been. *You don't know how things'll be once you get this out of your system.* He'd never really understood what she was trying to do, though he really had tried. *Why does it have to be so sudden? Let's get the wedding out of the way and make proper plans. We can go together, take sabbaticals.* She'd tried to explain, about the suffocating panic she could feel all the time, how it rose up at the thought of putting things off, about getting married, about the ever-present but no longer discussed question of children. If he'd given up on any idea of their picking up the threads, it would make this conversation easier anyway.

'We need to sort out what's happening to the house, for a start. And I'd like to have Bella back.' There, the words were out there. His reply was clipped, but it wasn't the nicest thing to be dealing with after all. Following a pause for what felt like ostentatious diary-checking, he suggested a date. She agreed, hanging up with the uncomfortable sense that she'd made some kind of faux pas.

It was Bob's idea for her to make the trip up the canal, brushing away her objections with ease. They were on the back deck, leaning against the roof, having just returned from filling the water tank. He'd let her do it without stepping in, even when she took three tries to get *Skíðblaðnir* lined up with the water-point tap.

'You've got a week,' he was saying, comfortably uninterested in what her meeting might be. 'Bugsworth's a two-day trip, no locks, couple of bridges to open. And it'll

99

be quiet this time of year.' He looked up at the sky, eyes squinting into the light. 'Your mother had some *Canal Companions*. Hop down and get the one for the Cheshire Ring, and we'll have it sorted.'

It was the first time he'd mentioned Britta directly, and he did it with his face turned away, whether out of consideration or an unwillingness to get involved in emotional talk, she couldn't tell. She knew better than to invite him in. After the first teaching session, she'd asked if he wanted some tea, beckoned to the door. *Keep your boat to yourself, lass,* he'd responded, with the same gesture of turning away as he was using now. *I'll have mine out here.*

She knew the books he meant, the pile of small, brightly coloured guides on the top of the bookshelf. There were seven or eight of them there, each with a cover in the style of traditional canal boat decorative art. She'd leafed through a couple, a little bit enchanted by the vivid artwork and gentle explanations. It was like stepping into a child's picture book, just one way to go and nothing complex waiting around the corner, each page a snapshot of a cosy, manageable world. Maybe that was exactly what she needed. She shuffled through to find the right volume before heading back outside.

Now she was actually on the way, part of the picture. The canal was a dark green lane unrolling in front of her, the boat's nose pushing the water aside in exploration. First, they were in a tunnel of overhanging trees, the water reflecting the dark mosaic of the leaves. The view down into the valley briefly opened up, only to disappear again behind a stretch of red-brick apartments.

100

Some of the balconies had chairs set to face the water, but there was no one out to watch the boats go by. On her other side, the ground fell away in ridges, down to open fields dotted with sheep.

Charlie tucked the tiller under her arm. She was probably just imagining it, but at that moment she could feel that *Skíðblaðnir* was happy to be working with her. Behind her, the troll watched over everything, the small, judgemental deity of the boat. She still had him turned to look behind, so she didn't have to feel him watching her, but today even he seemed less distrustful of her ability. She began to see individual moments, the panic of being in charge easing off just enough. The lone stump of a tree topping the rise of the bank, solid and defiant in its remains. The curving swoop of an improbably beautiful bridge. (*Snake bridge*, Bob's voice said to her. *Speciality of the Macclesfield canal.*)

Another boat was coming up. Charlie swivelled round, wondering if Bob was still in view. But he was long gone now, the twenty minutes or so of sailing taking her into a different dimension. He'd told her what to do, though. Her nerves began to settle, and she steered towards the right-hand side. The other boat was coming up quite fast and didn't seem to be moving over. Charlie reached for the throttle. It wouldn't hurt to slow down, even if this was quite normal. But had she remembered it right? What did Bob say? *Always pass on the right, the opposite of being in a car.* So she was doing it properly. *Skíðblaðnir* was almost at a standstill now, which made steering near impossible. Was this boat just going to stay in the middle and bash into her? She

101

could see the man on the back deck now, making some kind of gesture. She edged forwards. The breeze was catching her side-on, making the boat's nose drift across on a diagonal, at risk of colliding with the oncoming boat. Her body thought before her brain did, leaning into the rudder and bringing the boat round. She felt the resistance of the water and pushed against it as the boat began to turn. Not too much, ease it back.

'You on your own, love?' The other boater's voice broke into her thought processes. He was right next to her, then slipping past. She'd just managed to avoid contact. 'You want to make sure you keep over more.'

He was gone before she could respond, and her reply was lost in the combined engine noise. Then there was a bump and a scrape as she hit the far side, and she had to put her annoyance aside. Of course, there were people watching her now, a couple with a dog and an old boy clearly enjoying her struggles. She closed them all out, correcting her line, moving back into the middle of the waterway. It was bound to happen, she told herself. She just had to carry on moving, ignore the stares. She met a couple more boats before she stopped for lunch, both times each of them gliding to the right like a move in a well-choreographed dance. There was nobody on the towpath watching then, of course.

The whole thing was harder than she expected. Everyone else seemed to manage with no effort. The man – and it was almost always a man – would be standing on the back deck as if the boat was steering itself with just the slightest help from the tiller. *Skíðblaðnir* wouldn't keep to a line for more than a second. Bob had explained about over-steering, but whatever she tried, it didn't seem to work for long. And she couldn't let her concentration slip for a moment. She'd be going along with no trouble, move the tiller the tiniest bit and end up zigzagging from one side to the other, each adjustment making the turns worse until she couldn't be sure that she even knew what to do. At one point she got stuck on the offside, overhanging branches jabbing at her face as she did everything she could think of to get out into the channel again. She could get the bow away from the bank, but as soon as she tried to straighten, some kind of magnetic attraction drew the boat back in. By the time she got free, she was shaking with the exertion and wondering if it was worth carrying on.

A quiet lunch with views over the hills made her feel better. Libby had packed her some sandwiches (*You won't be wanting the effort of making your own, I can tell you!*) and knowing someone else had also found it hard helped. She studied the map as she ate, counting out the distance left. It showed the route in time, broken up into hours rather than miles. Less than six, which would bring her into Bugsworth Basin at the right time for tea. There was a pub there as well. She traced the blue line over the pages. A couple of bridges to open and a junction to watch out for. That was manageable, surely.

She'd almost changed her mind again a couple of hours on, thinking she might stop overnight when she reached the swing bridge, but another boat had just come through and they held it open for her, waving cheerfully as she went by. Then she fell into a state of near-stupor. It seemed easier to keep on going than

103

decide where to stop. The landmarks on the map ticked by: roads, pubs, a mill redeveloped into shops and craft studios. Libby had also made her take biscuits, and she ate them automatically, hardly tasting them other than to register sugar and the movement of her mouth. She began to feel stubborn, competitive. There was an end goal to reach and she was going to get there.

And then she missed the turning. Not the Marple Junction – that had been flashing in her head all day, a warning light to go right when the moment came. Knowing she'd done that made her relax, if that was the right word after spending so many hours standing and steering and making a hundred decisions about speed and direction. Bob would be proud of her. And either the way was easier here, or *Skíðblaðnir* was working with her, because everything was going smoothly. The biscuits were gone, and she was starting to fantasize about dinner. Something hot and spicy, topped with a bubbling layer of cheese and served with potato wedges. Or a pie, the pastry golden and crumbly and sitting on top of something rich and covered in gravy. And she was going to have wine. And dessert. A boat was coming towards her, not fast but with a steady purpose. She moved to the right automatically, *Skíðblaðnir* responding like a well-trained dance partner. As Charlie waved to the jolly couple on the other boat, she realized that the arm of the Bugsworth Basin was slipping past and out of reach.

104

Ten

It was a beautiful moment, with the golden light of the late afternoon sun flooding past her to pick out the warm tones of a curving stone wall. Charlie had just enough time to register the row of boats moored beyond a metal footbridge. They were like broad dashes of colour, red and yellow and lime, marking a line between the rich greens of the surrounding trees and the flat, smooth water of the canal. The scene was perfect, tranquil, and beyond her reach. For a second, she considered reversing. She wasn't far past, it wouldn't take long. Bob had shown her what to do, but if steering forwards was sometimes a challenge, going backwards brought in a whole new level of difficulty. By the time she'd thought about it, she was too far away.

Exhaustion flooded her limbs, making it feel as if her grasp on the tiller was the only thing holding her up. She went on, because she couldn't think what else to do. A line of boats moored to her left, leaving no place for her to stop. The low, white sprawl of a supermarket hiding behind a belt of trees. The sun had gone below the foliage, the shadows deepening the opaque brown tint of the water, light patterning through the leaves like lace on the surface. A pair of children ran by, shouting and waving sticks, a dog bounding at their heels. A road to the right, buildings ahead. And then the end.

The map showed this as another basin, roughly triangular. Charlie let the engine idle as she looked from the page to the scene ahead. There was clearly no space to moor, boats crammed along the outside edge in every spot. A winding hole was marked, so presumably she could turn. The thought made her want to cry. It wasn't that she didn't know she'd have to do it. A trip going out and then back would necessarily involve turning around. Canals didn't have turntables, like the friendly little piece on Poppy's wooden railway set. That would be too easy. Bob had shown her how to do it, stick the bow in the gap and keep the tiller hard round, to force the stern to swing. It was so simple, so logical. She'd even done one, with Bob at her shoulder telling her where to put things, when to make the engine work. This was different. She wouldn't mind so much if no one was watching, but the widened spot she'd be using was right next to a car park. Already there were people standing on the towpath, sunning themselves in the mellow light and waiting for boaters to make idiots of themselves. She didn't have a choice.

It was even worse than she'd anticipated. A breeze had picked up, but surely not enough to keep the boat from turning in this way. It didn't matter how hard she made the engine work; water was churning at the back of the boat but making very little difference at all to her position. In a pause, as she eased the throttle off to reconsider what she was doing, one of the children's voices rang out.

'What's she doing, Daddy?'

The parent's voice replying was too low to hear, but she could feel the ripple of laughter that went around the spectators. She was going to be here for ever, in this adorable, picturesque little canal place, polluting the loveliness with diesel fumes and engine noise until someone came and towed her away. Why the hell was she doing this anyway?

A different voice sounded, from the bank behind her. 'If you back out a bit and go beyond the turning place, you can let the back of the boat go in. Then the breeze'll push you round.'

She didn't stop to see who was talking, but followed the instructions with a relief almost as great as she'd felt the day she realized she didn't want to be a lawyer any more. As if she'd been hypnotized, *Skíðblaðnir* did exactly what she was told. Charlie stood on the deck, watching as the bow made a perfect arc, coming to a halt with the lightest of bumps against the side of the canal.

She'd been so focused on what was happening that she'd actually forgotten everyone watching. The round of applause breaking out from the spectators made her turn in such a hurry that she almost tripped over the mooring ropes coiled at her feet. Wishing she could disappear, she gave a half-curtsey of acknowledgement.

'Well done, you did it!'

She straightened up, recognizing the helpful man's voice. He felt like the closest thing she had to an old friend just then.

'Thank you so much. I honestly didn't know what else to do.'

107

'No worries. It's happened to most of us at some point.' He held out a hand and she wondered what he meant. The mooring rope? He must be offering to help tie up. But where? There were no empty gaps to use, and she couldn't moor on this side anyway.

'I think I'm going to have to move straight on.' She'd already picked up the rope and held the tangled mass uncertainly.

He laughed and made a grab for it. 'You can stop for a bit, no one's going to mind that.'

'Well, if you're sure.' She still didn't feel quite certain, but let him take the rope and shake it loose before looping it round a nearby bollard. 'I suppose they wouldn't have one of those if they didn't want you to tie up.' She paused, watching him secure the end. He was older than her, maybe forty, with a tanned face and greying hair slicked back with sweat. His running shorts and trainers showed what he'd been doing before stopping to rescue her. What *was* the etiquette for people saving you from eternal embarrassment? A cup of tea? It would have to do, she didn't have anything stronger on board. 'I was just going to put the kettle on if you'd like some tea?'

'No, you're all right.' He gave the rope a final tug and stayed squatting next to it, his gaze fixed on the boat, an expression on his face she couldn't decipher. Then he gave his head a shake and stood up. 'Where have you come from?'

'Macclesfield.' So far away, but she could probably get there in about half an hour by car. 'It's my first solo trip. First trip of any kind by boat, actually.'

He pulled the corners of his mouth down, nodding

his head in appreciation. 'Pretty good going. Are you living aboard?'

There was a definite sense of relief at being a newbie rather than inept. 'For the time being. I don't really know long-term. Maybe.' She waved towards the line of boats moored on the far side of the basin. 'Do you live here?'

'No, afraid not.' He stood up, running a hand over his scalp. 'I used to do some boating but, you know, things get in the way. I just run past them now, making plans.' They both laughed. In the middle of it, Charlie's laugh turned into a huge yawn. 'Look, I'd better not keep you up. You'll be needing to eat after your epic day.'

'No, I'm sorry.' She yawned again. 'It's just that I need to get back to Bugsworth Basin. I was supposed to stop there but—' She squeezed her eyes shut in what was now bemused acceptance, nothing like as soul-destroying as it had been before. It was almost funny, in fact. 'I was trying to keep out of the way of another boat and went straight past the turning.' She opened her eyes again, to find him keeping a smile back. 'No, don't! I'm so not looking forward to going all the way back. Is boating always this exhausting?'

'It gets easier.' He straightened his face, a thoughtful expression replacing the amusement. He seemed to be turning something over in his mind. 'Look, you're going to want to get sorted before dark. I've got to get back that direction anyway, so how about I come with you, take over a bit of the steering?' He contradicted himself straight away, stepping back with his hands out in front of him. 'No, forget I said it. That's probably the last thing you want.'

'Are you kidding? That sounds brilliant. As long as you really don't mind?' The thought of handing over even a bit of responsibility made Charlie's body sag in relief. She held out a hand. 'I'm Charlie, by the way.'

'Dave.' His shake was firm. 'Seriously, you'd be doing me a favour.' He bent to unwind the rope again, coiling it with practised movements before placing it on the roof. 'You go and make that cup of tea, and I'll make a start.'

Down in the kitchen, Charlie began to have doubts. Was it really a good idea to invite a complete stranger on board? She remembered Bob's strictures. But it wasn't as though he was coming inside. In fact, he'd deliberately not tried to bother her. Under her feet, the floor vibrated as the engine started up. It was unsettling, to be inside when *Skíðblaðnir* was getting ready to move. As she waited for the kettle to come to the boil she dialled Eleanor's number. She'd tell her where she was and get her to call back in an hour to check on her.

'El? Listen,' she said when her sister answered. 'I'm out on the boat and someone's giving me a hand with the last bit of the route.' She waited for the flood of questions, the endless dictates to think what she was doing and interrogation about who this someone was.

'Charlie? Look, I'm a bit busy just now. Can you talk to Martha?'

'Yes, sure.' There was a fumble at the other end as the phone was handed over.

'Aunty Charlie?' Martha's voice was breathless, and the words tumbled out. 'Guess what, Daddy gave me his old phone!' She barely waited for Charlie to make the appropriate noises in response. 'Can I have your

110

number? So you can text me? Mum says I can see where you're going on a map. I'm going to put pins in it, so we know where you are!'

They were all assuming she was going to go somewhere then, so she'd better start planning something proper. And Martha's enthusiasm made her smile. 'OK, your mum has the number. You can put Whaley Bridge as the first stop.' The kettle began to whistle. 'Look, tell your mum I'll call her back in a bit.'

The tea was lapping the edges of the mugs as she carried them up the back steps. Dave was standing at the tiller as if he'd always been there, and Charlie's doubts began to dissipate.

'She really likes you,' she commented, as she passed one mug over and settled down thankfully with her back resting against the closed door. 'Just look how straight she's going!'

'Ah well—' He came to a stop, paused, and gave a laugh. 'Nope, no way of answering that. Moving on.'

Charlie laughed with him. It was very relaxing, to sit and feel the sway of the boat beneath her, watch the canal stretch away behind. She sipped at her tea, wondering when she'd last felt this tired. Probably the day she came back from Thailand. The thought was a jolt, a poke in her synapses reminding her not to get too comfortable. The more she settled into living on the boat, the more it felt like she'd been given a new start. But that wouldn't come without strings from somewhere. Hugo, perhaps, the wicked fairy godmother furious at being kept in the dark about the boat, the money. Britta's plans, whatever they'd been, cut short before she

111

could carry them out. They were back in the tunnel of trees now, and the air felt chill. Charlie realized that Dave was looking down at her, as if waiting for her to say something.

'I'm sorry, half asleep down here.' She gave a little shiver. Dave must be even chillier in his running kit.

'I was just saying, I think you might have something wrapped around the propeller. There should be much more power than this.'

'Oh no, really?' And how were you supposed to deal with that? She tried to imagine what it could be. 'Like weeds or something?'

'More like rope. Or plastic bags.' He broke off to man-oeuvre away from a low-hanging branch. 'A mate of mine managed to tangle with a mattress, one of those things made of metal springs.' He waved to a couple on the towpath. The man called out some remark, which Charlie couldn't decipher over the noise of the engine. Dave shouted back over, 'No, just for the evening!' then carried on with what he'd been saying. 'Though I'd rather have that than a dead sheep.'

'Really? No.' She glanced up. 'You're having me on, right?'

'Happened to another friend of mine.' He caught her expression and started to laugh. 'Don't worry, that really doesn't happen very often. Hardly at all, in fact.'

'I could deal with it if I had to.' As long as she didn't have to. 'Though I haven't got the first idea how to go about checking.'

'Are you going to be around for the next couple of days?' The question made Charlie's sensors twitch. This had felt like such a straightforward interaction, with no pressure or expectation. It would be an effort to have to push back now. Maybe she should have brought the boat back by herself after all. Dave carried on, though. 'I've got stuff on tomorrow, but if you're here the day after I could drop by and introduce you to the joys of the weed hatch?'

They were back at the supermarket, the turning into the basin about to come up. It would be ridiculous to turn down an offer of help.

Dave was kneeling at the back of the deck. He'd taken a board out, opening up access to the bilge, where apparently she should be checking for water on a regular basis. Charlie vaguely remembered Bob saying something, but there had been so many somethings. Now she was listening, but she was also enjoying the scene around her. The basin was quiet, an old space with high, curving walls and a feel of industry halted, absorbed back into nature. She'd slept so well, reassured by the other boats pulled up nearby and lulled by the absolute quiet, and now it was another beautiful day, the sun warm across her shoulders.

'Any chance of turning the engine off?' Dave's question brought her back to the boat, and she blinked. It was really the perfect day for solar panels; then she wouldn't need to run the engine. Maybe Dave would know something about it. Anyway, the engine had been on for long enough; the batteries would be well charged by now. She moved over to reach for the key, grabbing on to the throttle post for balance.

'Watch out!'

The shout made her step back, unsure what she'd done. 'Sorry, I was just getting to—' She waved to where the key hung from its ignition panel.

'It was the throttle,' he explained. 'If you pushed it forwards and my arm was down when the propeller started to spin . . .' He mimed his arm hanging uselessly by his side.

Charlie stepped over with extreme care, keeping well out of the throttle's way, and turned the key. In the sudden silence, she was picturing the propshaft spinning, Dave's arm caught up and broken into a hundred pieces. 'I'm so sorry. God, that would be much worse than a sheep.'

'Speaking of which.' Dave finished unscrewing a pair of oversized wingnuts and eased a dripping metal plate out of the space. 'Want to come and have a look?'

The water in the hole was black, fathomless, and she realized it must open into the actual canal. This wasn't a contained amount of water. It was endless. She reached into it with an exploratory finger, ready for something down there to snap at her.

'What do you do next?' She twisted to look up at Dave, reluctant to relinquish her place now. She wanted to do this herself.

He was leaning on the tiller, happy to let her carry on. 'Stick your hand down, see if you can feel anything.'

She rolled her sleeve up and started to lower her arm into the water. It wasn't as cold as she'd expected and felt soft against her skin. Her hand seemed to be going down and down, out of the boat, out of reach. Then she touched metal. She let her fingers explore, letting her

114

mind visualize the information they were sending her. Smooth flanges flaring, angled out in the darkness. The propeller itself, the maker of the white surge of water when *Skíðblaðnir* was moving forwards. It felt intimate, somehow, reaching into her inner parts. She moved her touch further in. There was something there all right, a roughness twisted around the smooth surface of the propshaft. She worked her fingertips to get a grip on it, trying to find an end to pull, but it was wadded into a solid mass.

'Ah, arm starting to get cold!' She sat back on her heels, shaking her hand to get the water off before rubbing the skin. Dave squatted down next to her, leaning to peer into the hole, even though there was no way of seeing through to the obstruction. She moved back to give him some space. 'It's not an animal, but I can't get it to shift.'

'You might need a knife.' He was wearing a T-shirt with short sleeves today, so his arm was free to plunge straight in. 'There's something a bit veterinary about this, feeling around in a blind space to diagnose.' He looked round. 'Have you got anything sharp?'

'I'm not sure.' There were some tools in the engine room but she wasn't sure exactly what. 'Would a vegetable knife do?'

He nodded, and she climbed down into the boat. The knife was in the drawer, new and solid, the metal handle integrated into the blade. It felt heavy in her hand. Back on the deck, she hesitated before passing it over. 'Do you mind if I have another go?'

'Absolutely, your boat!' Was there the smallest hint of

reluctance there? He moved back readily enough, though. 'Watch out with the blade. Easy to cut yourself instead of the rubbish.'

She held the knife with her finger pressed against the flat edge of the blade, keeping her other fingers wrapped around the handle and sawing into the obstruction. Slowly, slowly, it started to give. 'Gotcha!' It gave way and she eased the blade further along, sensing the slight movement as the propeller began to rotate. The mass thinned, separated, and she brought the knife up to the surface, putting it to one side. Soon she had a handful of frayed and knotted blue rope on the deck next to her, intertwined with an assortment of shredded plastic bags. There was something else there, fabric, even more firmly caught. Back in with the knife and finally she had a fingerhold, then a loose end. When it gave up its grip, the whole lot came out with a rush, and she was grasping the remains of a sodden school blazer, embroidered badge still intact.

'Let's hope that's all he lost,' Dave commented, taking it from her and bundling it around the rest of the rubbish. 'I'll drop these in the bin on my way off.' He stood, watching as she fitted the covering plate back in, let her work out how the screws went together. Finally, the deck board went back on and the boat was once again in a fully dressed state. 'You'll feel a difference with your steering.'

'Thank you so much.' Charlie pushed herself up, kneading out a cramp in her shoulder muscle. 'You've been so kind.'

'It's nothing. And I got to go afloat, payment enough.'

116

He hesitated for a second and then stepped across to the bank. 'Let me know if you're ever back this way,' he said. 'Unless you've got time for a drink to see you on your way?' He half turned, looking over towards the pub.

It would probably be the right thing to do, as a thank you, if nothing else, but Charlie felt an urge to get going, try out the newly liberated propeller. 'I'd love to, but I really need to make a start . . .'

'No worries, I'll let you get on. Hope it all goes well!' He waited on the bank as she started the engine, giving a kind of salute as *Skíðblaðnir* edged out into the water. She still needed to be turned around, but there was plenty of space this time and the manoeuvre went without a hitch. As she pulled away, she heard Dave's voice behind her. 'Attagirl!'

She waved, giving a thumbs up, and then turned back to focus on where she was going.

Eleven

She arrived much too early. Max had said half two, and Charlie had vaguely planned to have a wander around the town and something to eat before meeting. Now she was there, though, she couldn't think of anything that she'd want to go and see. It wasn't even as if they'd spent much time there, not in the centre, anyway. What with work and travel in the week and getting the house sorted at weekends, they'd never had time to explore. It made her feel strange, coming back to the town she'd lived in and not feeling that she knew it at all. Instead of walking towards the shops, she followed a sign pointing to the canal.

She must have known it was there really. Had they talked about walking along it, perhaps? She didn't think so. Or maybe it had been Max's father, or one of his sisters. A conversation about potential holidays, the whole family in a fleet. As she walked, she let memories of his family play through her mind. Max was one of five, the only boy, and all of his sisters had children. For years she'd revelled in their closeness, the care they had for each other. She'd really believed that she was part of the circle, that they embraced her as one of them. Then one

118

year, just one year out of so many, she'd persuaded Max to go away for Christmas rather than join the gathering at his parents' home. They'd all been so understanding. Of course they needed to get away, how lovely to think of them in a cosy cottage with a log fire and no Wi-Fi. In the grind of the New Year, Charlie hadn't noticed the dropping off of calls, but she'd noticed brittleness over a family weekend, the conversations closing off as she came into the room. Max's youngest sister, the one Charlie felt closest to, was about to have her first baby, and Charlie's being a godmother had been part of the planning, spoken of as an absolute. Now it wasn't mentioned and Charlie, too proud to show how much she cared, had let the ceremony pass without comment, even to Max. She could still taste the rawness of the betrayal, though that was nothing to what happened that Easter. She still couldn't think in any detail of the things his oldest sister had said to her. She'd never told Max about it, but it was the final straw in her decision to leave. Would she ever tell him? Probably not. They were his family for ever, after all.

The footpath took her down a shabby passage, with a tall brick wall on one side and metal fencing on the other. Through the fringing sprawl of buddleia and ivy, she could just make out a yard, filled with old cars and piles of worn tyres. Underfoot, the gravel was damp and thinly spread. She walked with her head down, dodging the dog mess. Spots of rain started to fall. It had been warm enough when she left to gamble on her denim jacket's being enough. Now she wished she'd picked up that extra jumper.

119

And then she was there, the dank pathway opening onto a cobbled stretch of bank. In front of her was a lock, one big wooden gate open to let a boat emerge from inside the chamber. Charlie stood and watched as it came out. An older woman stood at the tiller, and Charlie felt herself plotting movements in her own head as she watched the boat being angled expertly towards the bank. She wanted to go and say hello, to align herself to the boats rather than the pedestrians. Was three weeks on a boat and one short journey enough to qualify, though? There didn't seem to be anyone with the helmswoman, and Charlie wondered about going to offer a hand, as Bob would have done, or Dave. She hesitated too long, overwhelmed by impostor syndrome, and the moment was gone. The woman on the boat had already lashed her rope around the waiting bollard and was on her way back to the lock to close it behind her. There was something self-absorbed about her movements as she leaned her weight against the long wooden arm, allowing it to move against the water at its own pace. There was no rush, just the natural rhythm of the process. With the same efficient air, she picked up her windlass, let a hidden sluice fall down and walked back to her boat. A flick of the rope, a step across and she was gone, the boat chugging away at the same unhurried pace.

Charlie found a bench tucked under the lee of an old brick building and sat there, watching the lock being worked another couple of times. There hadn't been any locks on the route up to Whaley Bridge, but Bob had taken her down to Bosley and they'd spent a couple of hours working the gates for passing boats. She knew in

120

theory how it all worked – lock filled, boat in, water out, boat down – but could she manage it herself? Seeing a solo boater had given her a little burst of determination, and she tried to pick out the stages that would be hard, single-handed. One of the boats had a family aboard, the two children clamouring over who got to do what as their father directed their energy and their mother concentrated on getting the boat in and out. That must be hard to do. The father cheered as the manoeuvre was completed, ruffling one child's hair and high-fiving the other. It was basically a language that Charlie knew she'd never be able to learn. She could manage to use it for short bursts, but was always on the edge of saying the wrong thing. Even when she tried really hard she came up short. Martha's texts, for instance, waiting for replies. It would take so little to tell her something nice. Take a photo every now and then, of a duck, or a funny boat name. That was what you did to build friendships: you put the time in, made the effort. Maybe that was the problem, that she was worried about building too much between them in case she let Martha down. Maybe that was the problem with her whole life. As if on cue, her phone buzzed in her pocket. She pulled it out to see a message from Max, not Martha this time, saying he was at the café.

She still didn't move, weighed down by a reluctance to set off the next stage in their long dance of separation. And the town felt alien, an enemy area. She wanted to stay here, where the canal linked her, however tenuously, to a different life, one where she didn't have to think about negotiations and bargaining. For the first time, she realized that this was literally true. The canal here was connected to the canal there. She could walk along the towpath and, sooner or later, find her boat. She could be here, in her boat. Maybe that was what she should have done, brought her boat here so that she had a place to retreat after the battle. Even the thought of it made her feel more positive. She stood, taking in one last glance before heading for the café meeting place.

He'd seen her. It was too late to disappear. She made herself carry on walking. The door of the café swung open in slow motion and each step felt like another moon landing. The terrain ahead was just as unknown.

'Hi.' He seemed as awkward as she felt, rising from his seat and half holding a hand out in welcome. He pulled it back just as she decided to respond. A slapstick moment without the laughs.

The café felt abandoned rather than quiet. As Charlie navigated the clumsy slide along the wooden bench, her hand went through a sticky puddle. And people wanted children why? She wiped the mess away with a discarded napkin, glancing over at Max and wondering again how much he really did want a family. During one of their more fraught evenings before the break-up, she'd accused him of sleepwalking into the decision, letting his sisters do the thinking for him. They all had children so of course he'd want children. She'd always known that he'd be a good dad, just from seeing him around his nephews and nieces. She'd known he wouldn't be like Hugo; she was less sure that she wouldn't be, and she couldn't take the risk. They'd ended that evening with both of them in tears, clinging on to each other with a desperate and, it turned out, futile passion.

It was odd, now, seeing him from the outside, a tall stranger with a suit that was slightly too big. He always gave the impression of being just a little undernourished, in a way that made people want to feed him up. It wasn't that he was thin, Charlie had always told him, more that his cheekbones and nose made a statement and the rest of him disappeared. He was looking well: a new haircut, a recent tan. Ironic, really. She was the one who'd gone away on – what had his sister called it? *Your self-indulgent escapade*, that was it. Anyway, she was the one who'd been away, and here Max was looking like he was just back from a cruise. She caught a glimpse of the two of them in a smeared mirror on the wall opposite. Strange that they'd been a couple. His first words went by without her hearing them.

'Sorry, what?' She heard the confrontation in her tone as it bounced from his face. Taking a deep breath, she rubbed her fingers against her eyes, realizing too late that she hadn't been as effective with her cleaning as she'd hoped. 'Look, I'm sorry, this is all, well . . .' She made a vague gesture to indicate her discomfort.

His reply was stiff, offended. 'I actually am, though. Sorry.' He was sounding impatient already. 'About Britta.'

'Oh.' Max had found her family incomprehensible. Every time they visited, he'd tried a new approach, unwilling to believe that he couldn't make a difference, couldn't fix them with a day out or a better line of conversation.

123

'Thank you. It was . . . unexpected.' She didn't know what else to say. Now was when she should probably ask about his family, but every approach felt wrong. It was as if she was walking along a glass path, and every potential step would break a little more of it away. The silence stretched out. 'How's Bella? I thought you might have brought her with you.'

'I came from work.' He sucked his mouth in against his teeth, the way he always did when he was trying to decide what to say. A waitress ambled out from a door at the back of the café and came to stand by them. Max waved a hand. 'We're all right for the moment, thanks. Unless you . . . ?' He half turned to Charlie.

Charlie shook her head. 'I'm good.' The waitress ignored the directive, standing with her pad open, not quite making eye contact. She was going to wait until they decided. Charlie gave in. 'I'll have some tea.' When she'd gone, Charlie turned back to Max, managing a smile, wondering how to start now the moment had come. It was just business, she reminded herself, and in both of their interests to get it sorted out.

'I can't stay long.' He checked his watch. 'I've got a meeting to get to.'

'OK.' Charlie was a little taken aback. 'We agreed you'd cover the mortgage payments while I was away.' She waited for his nod. 'Things have obviously shifted somewhat since then and, well, we need to decide how to take things from here.' That was it, really. Ten years of being together, and it came down to a house and a dog. 'We need to think about selling.'

Max was looking down at his hands, not meeting

124

her gaze. His fingers fidgeted with a napkin before tapping decisively on the tabletop. 'The thing is, I want to keep the house.' He still didn't seem to want to meet her eyes directly. 'I've been working it out, in fact. Taking into account the outstanding mortgage and the payments I've made over the past year, plus what it would cost in fees if there was a sale, that would mean paying you around twenty-five thousand. Finished. Done.'

Charlie looked up in surprise. He had it all worked out, whilst she was still approaching it as an exploratory discussion. 'OK,' she replied, trying to juggle figures in her head. 'What sort of valuation have you had done?'

He breathed out impatiently, leaning forward with an unexpected air of confrontation. 'I'm not trying to do you out of anything. I just want to get it sorted.' He glared for a moment, then sank back. 'I need to move on.'

What did he think she expected, that she wanted him to stay where he was? Moving on was the whole point, it was why they were here. What did it have to do with asking a question and expecting a rational answer? 'Look, why don't you email me the figures and we'll take it from there?' A basic response, and surely the one he'd expected. She was stunned, then, by the force he used to push his chair back.

'Fine, if that's how you want to play it.' The waitress had just arrived with a mug in one hand, teapot in the other. He stood up, knocking into the girl so that hot tea splashed onto Charlie's hand. 'I'll be in touch.' Charlie watched him walk out, unable to comprehend what had just happened.

'You still want this, right?' The waitress was standing there, seemingly uninterested in the scene.

'Yes, sure.' Charlie realized her hand was hurting and blew onto the reddening skin.

The waitress put her cargo down. 'I'll get your milk.'

She was back within seconds with the little jug, and a serviette filled with ice. 'Thought this might help,' she said, turning away before Charlie could answer. 'Stick to your guns,' she added, over her shoulder. 'He's out for what he can get, if you ask me.'

Twelve

The tea was surprisingly good, hot and strong. Charlie took her time with it, eking out almost three mugs from the pot. Had she been unreasonable? But how could he expect her to agree blind, without even knowing the figures involved? That made no sense at all. And it didn't feel exactly like Max, either. He was careful, never buying anything, however trivial, without double-checking quality, comparative costs, guarantees. Choosing the right fridge had taken weeks, and even then he'd sent the first one back after tracking the power usage over a twenty-four-hour period. That made her think of all the other joint purchases: furniture, television, car. She'd packed up her personal stuff before she left, an urgent impulse telling her to get it out, somewhere safe. Max had been emphatic, though. She had no need to worry, there was enough space, don't make any final decisions. Presumably it was still there, the boxes stacked in their compromise position at the back of the garage.

Every complication brought to mind another, the things she needed to consider swirling around, coming into focus, disappearing again. She rummaged in her bag for a pen and started to make a list on a spare napkin. If Max was going to be difficult, she needed to get herself organized. And the first thing was a trip to the nearest estate agent. As she left the café, she would have liked to have given the waitress an acknowledgement, some thanks for her brusque kindness. She'd disappeared again though, so Charlie left coins instead, hoping it would send the right message.

In the first place she tried, the only agent was caught up in a long phone call. Charlie sat for nearly twenty minutes, waiting for a glance, a gesture that they would be with her any minute. At least it gave her time to sift through a pile of recent listings. She took the sheaf with her when she gave up and left. The second agent refused to speculate on possible prices without visiting the property. Charlie couldn't even talk the woman into discussing houses in the same area of the town. In the third, however, she struck lucky. The young man behind the desk, Carl according to his name badge, was putting the phone down just as she walked in, and turned to her with a welcoming smile. An hour later, she was walking away with a clear picture of the local housing market, a list of options in dealing with joint mortgages, and an equally comprehensive list of possible pitfalls. Carl had echoed the previous agent in not committing to a valuation without a visit, but he'd taken her through all the recent sales in the area. It turned out that his sister had just been through a difficult divorce, and he was almost evangelical about how not to approach the problem. *She wouldn't listen to me, kept thinking her ex would be reasonable.* He'd tapped the topmost leaflet on the desk between them. *Your fella's working on a figure that's right at the bottom of the market. Even with all the variables, you'd be unlucky if this was all you got for it.*

As Charlie walked away, her mind was buzzing with plans for action. There was no way she was going to just fall in with whatever Max had planned out. Whatever else, this had to be fair. Without thinking, she had started walking in a direction that would, eventually, lead to her old home. She paused, weighing up time and effort and possibility. There was nothing she couldn't put in an email, except that she'd have to go out and find a computer with internet. And why not go now, whilst it was all straight and clear in her head? That way, at least they'd both know where they were.

It was weird, walking along her old road. Maybe it was because she was on the outside looking in, but she had the sense of things being invisibly altered. Like a spot-the-difference cartoon challenge. Different blinds at the Taylors', a new car at number 73. The rain, which had tailed off earlier, was now coming down again with a gloomy determination. At least she wouldn't run into anyone she knew. And here was the house, a neat red-brick semi with the bins out for the morning. Strange that it was, technically, still half hers. Max's car was in the drive, so she wouldn't have to hang about. Stupid idea, walking over in the rain without a coat or umbrella. She stopped by the driveway, almost ready to turn back. Then a figure appeared around the corner of the house next door. Mrs Crabbe, wheeling a bin almost as big as she was down towards her gate. Charlie watched her progress with resignation. She knew better than to offer to help, but she could make sure nothing went too badly wrong. The old lady made it to the pavement in one piece, however, positioning her bin with care and taking a final look under the lid before turning to Charlie.

'You won't have any luck there,' she said, standing with her head to one side.

'Hello, Mrs Crabbe. How are you keeping?' The rain intensified, a blustery wind picking up to blast it against Charlie's face. She wiped away the thin stream running down from her hairline. Her neighbour didn't seem to notice. It was hard to tell if she was aware of Charlie's recent absence, or even if she remembered her at all. She was regarding her with suspicion rather than acknowledgement.

'So many young people in trouble in these places,' she said, finally. 'I tell my granddaughter she's better off staying put. Poor Judith never liked the heat.'

'Ah, yes. Well, we don't have to worry about the heat here, do we?' Maybe the weather would cut the conversation short. Charlie had never quite learned the trick of breaking away from one of Mrs Crabbe's circular diatribes. She wiped her forehead again, slicking back the tails of wet hair that were now dripping water into her eyes. 'I'd better get on. You don't want to be outside in this much longer.'

'That's right, dearie. He's not been the same since his mother died.' Mrs Crabbe put her hand on the bin handle again, tipping it back and making a minute adjustment to its position.

'Whose mother is that?' The old lady was getting worse,

130

her comments more random than Charlie remembered. There was no chance she was referring to Charlie, because Max was particularly good at avoiding conversation with any of their neighbours, particularly this one. Charlie felt a stab of responsibility. Mrs Crabbe didn't have any family that Charlie had ever seen. Was there anyone looking out for her?

The woman paused in her bin positioning, looking over her shoulder before shuffling forwards to take a hold of Charlie's sleeve. 'All I will say is that there's no point coming here and expecting to get any money.' This was said in a confidential tone. Up close, her skin was pouchy and grey. Charlie wanted to pull away but the woman carried on, her voice little more than a whisper. 'If I was you, I'd cut my losses and save yourself the trouble.' She nodded, giving Charlie's arm what might be an encouraging shake. With the air of someone who has said their piece, she straightened up and made a move towards the driveway.

'Thanks.' It was like having a spirit consultation. 'I'll bear that in mind.'

'That dog, though.' The old lady came to a stop, her head trembling as if her neck were a coiled spring. Charlie's skin prickled. 'Barking and barking.' The woman turned back to Charlie with the jerkiness of a marionette. 'I told them, it's against the licence, leaving them outside like that. Barking all day.' She turned again, this time not stopping. Charlie could hear her muttering to herself as she went.

A light came on in the downstairs window of the house. Charlie shifted. Should she go and knock, or leave

131

it? It was the talk about dogs that made up her mind. The chances were Mrs Crabbe was talking about another dog entirely, probably from a long-distant decade past. Even so, she wouldn't rest easy until she'd checked.

She stood inside the porch, shivering in her wet clothes. There was no answer to her first ring, and she was just about to try again when the inner door opened a crack. A waft of floral perfume washed past, along with a billow of centrally heated air.

'Yes?' The voice was unfamiliar, and Charlie had a sudden thought that Max might have sold the house behind her back. But that was definitely his car outside. Surely he wouldn't have sold that as part of the exchange? Then she heard a flurry of excited barks and the sound of paws skidding along the wooden floor. 'Oh, for God's sake, will you just shut up!' As Charlie was processing the fact of a strange woman in Max's house, undercut with the thrill of Bella recognizing her just from some sense of smell or presence, the woman stuck out a foot. She shoved at Bella's small form with a brisk movement, almost a kick. 'Get back in there, you little—' With a lithe movement, she sidled through the narrow opening and pulled the door behind her. Holding it closed, she turned back to Charlie. She was tiny, barely coming up to Charlie's shoulder, and dressed in exercise leggings and a crop top. There was no way she could be more than, what, twenty? 'Sodding dog, never shuts up. It's supposed to live outside, but I said all right, just this once, because of the rain.' She shook her head, inviting Charlie's sympathy. 'Were you wanting to find out about the Pilates?' She waited for a response,

132

then pecked forwards, her head at an enquiring angle. 'Sorry, who did you say you were again?' After waiting for another moment, she tapped one finger against a card stuck to the porch window and raised her voice, as if Charlie was too stupid to have heard her. 'No cold callers,' she said, and made to close the outer door on her.

'Oh, I'm not selling.' Charlie was shaking with anger, barely able to control her voice to get the words out. 'And that's my dog, and she doesn't live outside.'

The girl drew back so that she was practically flat against the inside door. 'You must be Charlie.' She made the name sound like a disease. 'I think you should leave.'

'Not before I talk to Max.' Charlie nodded towards the door.

'He's got nothing to say. He told you what we decided.'

'Oh, what *you* decided? And what makes you think it's your decision?' Charlie moved a step closer. From inside the house, she could hear Bella whining and scratching.

'Uh, the fact that you walked out and left Max paying for it all?' Charlie barely heard the words, even though the girl's voice was rising. 'Because it wasn't good enough for you then, was it? Even with your precious dog. Left that behind quick enough when it suited you. And now you want to kick us out because it suits you. Let me tell you something—'

There were footsteps coming up the path and then Max was there, blocking her in, interrupting whatever words had been about to fall. 'What the hell's going on?' He was looking at Charlie. His shoulders were hunched against the rain, and he was holding a plastic bag giving

133

off the smell of Indian spices. Max, who had to be persuaded into buying chips on a day out to the coast.

'Anything else you forgot to tell me?' She was finding it difficult to breathe, adrenaline flooding her skin in an almost painful wave. 'Because—'

Behind her, the other woman's voice was breaking in, shrill with accusation. 'She was threatening me, Max, she—'

'Zoe, go in.' He squeezed past Charlie and held out the bag. 'And take this.' He herded the girl back inside the house. Charlie caught a glimpse of Bella trying to get out, then the door banged shut. Max leaned against it, his face weary. 'What do you want, Charlie?'

'I want my dog.' Charlie slumped against the side of the porch, nearly knocking over a bowl of miniature daffodils. 'Which is more than your new girlfriend does.'

'Bella's fine.'

'Really? Left outside all day so the neighbours complain?' Charlie shook her head. Her rage was making her feel very close to tears, but she wasn't going to cry. Not for this.

'Mrs Crabbe?' Max gave a humourless laugh. 'And you're going to listen to her over reason?'

'Your girlfriend,' Charlie responded, unable to stop herself from giving the word a heavy emphasis, 'said, and I quote, "the sodding dog's supposed to live outside". Since when has that been fine?'

'Zoe exaggerates,' Max said, shaking his head with his familiar show of impatience. 'She just doesn't like Bella on the furniture. She's got a perfectly comfortable bed in the utility room.'

134

'I want her back,' Charlie repeated. She thought of Bella snuggled up against her on the sofa, could almost feel the warmth of the skin beneath her shaggy coat. The thought of her kept on hard floors with no cuddles . . . She should never have left her.

Max was replying. 'This isn't the time to discuss it.' She was aware of him putting his key into the lock, signalling an end to the conversation.

'Oh, and when is?' She stood upright again, a hand out to stop the door opening. 'Because I'm ready now. And we can discuss your ridiculously low estimate of this place at the same time.'

'Really? You want to talk it over in the porch, when you're soaked to the skin?' Max sighed, his face drawn in planes of dark and light by the orange glow of the street lights. He looked exhausted. 'Look, I'm sorry it happened like this.' He tilted his head towards the house. 'It's not quite how it looks.'

One of those odd shifts happened, something she'd experienced occasionally in the weeks after her decision to leave. The emotional temperature suddenly levelled, and Charlie saw him again as Max, the person who had been closest to her for years. Distant now, maybe, but still the same person. 'I don't know how you think it looks,' she said, the surreal sense of calm removing them into a kind of parallel universe. 'I mean it, though. I don't want my dog living with someone who doesn't want her. And don't tell me it's my own fault for going.' She shivered. 'You can't just give me a price and expect me to agree. That's not how it works, and you know it.'

Max's mouth tightened, but then he nodded. 'So email me, Charlie. Don't turn up on my doorstep.'

She let the 'my doorstep' go as they stood for a moment, not quite exchanging glances. As she walked away, Charlie could sense Max watching her down the path. Whether it was with any degree of sadness or just to make sure she'd gone, she couldn't tell. She paused as she reached the pavement.

'I mean it. I want Bella.'

She didn't wait to hear his response, if he even gave one. It was still raining, if less violently than before, and she headed back to the station weighed down by her wet clothes, and something more.

It was properly dark by the time she got back to the marina, her head thumping and her heart sore with longing. Bella's frantic yelps had followed her to the train, had rung out again with every step from the station, and Charlie was still going through each moment over and over. She should have forced her way in, forced Max to hand her over. The walkway was slippery, her feet uncertain. She was afraid of finding that something had happened whilst she was gone, that she'd get to the water and find *Skíðblaðnir* lost beneath the surface. The boards swayed beneath her feet as she made her way along, with surely more movement than usual. Most of the boats were still and silent, but she spotted a few portholes glowing with yellow light, caught a whiff of smoke from a wood-burner. It made the area feel homely, welcoming. And there was *Skíðblaðnir*, waiting for her, still afloat. That was something, anyway.

136

Thirteen

The man was leaning against the arm of the lock gate, using his weight to close it behind her in a slow-motion swing. It penned her and the boat in, like sheep, and she watched the man move round to start letting the water out. Total luck that he'd turned up just as she made it to the first lock. He'd seen her standing on the bank, holding the mid-rope to keep *Skíðblaðnir* in place whilst she wondered if she'd bitten off more than she could actually manage, and taken the lock-work on as a matter of course. Now she eased forward, to stop the boat's back end grounding out on the cill. She'd visualized herself carrying out these steps so much that this didn't feel like the first attempt, but whether she could work the locks as well was another thing entirely. The boat's nose bumped gently against the gates in front.

The water beneath the boat gave a tremor, and she was dropping down. The first moments felt faster than she'd anticipated, the walls rising on either side to surround her with their dank and shiny stonework. Then the pace settled, the noise of the engine increasing as the walls reached up around them. At the front of the lock, she could hear the rush of water leaving the chamber, pulling *Skíðblaðnir* with it. Behind her, water plumed through the join of the gates. No good being so far back that it landed on her. And then there was the cill. Bob had told her, almost with relish, about boats caught on the stone ledge as the water dropped. Boats tipping head first as their bows continued to go down. Boats capsized by careless steersmen. There it was, just appearing out of the water, further back than she'd expected. It was far enough away from the boat to let her draw a breath in relief.

The final few inches took an age to drain. She was suspended in the dim light of the chamber, the man's boots visible above her head as he braced against the arm of the lock gate in readiness. Someone else had joined him; she could make out the sound of voices but not the words. Again she felt the pull of the water sending the boat sideways, knocking her into the slime of the walls. Then the world settled and a crack of light appeared between the forward gates, gradually widening in a slow reveal. Charlie put a hand to the throttle, ready to go, but as the gate swung out, she paused. Ahead was an Italianesque vista done out in English green, the tiny landscape of hills and trees framed by the flare of the walls on either side, *Skíðblaðnir*'s roof filling in the space below.

'Are you coming out, then?' The voice brought her back to the business at hand, and she set *Skíðblaðnir* going. There was a minuscule time lag before the propeller effected the move, and she was heading out into reality, wider but somehow less detailed than it had seemed when framed by the lock just the moment

138

before. It was like entering into a new world, from darkness into light. As the last few feet of the boat came clear, the sun broke through the clouds, bathing her in a warm light.

The decision to move on had been fully formed when she'd woken up that morning, the night having been spent revolving everything she wished she'd said to Max at the time. Her anger was physical enough to make the tapping out of an email to him from her phone a slow and frustrating exercise, but she managed it. And managed it, she thought, with an admirable restraint. In it, she laid out the findings from the estate agent, demonstrating how low his offer had been. Her counter-offer was pragmatic: not the highest amount the estate agent had been willing to suggest, but meeting Max halfway. And Bella. Non-negotiable. And whilst she waited for his reply, she was going to go boating. She might not know where Margareta was, or where the photograph with *Guillemot* had been taken. She might never know. However illogical it was, she felt that a journey would prove to the Fates that she was serious about finding her, about unpicking this hidden moment of her mother's life. And it wasn't as if she had anything better to do, after all.

She phoned Eleanor that night, walking away from her first towpath mooring to search out a signal. Partly it was to catch her up with where things were, more specifically where she was. It had been surprisingly easy to slip away without letting anyone know. Neither Libby nor Bob had been around, and there was no one else to see her leave. If Britta really had been planning to step

139

off the map, this could definitely have worked, especially if none of them had known about the boat. There was a little bit of Charlie that liked the idea of disappearing in a similar way but here, now, moored on a stretch of bank with no other boats or houses in view, it was making her feel a touch too disconnected already.

'Hello?' It was Martha on the end of the line.

'Hi, sweetie.' Charlie remembered too late that she hadn't sent a text message yet. Damn, what was wrong with her? 'Listen, is your mum there?'

'Ye-es.' The word was drawn out. 'But she's a bit busy.'

'OK.' Charlie took a deep breath. Eleanor was always busy. 'Look, I'm so sorry about the text messages. It's been really busy, and I'm just not very good at remembering.'

'OK.' Martha's voice was still flat, and Charlie felt a twinge of impatience. Was it really that big a deal? Then Martha spoke again, her voice sounding bruised and small. 'Aunty Charlie, when are you coming back?'

'I'm not sure, sweetie.' Charlie glanced at the phone, checking the time. 'But I'm going to be stopping in a lot of places now, and I promise I'll text you them for your map. And maybe you can come and visit in the holidays?' When were the holidays? Easter? Or had that already gone past? She hoped she hadn't just pledged herself to something starting the day after tomorrow.

'In the boat?' Martha's tone had risen. 'Really? Just me, not Poppy?'

'Yes, just you.' Charlie imagined being in charge of Poppy on the boat. That was never going to happen. 'I'll talk to your mum about it. Tell her I'll give her a ring when I've got a better signal.'

140

It seemed to have got dark very quickly, and there were no lights here. The edge of the towpath was indistinct against the hedgerow, and she couldn't see into the field beyond. It wasn't that she actually thought there was someone waiting there, ready to jump out, but it did make her want to get back. The canal was dark and smooth to her left, the water silent and indifferent. She wished there was another boat, someone to call on if anything went wrong. And the boat felt empty as she opened the door. Maybe not empty so much as hollow, its length filled with shadows and the possibility of hidden intruders. Telling herself not to be so stupid, she nevertheless went all the way down to the end, turning lights on to check in every corner. There was no sign of anything unusual. Of course there wasn't. But she still couldn't shake off the sense of unease.

It was when she went to check once more that the door was locked that she noticed something odd about the steps. The top tread moved, so little that she'd missed it before. She squatted to look more closely. With careful fingers, she gave the board a wiggle. It moved, just enough for her to sense the space underneath. The whole thing was very carefully done, with a recessed bolt on the far side holding it in place. She released the catch and opened up the step. Slotted in the neat space below was a cardboard filing box.

Charlie's hands were shaking as she eased the box out. The sense of secrecy, the promise of discovery at last, was making her feel slightly sick. But when she had it in front of her, she felt a reluctance to take the next step. Eleanor should be here as well, should be a witness to this alongside her. It was no use phoning her. She'd be too busy, or someone would need her halfway through the call. Better to see what was there and arrange a time when she could actually sit down and talk. The front clip was awkward and took her some time to work open. She was almost ready to rip the whole thing apart. But then it gave, and the yellow concertina folder fell open, letting out the smell of new cardboard and stationery. Charlie riffled her way through the spaces. A handful of items to do with the boat: a handwritten receipt, insurance papers, some kind of safety certificate. Interesting, in a way. At least they'd know when the boat was bought, and the names of the previous owners were there. Would Britta have shared anything about her plans with them? Probably not, but it would be worth a try. She went back to the file. There was another page in the same pocket. It was headed with the Canal & River Trust logo and looked like another bit of bureaucracy. That was all, the rest of the pockets stiff and empty. Charlie went through them twice, even turning the whole thing upside down and giving it a shake. Nothing. She sat back on her heels, her excitement dissipating into anticlimax. Then something caught her eye at the top of the final sheet. She checked it twice and then took it over to the light to make sure she'd seen it properly. The words stayed the same. *Skíðblaðnir* was registered in the name of Charlotte Nilsson.

142

Fourteen

The owl called for a second time, an imprint of the sound lingering in her ears long after the reality of it had died away. So unfair. She wanted to enjoy hearing it, instead of feeling cross at being awake, fed up of trying to make her mind calm enough for sleep. Once again she turned, thumping at her pillow. Not that the action would make it any more comfortable, but it was the middle of the night, her head had stopped working, and she couldn't think of anything more productive to do. In a totally off-piste way, it made sense that Britta had bought the boat in her name, well, sort of her name. She'd opened the bank account in Eleanor's, so this was a balance. And she wouldn't have been able to tell Charlie, because she'd been on the other side of the world. What was really throwing her was the use of Nilsson, Britta's maiden name. Assuming she hadn't used it by mistake, it must mean something particular. A signal that she was separating herself from a marriage she no longer wanted, had maybe not wanted for years? That at least would fit in with the boat, and the secrecy surrounding it. Had she been escaping or running away? There was, Charlie felt, a subtle difference between the two. Charlie tried again to remember their last conversation, to dig out a hint of what was coming.

It was all caught up in the argument of the visit, with Hugo dominating the scene and Britta, as always, disappearing into the background. What if her mother had wanted to talk to her, to tell her something, but hadn't had the opportunity? But she could have emailed or written. No, because Charlie had deliberately not given anyone a postal address, and her mother couldn't use a computer without someone else doing pretty much everything for her. It all came back to one thing: Charlie choosing not to notice that anything was wrong, being so caught up in her own drama that she didn't have time to find out what was on her mother's mind. And yet the boat was there, owned by Charlotte Nilsson. A gift she had no right to. A name she was being given, but for what purpose? It was ironic, really. She'd spent hours trying to decide what to do about names when the wedding had still been on. Change her name to Max's? Keep her own surname? And what was the point of that anyway, when it was just the symbol of another line of male forebears? This at least could be seen as a gift from her mother, the honouring of another, if previously withheld, history. But 'Nilsson': didn't that mean 'son of Nils'? So it would be a mother giving a daughter something that in its very definition was for a father to give to his son. And where did that leave either of them?

In the end she got up, desperate to stop the circling questions. *Skíðblaðnir* shifted under her feet, the slight bounce in the water more exaggerated in the dark. It was as if the boat was twitching, a sleeping dog ridding

144

itself of a fly. Charlie stopped in the kitchen for a drink of water and then moved along to the living room, navigating by touch. She picked a book from the shelf at random and took it back to bed. There was a tiny electric lantern hanging on a hook by her head. Strange to think of her mother being here, maybe reading the same book by the same light. *Why did you come here? What is it all about?* The questions prodded through the underlayer of her consciousness, interrupting the passage of words from the page to her brain. Over and over, she had to re-read a passage, getting to the end to realize she still hadn't followed it. She gave up in the end, allowing her brain to wander, trying to let the thoughts travel through without holding on to them. What happened to her mother's wider family? Why did she never talk about it? Where had the money come from? Why did she want Charlie to be a Nilsson?

She must have slept in the end, because she was suddenly and abruptly awake, straining for the noise to come again. She knew there was one, pulling her out of sleep on full alert. Now it was quiet, though, just the squeak of a rope stretching and then easing back. No footsteps or voices, no breaking of glass. Her heart rate started to slow, only to race again at a new sound. A patter, heavier than rain and seeming to run backwards and forwards across the roof. She strained after it as all went silent again. There. A picture jumped, fully formed, into her head. Rats, dozens of them, scampering over the boat, using it as some kind of rat playground. The thought made her shudder. If it was a thing, how had she never heard of it before? She'd have thought it would be something Libby Rae might have mentioned, for a start. Maybe it just didn't happen in marinas. Eventually she had to get up and see for herself.

The sky was covered in cloud, keeping any moonlight to a dull glow. Far away was a faint wash of street lights. Behind the hedgerow just next to her, open fields lay quiet. Charlie shivered. The night air was cold, but the dark wasn't threatening. She felt better, soothed somehow by the silence. And it was silent. No rats, no tiny feet. In the distance, she heard an owl call. Finally, reluctantly, she went back inside, the mystery of the noise unsolved. Maybe she'd imagined it. But then, just as she closed her eyes, there it was again, this time along with a conversational quacking. Now sleep came easily, accompanied by the gentle sound of ducks working their way around the hull, picking at algae.

She woke up with a stiff neck and a dull pain behind her eye sockets. Her face in the mirror was wonky, not quite real. Nothing was quite real. When she went outside, even the breeze felt contrived. There was water in the bilge, under the back deck. She squatted by the access hole, trying to get her mind to work. It wasn't much, but enough to have spread right across the metal flooring. She tightened the stern gland, just as Bob had shown her, hoping that would be enough. All she could do was keep an eye on the level. And hope she didn't sink.

It was a morning's work to get to the next town, where the guide reported a small supermarket. There were no locks on the way, and just one road bridge to swing open. She felt herself in a different world as she tied *Skíðblaðnir* up and jogged towards the control box. The car drivers – waiting with impatience or acceptance as she worked the mechanism, returned to the boat, brought her through and finally wound the bridge in to close it – might as well have been holograms. It was warm, too: one of those early summer days when resistance to the weather could soften and retreat. Usually it was her favourite kind, where she would stand and soak it in and wish that it could stay exactly the same for the rest of the year. This morning, it just made her headache feel worse.

Her phone pinged as she got back on the boat, and she glanced at the screen. Notification of an email arriving: that must be Max. It was ridiculous how edgy the knowledge made her feel. Exam results edgy. Bad news edgy. But why was she assuming it was bad news? Maybe, now he'd had time to think, he would see that his offer was unreasonable. In her heart, she knew they were both laying out a starting position, but they were adults, and they'd always tried to be reasonable. Surely he would have come to the conclusion that meeting in the middle would be their best option. And then they'd both be able to move on. Steering with one hand, and with more than half of her attention on the water ahead, she went through the pattern of codes and options to open her email. The sun was bright enough to make reading the words hard, and then her eyes didn't want to focus. The message, when she managed to see it, was brief and to the point. *No. Figures way out. My offer or no deal. You can have the dog if you agree to the terms.*

*

147

The moorings in the town centre were full. Four or five boats were lined up, one busy at the water point, a couple with owners carrying rubbish to the bins or waiting for their turn at the hose. There seemed to be one free mooring bollard with space for maybe half of Skíðblaðnir right at the end of the row. Charlie hovered in neutral, wondering if it would work to go in with her tail sticking out. It seemed possible, but she wasn't really in a state to decide. A woman appeared on the deck of the next-door boat.

'Are you wanting to stop?' she asked, with the hint of an Irish accent. Her face was set in a comfortable smile.

'I was hoping to.' Charlie felt herself drifting and gave the engine a quick blast to come back level. She thought about what she was trying to do. 'I need to get some supplies.'

'Just come up against us, lovey,' her new neighbour said. She was elderly, with short grey hair and soft wrinkles. 'You can tie on there and go and get your shopping. Come far, have you?'

'Yes. No.' Charlie wasn't sure. Come far from which point? She needed to concentrate so she didn't scrape the other boat's paintwork. What if they needed to go out before she got back? 'You're not about to go anywhere?'

'Ah, bless you, we don't go far these days.' The woman chuckled. 'Just tie yourself to us and come across the deck, now. We came out for a little spin, that's all, remind us what it's all about.' A shout came from the far end of her boat, and they both turned to see a small man with a red face waving an arm. 'And there's himself telling me to get along. All right, all right, and there's no need for panic.'

148

Charlie watched her trot off then went to fetch her bag. She'd passed a test of some kind, in her own head if nowhere else.

It wasn't a big town, but the roads and pavements were still a mild shock after the narrow quiet of the towpath. She lost her way twice and her nerves jangled at the traffic and the people. The words from the email thudded in her mind, over and over, the rhythms landing in time with her feet. *My offer. No deal. You can have the dog if you agree to the terms.* A car reversed at speed out of a parking space, making her jump sideways into a puddle. The driver gave her an earful of abuse as he accelerated away. Fuck him, fuck Max. The shop was busy as well, more so than she'd expected. She stopped just inside the doors, wondering if a bank holiday was coming up. She couldn't even be sure which day of the week it was, let alone where she was in the month. Giving up, she eased her way through the trolleys and shoppers, all of them a little too large, the space between them inadequate.

She picked up bananas, carrots, and then came to a stop in front of the cheese. What did she even need? Her mind was blank, overwhelmed by the choice. It was a few days on the canal, not a trek in the great wilderness. Though everyone else seemed to be buying for the apocalypse. A trolley was pressing into her and, behind, a towering cage of new produce blocked her exit. She grabbed at a wedge of Edam and wriggled her way out, escaping to the relative quiet of the toiletries. Nobody needed toothpaste or shampoo, apparently.

149

Which reminded her she needed toothpaste. And tampons. She closed her eyes to think what else. Bread and fresh milk, pasta, butter, something different for tea tonight, a pizza maybe. And something green: kale, spinach. Too many things. The names revolved in her head, each in turn pushing the others out so she had to keep starting again. She should have made a list.

A small girl came up beside her, giving her a questioning look. Who was she with? Charlie was still looking around when she dropped to her knees to peer underneath the shelves. A woman with an overflowing trolley, baby wedged in the seat, zigzagged up.

'Get up, Sammy,' she said, her voice a balance of irritation and frayed patience. She gave Charlie a suspicious look, as if she'd put the child up to it.

'But there's a penny under there!' The little girl was on her stomach, still wriggling in pursuit.

The mother reached down to grab at an arm, her voice rising in frustration. 'I don't have time for this!' Keeping a firm grip, she tried to manoeuvre away but the trolley veered off, knocking into a shelf stacked with nappies. The girl took her chance to run back to the treasure hunt. Charlie began to edge away. It was all a bit much, the noise, the stress. Would she have been any different if things had worked out the way Max had wanted? She sneaked a look at the baby, who was lying back in his seat and gazing into some cheerful oblivion. Martha and then Poppy had been solid babies as well. She could remember them both curling into her shoulder with an unexpected heft and density when she'd gone to visit after their births. That was one thing she'd

150

liked, that twist of protective delight as they'd clung on to her finger. She gave herself a shake, remembering how they'd also fought to be free of her, stretching themselves into outward curves to get back to Eleanor or Jon, they hadn't been fussy which. She just wasn't a baby person, that was all there was to it.

The mother was staring at the packs of nappies, scattered all across the aisle, as if she didn't know how they'd got there. The baby gave a start, as if just catching up with events, and began to wail. The girl, her mission accomplished, skipped past, only to be grabbed in what must have been a painful grip, if her yells were anything to go by. Charlie began to pick up the nappies and stack them back in place. An assistant put his head round the corner and stared at her, his expression labelling her the cause of the disturbance. Charlie waited for the mother to explain, but instead she gripped her trolley, gave her daughter another shake, and managed to turn round and lead them all away. As she went, she gave Charlie a critical look up and down, mirroring the assistant.

Left on her own, Charlie glanced down at herself. So she hadn't washed her hair for a couple of days, and her clothes weren't exactly stripy boating chic. Her jeans were ripped, and not in an artful way, and she'd picked up a long smear of oil on one knee. She was wearing a pair of old sandals she'd found in the locker on the front deck, curling leather flats that weren't at all right for the weather. They fitted her though, which would make them too big for Britta, so they must have been left by the boat's previous owners. The strap was coming away on one side, and her feet were grubby. That was

151

who she was, the sort of person mothers herded their children away from. Because that was what mothers did. They were cross and impatient and sometimes they shouted, but they were always there, always ready with arms to wrap you up in, and they stood up for you against people who weren't nice. And what had Charlie had? A mother who whispered and backed down and was always telling her not to say things. Who planned to escape but without telling anyone, who expected her to change her name but didn't tell her why. And the sadness grew and grew inside Charlie's chest, because she hadn't asked, she hadn't stayed. She'd left her mother behind, and now her mother had left her behind and she didn't know what to do.

Fifteen

'Charlie, you have to breathe.' Eleanor's voice was steady down the phone. 'I want to help you, but I don't know what the matter is.' Charlie could hear the words, but she couldn't remember how to respond to them. She was trying to do what Eleanor wanted, but her chest wouldn't let any air in. The tears that had started inside the store were still shuddering through her and she wasn't sure how to make them stop. A man came round the corner of the building with an empty trolley, turning away abruptly as he saw her standing there. She moved further along, sinking down onto the line of gravel that bordered the wall. 'Charlie?' Eleanor's voice came from her phone. 'Charlie, talk to me.'

'I'm here.' She lifted the handset up again. It weighed so much. She wasn't sure Eleanor had heard her.

'Charlie, listen. I want you to tell me what you're looking at.'

Charlie let the words filter into her brain. What was she looking at? She gave a gulp. 'There's some grass.'

'Good, what else?'

'An empty Coke can. And some flowers.'

'That's good. What kind of flowers?'

153

'I don't know. Yellow ones.' The world was beginning to settle down around her, getting back to manageable proportions. What had she done with her shopping? It wasn't with her, so she must have left it inside. She didn't think she'd paid for it. On the other end of the phone, she could hear Eleanor telling Poppy to be careful on the climbing frame. Then she was back.

'Sorry, she's all over the place today,' she explained, her tone calm and unruffled. 'Are you going to tell me again about the name? I didn't really understand what you were saying.' She listened in silence as Charlie went through the previous evening.

'And I told Martha she could come and stay,' Charlie finished, giving a last hiccuping sob. 'Though you probably won't want to send her now.'

'I can just hear what she'd say if I tried to stop her. She hasn't shut up about it yet.' Eleanor's voice was so normal. 'Look, I'm going to have to go. The park just filled up with about a million kids, and I can't see Poppy. Are you going to be all right? Have you had anything to eat?' She didn't wait for a response. 'It's a nice thing that Mum wanted you to have her name, you know. Maybe she was trying to make up for something.'

'I don't know.' Charlie watched as another shopper came round the corner, paused, disappeared, though she wasn't really thinking about them. 'Sorry for calling like this. Is everything all right your end?'

'Not bad. We're due to exchange next week.'

'Exchanging?' Charlie realized she meant the house, with all the space and garden, the annexe. She had an uncomfortable feeling about the whole thing, but what

154

did she know? For some reason, she remembered how crushed Martha had sounded the day before. Was that anything to do with tensions at home? Maybe she should at least mention that she wasn't sure Eleanor should be doing this. 'About the house—'

But Eleanor was adamant. It was the right plan, they were doing it and everyone was on board. Martha was getting to that age, surely Charlie could remember what it was like.

With that last, slightly barbed, rebuke ringing in her ears, Charlie let the call end. It was only afterwards that she realized she hadn't mentioned Max's email.

Back on the boat, she wandered about, unable to settle. She had a glass of water, wondered about heating up some noodles. It felt like too much effort. She continued to pace, picking things up and discarding them. There was a guitar propped up in a corner of the living room. She'd thought at first that it was her old one, rescued from years of neglect. That, though, was currently in a charity shop somewhere in Derbyshire, if it hadn't already been sold. This one was a beauty, the polished veneer deep in colour, unscratched, expensive. An odd purchase for a woman who'd never shown any interest in music. There was a book as well, neatly placed on the floor next to the instrument. *Classical Guitar for Beginners*. Charlie tried to picture Britta sitting in the quiet space of the cabin, practising each tiny step, over and over again.

She lifted the guitar up, taking some time to remember the knack of tuning. It was years since she'd played.

The first few chords made her shudder with a discomfort that matched her mood. Then muscle memory kicked in and one perfect sound hung in the air. It made the back of her throat ache. She stayed where she was until the last shiver dispersed, before placing the guitar back, a little further behind the sofa. She didn't feel like playing after all.

The guides were still scattered across the floor from her planning the night before, alongside the boat paperwork and the accordion file. She picked the books up first, tapping them together so the edges were straight and placing them carefully on the shelf. It felt important to get it right, to make them sit there in a perfect stack. Once she was satisfied, she moved on to the papers. Each went into a separate compartment, the one with her name on going in last. She stroked her finger across the top line as she slipped it in. Charlotte Nilsson, daughter of Britta Nilsson. The box had better go back under the steps.

As she manoeuvred it in, she realized that the space went back further than she'd realized on her first investigation, right under the front deck by the feel of it. If she knelt down and got her whole arm in, she still couldn't feel the back of it. With her breath held in, she inched her fingers across, not wanting to miss any other hidey-holes. It wasn't until her hand was right in the back corner that she felt the envelope.

Her fingertips were black and she had to stop to sneeze before she could look at it properly. A5 size, and old. She knew that without thinking. It was in the soft feel of the paper, the way the flap was curling out, the gaps in the sides where the edges had given up the struggle to stay together. Nothing written on the outside. Charlie put the tread back onto the step and sat down, her legs not quite up to the job of standing. The envelope, stuffed to capacity, gave way in her hands, and the contents spilled onto her legs, dropped to the floor.

A newish page with figures in a column, costs for something now beyond understanding. A pencil sketch of *Skíðblaðnir*, crude but recognizable. She looked festive, with flowers on the roof and bunting looped along the handrail. There were odd words written in what Charlie assumed was Norwegian. They were clumsily formed, somehow childish. The change in alphabet, she supposed, maybe reflecting the time Britta had last used it. She'd have to look them up later, find out what they meant. Below, this time in English, was a sentence, finished off with an exclamation mark. The words ran along in wavy lines, bouncing cheerfully: *One day we shall sail to London!* Charlie's throat squeezed tight, a wave of sorrow cutting off her airway. Why had there not been time for her to get there? She wanted to howl it out, to bellow it to the world. Instead she whispered, just to the silent boat, 'I'll go for you. I'll go to London.' What was she expecting? Some sign of recognition, or forgiveness? If she did, nothing came back.

Then Charlie noticed something tucked into the back, a fragment of newsprint, faded and yellowed and fragile. She eased it out slowly, afraid of damaging it.

It was a quarter-sheet from a newspaper, the edges showing where it had been torn along the bottom and the left-hand side, the date along the top line shown as 26 June 1965. The *Sneasham Gazette.*

157

The first side was dominated by an advert for Nescafé, picturing a smiling housewife holding out a steaming cup. Beneath it, an article was headed *Waterways group in quest to keep local canal open.* It seemed like an odd item to have treasured for so long, about a threat to the canal from a planned motorway. The campaign was for a bridge to be built over the canal, saving the navigation. Under the article, and taking up about as much space, was a grainy photograph of the determined group. Charlie didn't spot the face until she read the accompanying text: *Norwegian boater Margareta Sørensen leads the charge for canal preservation. 'This is my home,' she told our reporter, 'and I will fight for it.'*

The dots of the photograph came together better if Charlie held it at arm's length. Even then it was hard but, with her eyes slightly closed, she could make out the same features as the woman in the photograph with Britta. Almost as an afterthought, she turned the page over to see what was on the other side.

More advertisements, a reminder to get entries in for the summer fete, and a short column with a subheading in small capitals: GRANDMOTHER LEFT TO DIE IN VILLAGE TRAGEDY. There wasn't much detail in the story, which was strange given the dramatic potential. The body of a woman had been discovered in a house. She was thought to have died several days before, of a seizure. With her was her daughter, a new mother herself with a baby of just a few days old. The girl was reported to be in a state of shock and would be questioned in due course. Long-distant dramas, small-town happenings. Charlie went back to the canal story. Bob had been right, and Margareta had at least been to this place, Sneasham. And Sneasham must be on the canal, so it was a possible place for her to start her search. That would sort her route out, anyway. She could even try and spot where the original photo had been taken, ask around for people who might remember a young Norwegian girl coming to join the older woman, perhaps for a holiday. The segments began to form a shape in Charlie's head. That might be it. Britta had come over for a brief visit, whether Margareta was a sibling or cousin, or even just a friend. Then she'd gone home, coming back several years later to stay. It would make sense for her to count her residency from that second date. It would be the more significant one, anyway. If only she'd kept in touch with her family. Then Charlie might already know this Margareta. She stopped, imagining a different life where foreign relatives had come to stay with them, or they had gone on trips to Scandinavia for their summers.

Whilst she'd been reading, the sun had gone down far enough that she was finding it hard to read the small letters on the page. She got to her feet, stretching out. Her legs were stiff, and she hobbled across to the window. *Draw the curtains and put the light on. Make some tea, find something to eat.* As she went to pull the thin fabric across the windows, a pair of feet walked past. She could see them – battered old desert boots, she hadn't spotted any of those for a while – and legs in faded jeans, but the top half was cut off from view. She was more or less used to having people passing at close quarters now, so would have ignored whoever it was.

159

But these feet slowed, then stopped. Again, not entirely unexpected. People did stop – to look at the canal, take in the view. Sometimes they went as far as discussing the boats, making judgements in loud voices. One or two went further, stooping to peer inside. Libby Rae had a store of anecdotes: the couple who'd sat their toddler on the roof to take a photo; the elderly lady who'd put her head through the bow doors and asked if they did tea and coffee.

This person, whoever it was, came up to the side of *Skíðblaðnir* and rapped on her metal hull.

160

Sixteen

It was ridiculous to feel threatened. Even so, she stood a little way back from the window, her skin buzzing with alarm. If she held herself at a certain angle, she could see through the gap in the curtains without, in turn, being seen. Not that it helped much. The figure was tall, a shadowed bulk in the dim light. There was no way of seeing his face without making herself visible, and she wasn't sure she wanted to let on that she was in. Mustn't move so that the boat rocked. At least she hadn't put the lights on yet.

The rap came again. No different from someone knocking at her front door. But who knew she was here? She went through the list in her head. Eleanor. Maybe Jon, if he'd listened to Martha's chatter. Martha, of course, though she surely wouldn't have much concept of where the location actually was. For a moment, Charlie wondered if it was Max. No, she'd know him, even from the sight of his feet and the outline of his shape. And he didn't know where she was anyway. Someone checking about the mooring? Maybe she wasn't supposed to stop here, or she'd taken someone else's place. She sat for a moment longer, waiting to

161

see if whoever it was would go away. The trouble was, the longer she left it, the more idiotic she'd seem if she did go out. Though there could be reasons for a delay. She'd been in the shower; asleep. How about that for too much overthinking. Impatient with herself, she scooped up her phone and made her way to the front of the boat. She pleaded silently not to be told that she'd have to move, not now, not in the dark.

'Hello?' It was no use staying inside the boat with the door open a crack. She had to go out onto the front deck to unzip the cover. Too late, she realized she could have opened the side hatch in the kitchen, had this conversation from a much safer place. Her position, down below the waterline, made her feel instantly at a disadvantage.

'Hi, wow, it is you!'

The voice was almost familiar, though Charlie's first response was to demur. 'Sorry, I think you must have—' Then she stopped as the visitor squatted down to her level. 'Dave?'

She invited him on board. She had to, really. It had started to drizzle, for one thing, and she could hardly leave him standing on the bank getting wet. And she was pleased to see him, in a way. It was just being in a different place, that sense of being off-grid, out of the loop. She hadn't really expected anyone to find her.

'I'm sorry to turn up like this,' he was saying. He was wearing a fisherman's jumper, the surface speckled with shining drops of water. It was weird, seeing someone where you didn't expect them. Like bumping into someone you worked with in the swimming pool. Dave

162

belonged in running shorts, up in the sunshine of Bugsworth Basin.

'That's OK.' He wasn't a big man, but this was the first time she'd been on the boat with another person. It made the room feel smaller. Charlie sensed that he was looking around, taking note of what was on the walls, the shelves.

'Look, I've come at a bad time,' he said, taking a step back towards the doors. 'I hadn't realized it'd got so late.'

'No, really.' Despite the oddness, it didn't feel wrong that he was there. As she'd felt when he helped her with the boat, he fitted in. 'It's just I wasn't expecting anyone to know where I was.' And that made it sound like she was on the run.

'I didn't,' he said, with a lop-sided smile. 'It was complete chance. You see, I've been staying with a friend in the town, and they mentioned that the boat was here.'

'Coincidence,' Charlie said. Then the flaw in the explanation struck her. 'But how did they—'

'Know that I knew you?' Dave gave another quick smile. 'They didn't. It was the boat they knew.'

He explained more as she made tea, talking through the opening between the rooms as she clicked on the gas, chose the mugs. She gave herself the one called *bluestocking*, pausing for just a moment before selecting *secret agent* for Dave.

'I should have told you back at Bugsworth,' he was saying. 'But I was still trying to pretend it didn't matter.'

'Didn't matter?' Charlie held up the milk, waiting for his nod.

'The boat,' Dave said. 'It belonged to my mum, you see.'

163

'No way?' Charlie came back into the room. He took the mug she offered, waiting for her to sit before lowering himself to the sofa. She tried to remember what they'd talked about on the back deck, her up to her armpit in canal water. Nothing about the boat, she didn't think. 'That's odd, actually, because it was my mum who bought the boat. I've only been on board for a month.' She thought of the licence, with her name on it. Charlotte Nilsson. Would she claim it as hers now, if Dave asked the question? She pulled herself back to the moment. 'Had she had it for a long time?'

'About ten years. How come you're here, not her?' His swift change of direction pushed them away from the question of his mother, and towards hers.

'It's kind of complex.' She paused, wondering how much she really wanted to get into it. On the one hand, here was an opportunity to find out more about Britta and the boat, but she could hardly jump straight in with all the details at once. 'Look, did you want to stay for something to eat? It's only going to be cheese on toast or something, but you'd be very welcome to share.'

'If you're sure.' He gave the lop-sided smile again. 'Thanks, I'd like that.'

'Where are you heading next, then?'

Dave was leaning against the opening between the living room and the kitchen. Charlie put the last plate into the bowl and turned the tap on. A trickle came out, followed by a burst of air that sprayed the last of the water over her T-shirt. 'Dammit.' She turned it off and reached for a towel. 'I'll be going to get water, by the

164

looks of it.' From the front of the boat she could hear the sound of the water pump, straining to get more water out of the tank below the deck. 'Let's go through. I need to turn that off. And then let's have some wine.'

Conversation had drifted over the evening from one area to the next: music, food, politics, schooldays. It didn't matter where they went, each choice led to a mutually experienced cultural moment. None of it was deep, as if they'd made a shared decision to keep away from that corner, but Charlie couldn't remember the last time she'd laughed so much. The boat became warm and vibrant, a glowing spot in the darkness.

'But no speakers? How do you manage without them?' Dave was sprawled back on the sofa, his arms spread out along its top edge. Charlie had curled into the armchair, her head leaning against the winged side.

'I haven't noticed not having any. And I haven't got anything to play through them anyway.' He reached over to where her phone was sitting and held it up. It took her a while to work out what he meant. 'Nope, I haven't got any downloads, either. Or enough data to stream. Back to basics, remember. Got to make your own entertainment.'

'Oh well, in that case.' He turned slightly to grab at the guitar, still resting against the sofa where Charlie had left it earlier in the day. Really just that day? Realizing that her vision was slightly hazy, she watched as he settled it in place across his knees, testing the strings.

'Nice.' He glanced up with a smile before focusing on making tiny adjustments to the tuning pegs, pinging the strings gently as he wound them to the right place.

165

She vaguely expected him to play something from the classic rock songbook, Springsteen, perhaps, or even Bon Jovi, Van Halen. The imagined soundtrack of all of the beach parties she'd missed in her life. Instead, after an initial pause, he took her completely by surprise. It was a delicate melody, transporting her to another time, though she couldn't place the period. Dave curved over the instrument with intense concentration, his fingers moving with complete control. Single clear notes sang out over the rippling, complex bassline. Charlie let herself sink back into her chair, the long day and the wine together making her head feel as if it was about to float away. The music built, layer upon layer, filling the room with tension as delicate as the skin of a bubble. It felt as if every cell of her body was being filled, every nerve soothed. And still his fingers kept going – long, sensitive fingers with wide tips and square nails. Their movement was hypnotic, compelling. Just as it almost became too much to bear, he ended with a triumphant run. His hand remained lifted in its finishing position whilst the final sounds hovered in the air.

'That was incredible,' she said at last. 'Really . . . I'm just—' She couldn't find the words to say what she wanted. 'You must play professionally, right?'

'I wish!' He gave a laugh as he swung the guitar back into its hiding place. 'Once upon a time, maybe, but that ship has gone, I reckon. The odd open mic is about all these days. It's a nice guitar, by the way.'

'My mum left it here,' Charlie explained. She swished the remainder of her wine around, watching the way it coated the glass. And suddenly she was telling him about it all. How no one had known about the boat until after her death. How Libby Rae had let drop hints of a different woman from the one Charlie had known, with new goals, new priorities. 'I wonder how long she'd been wanting to do all this.' Charlie waved a hand to take in the whole interior of the boat. 'The guitar, the books. It's all a bit strange. And she was exploring where she came from, I think, getting back to some connection with her roots.'

'And it was a completely secret life?' Dave's face was alive with interest.

'Apparently. Nobody knew anything.'

'That's pretty cool. And she left it all to you?'

'In a way.' For a second, the glamour dimmed. 'My sister's moving to a new house and our father's going to live with them. It made sense for me to take the boat for a bit. There's no timescale, as such. I'll have to make the most of it while I can.' But the boat was hers, not a joint possession, after all. And what would the legal position be if she chose not to take on Nilsson as her name? She shook the thoughts away. 'Enough about me. What made your mum decide to sell? I'd really love to talk to her about it, actually. Find out what my mum said.'

The pause stretched out, Dave staring down at where his hands were folded on his knees. What had she said? Finally, he spoke. 'Sorry, it still catches me, you know? I mean, of course you know, it must be the same for you.' He lifted his hands, rubbing them along his chin and cheeks so that Charlie heard the rasp of stubble. 'She died at the end of last year. It was my dad who sold the boat. And I've not been in contact with him much since then, sorry.'

167

'Oh, don't apologize, please. It's me that's sorry.' From somewhere in the town, a clock began to strike. Charlie waited to count the chimes, but there was just the one, its vibration dying as she listened for the next.

'Wow, didn't realize how late it'd got.' Dave made a move to stand, stretching across to reach for his bag. 'I'd better let you get to bed. And get my mate out of his to answer the door. And I was going to offer to wash up.'

Charlie moved in response, levering herself out of the chair. 'Don't worry, there's no water anyway. I'll do it tomorrow when I go to fill up.' She yawned suddenly. 'Sorry, long day.'

He yawned as well, covering his mouth with one hand and at the same time giving the impression of a rueful smile. 'Apology accepted and reciprocated.' He yawned again, and they both began to laugh. A spatter of heavy rain sounded on the side of the boat. It made up Charlie's mind for her.

'Look, why don't you stay? There's a spare bed at the back, and a sleeping bag. You can't go out in this.'

Dave paused as more rain rattled down. 'Well, if you're sure. I don't want to—'

'No, honestly.' Charlie made a move towards the kitchen. 'Let me show you where everything is. And you can give me a hand with the next lot of locks tomorrow, if you like. I've got a lot coming up, and I've heard that's hard work.'

'Deal.' He held out a hand, giving a little bow of acknowledgement as she took it. His skin was pleasantly warm, the long fingers curving around hers. She pulled back with a laugh. No point in complicating things, though he gave no indication that it was anything more than a friendly gesture. Still, the sense of his touch lingered after they'd gone to their separate rooms. She could tell where he was on the boat by the movement of the hull. There was a slight sense of instability as he moved around in the bathroom, a more definite rock as he went through to the back bedroom and climbed onto the bed.

Seventeen

Charlie slept deeply, whether as a result of the late night and the wine or the reassurance of having someone else aboard, she wasn't quite sure. She didn't know if it was the boat moving that woke her, or the noise of Dave in the bathroom. She'd drawn the dividing curtain in front of her bed the night before and, as she lay there wondering what time it was, she heard the bathroom door on her side open. The curtain fabric bellied in very slightly as a shadow made its way past. A minute later, there came the pop of the gas being lit. So very domestic.

They negotiated the water point with ease, the extra pair of hands making for far less guesswork, and were on their way by mid-morning. The rain-washed sky was clear and pale overhead, and everything glistened in the aftermath of the night's downpour.

'Which way are we going at the junction?' Dave asked, as they pulled away. A hand came out of the neighbouring boat's window, waving them on their way, and Charlie waved back, though she wasn't sure either of the boaters would be able to see her.

'Junction? What junction's that, then?' She looked over

to Dave from her place at the tiller. The excitement of moving was back again, the thrill of what was to come, even if she didn't know where that would be.

He grinned across at her, his face relaxed. Moving must be having the same effect on him as it was on her. 'In about an hour, we'll be reaching the end of the Macc. You can turn left for a tunnel leading south, or right to go up a whole bunch of locks to the north.'

'Maybe I should flip a coin?'

'A tried and tested approach. Boat coming, might want to go right a bit.' He waited for her to manoeuvre across, then picked up the conversation. 'Were you planning on a short trip, or something a bit longer?'

'I don't know really.' Charlie shifted the rudder arm so that *Skíðblaðnir*'s bow edged closer to the bank. The oncoming boat was coming down the centre of the cut, and it didn't look as if the steersman was planning to move. It didn't matter. This part of the canal was wide and straight, and the breeze was both gentle and blowing from behind them. The whole steering thing felt easy. 'I want to go down to Sneasham at some point, to follow up on the woman in the photo.'

'Margareta?'

'Well remembered!'

'I was listening.' He gave a little bow. 'That would be down to the left, then.'

'But then I was thinking about—' She cut the sentence short. She was as far across as she could get, but the line of the oncoming boat was still too close. 'Have these lot even noticed we're here? Can you give them a blast on the horn?'

171

Dave obliged with the klaxon sound. A head popped out from the other boat, wearing a peaked captain's hat, and whoever was steering made a sudden turn, too much of a turn. Charlie winced as she heard the crumple of branches on the far side. It didn't seem to bother the other boaters, though. They waved as *Skíðblaðnir* edged by, a gang of cheerful young men, all holding cans of beer.

'Idiots,' Dave commented, with a tolerant shake of his head. 'They send 'em out on those hire boats with no instructions at all. It's a wonder they don't capsize.'

'The state they were in, they'd probably not even notice.' Charlie felt *Skíðblaðnir* settle as the disturbance made by the other boat died away.

'Anyway, you were saying . . .' He waited for her to say something, but she'd forgotten where they'd got to. 'About somewhere other than Sneasham first?'

He was silent after she told him about Bella, about the visit to Max's house and the meeting with Zoe.

'And have you answered his email yet?'

'Nope.' Charlie hadn't realized how much talking about it would upset her. She stopped speaking to concentrate again on where she was going. There was a bridge ahead, and she was aware of Dave's attention as she steadied up to go through the stone arch. She knew she had plenty of space on either side, but it was still far too easy to get it wrong and end up scraping along the edge. For once everything went as it should and they got through like a slow, elegant pea through a shooter.

172

'So,' Dave said, as if their conversation had never been interrupted. 'Why is it you want to go there in person? What's your plan?'

'I don't know. I might not even contact him. But I've just had it in my mind that the canal goes right through the town, and Bella's there . . .' Her voice trailed off. It sounded pretty stupid, said out loud like that. She gave the rudder a vicious jerk, then had to correct herself before they went into the bank. She'd pushed it too far, though, and *Skíðblaðnir* began to weave, every attempt to bring her back in line taking her further off track. 'Just let me concentrate a minute, OK?'

Finally, she had it all under control again, and just in time. They were coming up to a line of moored boats on the offside, and another boat was coming into view from the other direction. If she'd been a minute later, she'd have been bouncing off everyone. Dave seemed to pick up on how she was feeling. He moved until he was just off the deck, standing on the narrow gunnel that ran down *Skíðblaðnir*'s length. With one hand holding lightly on to the railing, he stood close to the boat's side, ready to fend off from any bumps if they went too close to the moorings.

'You've got to love boat names,' he commented after a while. 'They're heavy on the puns along here.'

The boat they were passing was brand new, painted in a mirror-smooth coat of bright green paint. The name stretched along the whole of the mid-section, proclaiming *WearyTired!* in foot-high red letters. Next to them was a painting of a pair of rag dolls, leaning in to each other. 'Do you remember them? Rosie and Jim?'

'You can't forget them on the canal.' He wrinkled his forehead in thought, then started to hum. 'How did it go again? I can't believe I've forgotten it.'

'No, please!' Charlie flapped a hand. 'Please. You start it off, it'll be in your head for days. I'm telling you. I've been there! Every time I see their smug little faces squashed in a porthole!' It wasn't as if it was that funny, but she could feel laughter bubbling. 'Watch out, they're everywhere!' She pointed at the next boat, this one a little older, a little shabbier. And with a doll in each of the two front portholes, spreadeagled as if trying to escape. One a boy with floppy red woollen hair, the other a girl with long black hair tied up in a red bow. 'They're going to get you!'

It was when the painful gulps of hysteria died down that he said it. He was back on the deck, squatting by the door, and he looked up with a serious expression.

'You should go and take your dog back.'

'What?' Charlie couldn't work out at first what he was talking about. She took a moment to untangle herself from childhood TV memories. 'Bella? What do you mean?'

'You should go and get her.' He pushed himself to his feet, taking the step across to stand next to her. 'If what you're saying is right, this new girl, this—'

'Zoe,' Charlie supplied. She'd shared the fact of the younger woman being at the house, but not how it had made her feel. Old, ugly, surplus. It didn't matter how many times she reminded herself that she had been the one to go, Max's replacement of her still felt – well, like a betrayal. She wondered how his family felt about it.

174

Relieved, perhaps, that he was finally with someone who could give Max what he wanted.

'Zoe, right. Well, she leaves your dog in the garden, yes?' He waited for her to agree. 'So we go round and find her there. That proves both your point, and that your ex is either lying or deluded in saying she doesn't get left there. Which gives you ample justification for taking the dog back. And once you have the dog, most of his bargaining position would disappear, see? It's a win-win.'

He was right. Or was he? Charlie focused on where the boat was going, yet without really seeing what was in front of her. One thing rang out in her head, loud and clear. The one point he was spot-on about. If they went and found Bella shut out in the garden, she would take her. She thought about the email, about Max using Bella as a bargaining chip. *Let's see what you do about that, mate.* She was brought back to the present with a jerk. What was that noise? She eased off the throttle so that the engine quietened enough for her to listen more carefully. Nothing. She waited for a few seconds, then pushed it back into gear. And it came again.

'I think you might have run out of fuel.' Dave sounded annoyingly calm, his words a simple observation with no hint of what she should do. Why hadn't she checked the tank? Stupid, stupid. She started looking around to see where they could stop. The bank by the towpath was full, boats packed in nose to tail. The end of the line wasn't too far ahead, but would she be able to keep *Skíðblaðnir* moving forwards for long enough? And would she be able to coax the boat into the space with no power to steer her?

175

Dave was already making his way along the gunnels to the spot where the mid-rope was coiled neatly on the roof. 'Keep her going as long as you can, I'll jump over and pull her in,' he said.

'We're not going to get far enough for you to reach the bank,' she said, an absolute certainty washing over her. The breeze was still behind them, pushing them along, but without any way to steer they were going to end up on the wrong bank, unable to get back. And that bank was thick with a margin of reeds, the ground beyond inaccessible and covered in new growths of bramble.

'Come on, just a bit further.' Dave was poised, ready to jump.

Charlie risked a little acceleration, easing *Skíðblaðnir's* bow over to the right. There was a final-sounding cough from the engine, and a sudden gust that caught them side-on. That was it. All she could do was stand there whilst the boat moved on with her inexorable trajectory. Then she heard a shout from the side. Dave had somehow managed to jump onto the gunnel of the nearest boat, mid-rope in hand. She watched as he made his way along, fending away from the side of the moored boat, then clambering round the front and making it to the tow-path. There was another boat to cross before a gap, and *Skíðblaðnir* was still trying to move in the opposite direction. Charlie felt the tension as the rope tightened. Dave was leaning into it, at the same time twitching it along over the roof of the next boat. Slowly, almost imperceptibly, they began to shift in the direction he was pulling.

'Keep going, we're getting there!' Charlie edged her way out, ready to fend off as they came in closer. A head had come up above the edge of the boat they were man-oeuvring past, but not to make trouble. Instead, the man – grey-haired and bearded, with braces over an old-fashioned white shirt – went along to where Dave was trying to adjust the angle of the rope.

'You go along there now, try and get your other rope,' he said. 'I'll have this one.'

Charlie crab-walked to the bow and picked up the bow rope. Dave was standing ready to catch it as she threw. It landed short, with a splash. With red cheeks, she coiled it in, dripping, to have another try.

'Wind it up, that's the way.' Another voice was calling out, and she looked up to see the friendly little lady from the town moorings. But it couldn't be her, because they'd left her behind only that morning. 'Divide it into two, now,' she was saying. 'One half in each hand. That's right, now let's be having it.'

This time, the rope flew over with no trouble. There was nothing left for Charlie to do except stand and watch as she was reeled in, with great efficiency, by a couple of small pensioners. Her only comfort was that Dave had nothing more to do with the rescue either. She caught his eye and he winked. She winked back, and suddenly felt a lot more cheerful.

177

Eighteen

Vincent and Mary loaned them some spare fuel, Vincent insisting on pouring it into the tank for her. Charlie stood on the bank with Mary, watching as the old man organized matters on the back deck, giving out orders to Dave as assistant.

'And sure, you'd have seen my sister up there.' Mary was maybe a little younger but had the same smile. 'Will you be telling her to come out for a cruise, then?'

'I'll pass on the message if we see her,' Charlie said. 'On the way back, perhaps. Thank you so much for this. I'm not sure what we'd have done otherwise. How much do I owe you?'

'Dear God, no need to pay us just now!' Mary shook her head, patting Charlie's arm as she spoke. 'You'll be going to the marina down the way for more. Have Mick fill the cans up and keep them for us to collect. We'll be away there in the next couple of days.'

Charlie was about to ask for more detailed directions to the marina when Mary spoke again. 'He's a nice young man you have there, now.'

Charlie turned automatically to look at where Vincent and Dave had just finished with the fuel. Dave was

178

bending over, screwing the brass fuel cap back in, whilst Vincent stood by, in the middle of what must be a funny story. He came to the punchline, slapping Dave's shoulder and repeating the last line. Dave grinned up at him, then, catching Charlie's eye, gave her a wink. 'He's just a friend,' she said, turning back to the little lady and nodding. 'Here for a few days, helping me up the next lot of locks.'

'Ah, well, there's enough of them for all that,' Mary replied. 'Now that's them done and you'll be away.'

There was a flurry of thank yous and goodbyes, and Charlie swapped places with Vincent and stood on the side, waving, as they moved away. It felt a little as if she was leaving her own grandparents behind. Not that she remembered them, or at least very little. There had only been her father's, and they'd both died when she was very small. She could just summon up the memory of a musty room, an old man lying flat in a hospital-style bed. She and Eleanor had been given a battered tin of broken crayons and some brown paper bags to keep them busy. For a second, she was back there, old carpet dust in her nose and her father's voice becoming suddenly loud. *It's the best arrangement we can manage.* And then – the same visit? The room seemed different somehow – *No, Britta can't do that. This will have to do.*

'Right, what's the plan then?' Dave was next to her, jigging on his toes to keep warm in the fresh morning breeze. It was bright, at least, the banked clouds on the horizon looking as if they were going to keep their distance.

'The marina first,' Charlie told him. 'You can steer until

179

we get there. And then we've got all of those lovely locks to do.'

Dave took a turn at the tiller when they left the marina, giving Charlie the opportunity to stand and watch as the banks slipped by. Reeds gave way to tangled undergrowth, then to a tree dipping its branches into the water. For a while, the edge by the towpath was bare, the grass trodden short on the path itself but thickening into clumpy tufts to form a line between water and land. A grey shape, hunched in meditation, caught her eye. As they drew closer, she took a sharp breath in at the sight of the long thin legs, the crooked shoulders. One of the scraps in Britta's envelope: *Three herons!!* The handwriting had fizzed with pleasure. *Unless it was the same one three times* . . . At the bottom of the page was a sketch, the few lines capturing perfectly the dismissive look Charlie now saw in front of her. With a last glance, the bird gave its feathers a shake and lurched forwards, taking flight in an effort of will against gravity. Charlie watched it make a line across the neighbouring fields, an ungainly bundle with legs trailing. Then it made a turn, tucking its feet up as if making a conscious effort to tidy itself. Its neck was bent at an angle that couldn't possibly be comfortable. The bird rejected her sympathy.

The first lock of the day was the last obstacle before they moved out onto the Trent and Mersey. Dave turned, letting go of the tiller and holding out his hands, palms upwards, to offer control back to her.

'No, you stay with it.' Charlie grinned as she stepped

over to reach for the windlass. She waited at the side for the bank to come close enough to step off.

'Are you sure you remember what order to do them in?'

'Boat in, water out, boat out.' She gave a mock salute, then wheeled round before breaking into a brief jog. The pound was at its lowest, meaning a boat had gone through before them, taking the water down. She could hear her boat engine running in neutral behind her, could feel Dave watching as she wound the lock paddles up, shoulders bunching with the effort. It was her turn to watch once the water was up and the gates opened. He took *Skíðblaðnir* in with ease, not touching the sides at all, his expression focused and absorbed in the action. There could be worse companions to be landed with. He turned as if he had heard her, and flashed a fast, companionable smile. Charlie felt her cheeks heat up, as if she'd been caught out in something, and she hurried to swing the gates shut. 'Let's not get carried away, hey, girl?' she whispered, either to herself or to the boat.

They took turns steering and opening locks after that, glad of the biscuits and chocolate they'd bought at the marina along with the fuel. It all made do for lunch rather than stopping to see what food there was in the cupboards. The day was tiring, though sometimes boats were coming down, leaving the gate open for them to go straight in. One of the boaters stopped to warn them of someone ahead who kept forgetting to close the gates properly, draining the pounds; they'd been held up for over an hour waiting for one to refill.

There was an incident halfway through, when they

181

were on a stretch between locks. Dave was just bringing out mugs of tea when they came up alongside a man on the bank. He was young, dressed in jeans and a hoody, a fishing line jammed under one arm as he bent his head to light a cigarette. Charlie was reaching out for her mug and wasn't quite quick enough to catch *Skíðblaðnir* as a gust sent her sideways.

'Watch where you're bloody going!'

Charlie was too busy with the boat to pay much attention, but Dave reacted with unexpected force.

'Have you got a problem?'

She turned to see him move out onto the side of the boat, hanging with one hand on the rail.

'Yeah!' The man was walking now, keeping pace with them. 'With bloody women drivers cocking up my lines. You need to get her in her place, mate.'

For a second, Charlie thought Dave was going to try to jump over to the bank. 'Just ignore him,' she said, shifting the engine to a slightly faster speed. The gap was too wide for him to get across, but he stayed where he was, holding eye contact with the other man until he gave up and went back to his pitch.

'Arsehole.' He was still on alert, hackles raised.

'He's a fisherman.' Charlie had listened to a few choice opinions on fishermen from Bob and Libby Rae. 'They can't all be woke, what you gonna do?'

To her relief, he gave a laugh and turned back to the deck, settling himself down against the door-frame and picking up a sandwich. A clutch of ducklings came into view, five or six of them strung out close to the bank. Not tiny fluffballs as she'd seen on previous days, but with

182

the tracery of adult feathers starting to show on their active little bodies. The mother was still with them, circling as the wake from the boat jolted them up and down. Charlie chucked a crust across to them and watched as they swam across the surface of the water towards them. She could feel Dave watching her.

'What?' she asked, relieved that his momentary anger had subsided.

He shook his head in response. 'You should eat your crusts, didn't your mother ever tell you?'

Charlie lifted her eyebrows. 'Quite frankly, if you can resist ducklings, you're beyond human help.'

'Oh, I can't resist them at all,' he replied. 'Shredded with crispy pancakes, roasted with a honey glaze . . .'

She aimed a swipe at his shoulder. He was out of her reach, though, laughing as he threw his own crusts out to the brood. It was good for both of them, she thought, that mothers could still be mentioned in a light-hearted way.

The plan had been eighteen locks by the end of the day, but in the end they stopped after twelve. As Charlie guided the boat out of the last one, Dave was pointing towards a white-painted pub standing side-on to the water.

'Dinner!' he called, as soon as she was close enough. 'And I have an idea.'

He helped her to tie up to the bank, then disappeared inside. Charlie was too tired to really wonder what he was doing. She just hoped they wouldn't get to the pub and find that they weren't doing food. Now that they'd stopped, she wasn't sure she'd be able to do anything else, even eat. Left to herself, she'd be in bed.

183

They didn't talk much whilst they waited for the food. Charlie sipped slowly on her lime and soda. Alcohol had been tempting but would have made the possibility of falling asleep before she'd eaten into a probability. How could standing on the back of a boat, or walking round from one side of a lock gate to the other, be so very tiring?

'Is it always this hard?' she asked.

'What, locks?' Dave shrugged, taking a mouthful of his beer. 'Sometimes. This stretch does have a lot in a row, but they're spread out a bit. Tardebigge's got thirty in just over two miles.'

Charlie sat up. 'We don't have that coming up, do we?'

'No.' He laughed across at her, giving his head a shake as she collapsed back down in her seat. 'But that is what I was thinking.' He put something on the table, spinning it round so the title was level between them. 'Map of the waterways.'

'Can we get this bit out of the way first before we plan the next stage?' *Bella.* Her mind thrust the thought into her head, up from the secondary layer she'd pushed it down into. The plan bobbed up as well. In this setting, with a couple of guys leaning on the bar to her left and a family settling in for a meal on the far side of the quiet room, it seemed ridiculous. They'd drag their way through all thirty locks, or whatever it was, and find the house closed and no sign of Bella. Or, worse, they'd hear her through the door and be unable to do anything about it. Or Max would be home and the two men would get into an argument. Charlie thought briefly of Dave's reaction to the fisherman. Was she making a fool of herself?

Dave was unfolding the map, manipulating it into the shape he wanted. 'We're here, OK?' Charlie nodded. She'd have to trust him on that. 'And we're heading up here.' His finger landed on a diagonal point up and to the left. In between she could see the canal, bristling with the little arrowheads which signified a lock. They'd hardly made a dent in the number. 'It's going to take at least another day, possibly two, to get up there, and then three more to get back to where we started.'

Charlie blinked to clear her vision and tried to take in what he was showing her. Was he about to say he couldn't come with her after all? But it had been his idea! Her doubts about the plan grew, yet at the same time she felt more determined that it should be carried out. How could she not, now? With him or without him. 'If you have to get back— I mean, I can get there, don't feel you have to stick around.'

'No, it's not that.' He came to her side of the table, sitting on the other chair and straightening the map so that it was in front of them both. 'You want to get up there, check things out, and then go straight back down, right?' She took a moment to let the statement run through her tired mind and then nodded. 'The thing with locks is that they take up time without necessarily getting you much further forwards. There's a winding hole here.' He tapped a spot just along from the position he'd said was their current location. 'We can turn in the morning, leave *Skíðblaðnir* tied up, and walk the rest of the way. I reckon it'll take, what, an hour? Then we can be back on board and on our way down again, get to the tunnel for the evening. It'll save time, energy, all the good things, right?'

185

'Steak pie?' The waitress's words took a moment to filter through. Charlie heard Dave thanking the girl, smelled the fragrance of the gravy coming from his plate. Her own food arrived as well, and she dug her fork in but then stopped before lifting it up.

'So we just have the locks we did today to go down?' The futility of the journey struck her. Maybe she should just turn back altogether. Everything she tried turned out wrong. She put the fork down, hopelessness building up behind her nose and cheekbones, the pressure salty and cutting.

'Well, there is that.' Dave wasn't sounding as though it was all an unmitigated disaster. He spoke through a mouthful of pie. 'But think about it positively. You get your dog and only have to do twelve locks. If we go all the way through, we'd have to be coming down through thirty to get you back. You don't want what's-her-name coming and finding us halfway down a lock, right?' He glanced up at her and noticed the tears that had finally spilled out. 'Hey, no need for that!' He took a napkin and dabbed at her face. 'You're just tired and hungry, OK? Go on, get stuck in. You don't want it getting cold.'

Nineteen

A chunky yellow retriever snuffled outside the open side hatch, stopping to cock his leg against the centre mooring pin. She turned to Dave, about to make a joke, say that he could get that pin out when they got back. He was looking at her, an expression on his face that she didn't want to analyse. It was only there for a second anyway; almost before she'd seen it, he'd turned away and was filling a bottle of water at the sink.

'Don't want to be getting dehydrated,' he said, turning back and gesturing to the front of the boat. 'OK, Operation Bella. Shall we make a start?'

Charlie closed the hatch doors and led the way out.

The sun was staying put behind a stubborn, flat layer of cloud. Charlie could feel a buzzing in her feet, almost like a tiny electrical current preparing her for the task ahead. *Skíðblaðnir* was a fair distance behind them now, bobbing at her moorings with the canal stretching before her like an escape route. Would they need it? She had a picture in her mind of them both making a run for it after whatever was about to happen. The little figures in her imagination jumped on board and started the boat up, heading away at the vessel's ponderous walking speed before having to stop at the next locks, held stationary whilst the necessary openings were done. Not the best getaway vehicle.

'Is it still a penny for them, or has inflation changed it for ever?'

'What?' She belatedly realized Dave was talking. 'Sorry, miles away.'

'No worries.' He didn't carry on with whatever it was he'd been saying, and they walked along in silence for a while, the sound of their feet falling into rhythm with each other.

'You've never said, you know, about the boat.' Charlie looked round at him in the end, suddenly curious. They'd talked about a lot of things, but more about her than Dave.

'What about it?' Dave seemed relaxed, but his pace sped up a little at her question. Charlie reached out and snapped the head from a strand of cow-parsley. The umbrella of tiny blossoms spun as she twirled the stem.

'Why have I got it rather than you? I mean, you said you wanted a boat.' For a moment, she thought she'd gone too far. Then he shook his head and picked a flower-head for himself, systematically stripping off the petals as he spoke.

'Bad timing, really. I mean, it wasn't anyone's fault.' He was down to the last few, the elderflower a mass of tiny stalks. With a flick, he tossed it into the water. 'The boat was their thing, my mum and dad's. A retirement thing, you know. But when Mum got ill, they couldn't use it any more. They even offered it to me.' He gave a brief,

188

humourless laugh. 'But I'd just met someone, we were making all these plans. I didn't have the headspace to see ahead. And then . . .' He reached for another stalk, began to strip that as well. 'Mum died, the relationship broke down. Everything was a bit of a mess. I think on one level I was waiting for Dad to suggest it again, but he didn't.'

'I'm really sorry.' Timing. Charlie could appreciate how that played out.

'Not your fault.' He tossed the second stalk away as well and gave her his half-smile. 'It's the way it goes, isn't it? Maybe you needed it more than I did. The universe works it out in the end.' There was a pause. 'Look, it's really helped being able to do this with you, to help you. I've been in a bad place, and this has made a difference.'

The road was quiet as they made their way along to the house. Charlie pointed it out, checking the drive as she did so. There was no sign of Max's car. Dave nodded and moved ahead. Charlie was going to peel off early, taking the alley a few houses short to make her way around to the back. From there, she'd be able to see into the garden. Dave would go to the door, pretending to be checking for a misdelivered parcel in order to see if Zoe was there. Charlie watched him walk away. This was ridiculous. They were acting out a very bad pilot episode for a series that would flop. Dave turned, giving her a quick double thumbs up. She was on the edge of calling him back to say she'd changed her mind.

'Hey, Charlie?'

The sound of the voice behind her made her jump, in the way that never convinced her on television: one

189

hand to her chest, an exaggerated breath out. It was Steve, a neighbour from a couple of doors down, walking down the alley towards her.

'Oh, hi, how are you?' She could see Dave going up the drive, waiting at the door. It was all going to descend into a horrible, second-rate cliché.

'I'm good, yeah, all good.' He stood there, a slightly overweight guy dressed in clothes that were just a bit too young for him. She could spot the moment when he became embarrassed. He looked round to check that Max wasn't there, then down at the ground. She'd only ever met him properly once or twice. He was divorced, had spent one very long evening at another neighbour's housewarming telling her about his battle to have his sons spend more time with him. 'So . . .' The pause lengthened. 'You're back in England.'

'Yep.' Charlie glanced down the road again. Dave would be coming back any minute. It didn't look as if anyone had come to the door. 'Steve, can I ask you something?'

'Sure, yes.' He looked uncomfortable. If he'd been wearing a shirt and tie, he'd have had to run a finger around the collar. He must be expecting her to ask him about Zoe.

'Mrs Crabbe, you know, on the other side of us?' He gave a cautious nod. 'She was saying that Bella gets left outside a lot. You know, our dog?'

'Look, I don't want to get involved.' He glanced about him, as if expecting to see Max hanging over him, hearing him take sides. Then he took a deep breath. 'There is a lot of barking sometimes.'

190

Charlie barely waited for long enough to respond. She ran down the alley, almost falling into the narrow path that ran along the back of all the gardens. People kept their bins here, children's toys that were OK in the rain. One house had a motorbike chained to a concrete post. Breathing hard, Charlie slowed as she reached her old gate. She didn't want Bella to hear her and be jumping at the fence in excitement. That would only tell her the dog was outside now, not how often. Here was the familiar blue-painted wood, the gate with a circular porthole shape cut out in the top half. She sensed rather than heard Dave come up behind her, and held up a warning hand.

Bella was sitting in a forlorn bundle just short of the back step. There was a plastic dog bed some distance from her, a thin blanket hanging over its edge. As Charlie watched, she got to her feet, trying to go towards the back door. Something was stopping her though. She was on a chain, the end attached to one of those corkscrews that dug into the ground. As they stood there, it began to rain.

'Right, that's it.' Charlie turned to Dave. 'There wasn't anyone in, was there?'

'Nope. I rang a couple of times and knocked.' He gave the gate a nudge. 'This is locked, right?'

'I think so. Give me a foot up?'

Bella spotted her before she'd even got one leg onto the fence. Charlie fell over the wall to the accompaniment of wild yips and whining. She stumbled across, calling out calming words as the little dog leapt against the restraint of the chain. When she got to her, it was all

191

she could do to contain the mad jumps and frantic licks. The confusion made her struggle to unclip the chain from her collar. Her hands were trembling almost too much to work, and she kept expecting to hear someone coming to intervene, Zoe arriving back. She'd almost have welcomed that, mind. She had a few things she wanted to say.

It wasn't until, dog in arms, she'd got back to the gate that she realized she didn't have a lead. There was nothing lying around either. She'd just have to look out for something on the way, carrying Bella in the meantime. Dave took Bella, and Charlie followed, tears of emotion blurring her vision. And then Bella was squirming back to her and they were running away, back to the canal, back to the boat.

'So, tell me again what kind of dog she is?'

They'd found a corner shop which sold all sorts of stuff, including leads and dog toys. Dave was carrying a plastic bag filled with purchases, and Charlie stopped to grab another handful of treats from it.

'She's nothing definite.' Squatting down, Charlie let Bella jump up on her knee and lick her face again. 'Some kind of terrier, though it's hard to know which one. Something else that was black and white. The best kind, in fact. Big enough to keep up, small enough to sit on your knee.'

The sun had made its way out, though the ground was still wet underfoot. They were about halfway back to the boat, and Bella was beginning to make wider forays around, going after interesting smells. She didn't

192

venture far, though, and kept stopping to check that Charlie was still there.

'Let me try her with a biscuit again.' Dave held it out towards her, but she wouldn't come up to him. 'Nope, still not having it.'

'Give her a bit longer,' Charlie said. She felt like a mother whose child wouldn't say thank you. 'It's been a strange time for her.'

'How do you think she'll be on the boat?'

Charlie stood up, clicking her fingers at Bella to get her moving in the right direction. 'I haven't even thought about that. Do you think she needs a life jacket?'

'I don't think she's going to go far enough away from you to worry about the water,' Dave said. 'So looks like I'm on lock duty this afternoon.'

'How far do you think we'll get?' Charlie was glad to hear that he wanted to be moving straight away. She felt edgy alongside the pleasure of having Bella back, and aware of an anger she wasn't letting herself acknowledge completely. Because, although the straightforward rage at how they'd found Bella was enough to keep her walking, it wasn't as simple as she'd hoped. However easy it was to build up a head of steam against Zoe, and however furious she was at how Max had let her down, she couldn't quieten the voice that told her it would never have happened if she hadn't left.

She managed to keep it all in until the evening. They'd made their way back down half of the locks and moored up for the night, with Bella adapting to the new way of travelling without any obvious trouble. They'd eaten as

193

well, and had just come back from a last little walk for Bella on the bank when it happened.

Three mallards were circling a female. The duck paddled in a circle, making a break for the bank, but one of the drakes jumped on her, holding her head down under the water. She broke away, but her assailant was too fast, grabbing her neck with an outburst of noise. Charlie looked around for something to use, a rock, a branch. There was nothing there, just clumps of grass, twigs of spindly hawthorn. Nothing on the boat roof, or at least nothing she wanted to throw into the water. Then she spotted the mid-rope, coiled in its place, but on the near side. It might reach. She stepped onto the gunnel, lifting the coil as she'd done when throwing it out to Mary, one half in each hand. Leaning as far across as she could, she let it go. The tail end fell a little short of the still brawling group of ducks. It created enough of a splash to make them break apart, though, and just as the female got away, batting at the water with her wings before taking off in flight, Charlie's foot slipped and she lost her balance. She didn't go all the way in, just one leg, but her arm was wrenched where she was still holding on to the boat, and the pain made her cry out.

Dave reached her just as she jumped over to the bank. 'That's enough rescuing for one day.' She felt his hand feeling over her damaged shoulder. 'It's all right, nothing broken.' It was, though. It felt, just at that moment, that everything was broken, and she turned to bury her head into his shoulder. 'Hey, what's all that about?' He had an arm around her now, his voice gentle in her ear. And the gentleness made her cry even harder.

'I'm sorry, I don't even know why I'm crying.' She clung on, too tired suddenly to stand without his support. Bella was scratching at her leg, wanting to know what was wrong. Charlie put a hand down to pet at her head, to reassure her. She needed to get herself together, but it was hard to move away from the warmth of Dave's arm. It was so long since she'd been like this, with the feeling of a hand pressed against her back, shoulder bone and T-shirt against her cheek. The soft skin of a neck. It was always so untouched there, under the chin. She wanted to reach up and stroke it, but then the moment would end. It would end any minute anyway.

Twenty

The sounds of the canal carried on around them. A splash and some final quacks from the ducks, still trying to work out where the female had gone. A late blackbird, giving one final chorus of joy from the hedgerow. Dave's heart, beating against her. Was it beating as fast as hers?

'I need to get that rope in,' she whispered at last.

'I'll do it.' His voice was husky, and he didn't move at first. When he did, the emptiness was a shock, and she couldn't move to do anything. Instead she waited, the inevitability holding her in place. Bella had moved away to investigate a smell in the long grass, and Charlie watched her snuffle as she listened to the sound of the rope leaving the water, being coiled and placed on the roof. Then Dave was back, standing in front of her with a question in his face. She nodded, a tiny movement, and led the way back into the boat.

They were moving together, an almost imperceptible rocking motion, and her brain was closing down. She pulled away for a moment, unsure if she wanted to give herself a chance to draw back or offer that opportunity to Dave. He showed no sign of wanting to retreat,

196

though he wasn't charging in either. She felt his thumb very gently rub against her neck. A small gesture, opening up for the next move to be hers. In response, she leaned very slightly closer in.

His heart was beating against her again, this time with a fast and jerky rhythm. His T-shirt was warm, the cotton slightly damp and smelling faintly of fresh sweat. Her skin bloomed into a million tiny explosions as his palms moved, fingers spreading out across the small of her back. She made her own exploratory move, slipping one palm down over his shoulder blade, and then round to the front, moving up to his chest. Her touch snagged on his T-shirt, grazing the nipple underneath. Dave made an inarticulate sound and any rational thought left her.

They stumbled through the kitchen in an awkward, three-legged gait, clothes coming off, skin not losing contact. Charlie couldn't recall the last time she'd kissed with this intensity. It was as if her whole being was there, in the stretching of her lips, the squirming contact of their tongues. And then they were on her bed, Dave bare-skinned beneath her. She had never been this wet, never been this ready to explode. His fingers brushed down her stomach, strayed into her pubic hair. She was so ready. Just a touch lower and she'd be gone. She could already visualize the waves of response, the feel of him inside her, building to his own climax. And then, just as he was about to get there, he moved his hand away.

The pause was momentary. She could feel the inside of her knee against his thigh, his fingers curving around her bottom. And then, without warning, he pushed

197

her over, swapping their positions with a grasp that was both possessive and urgent.

'Condom?' His voice was ragged and croaky.

It took a moment for the word to make its way through. She just wanted him to keep going, to keep touching. She wanted to close her eyes and let the senses take over, but also to see where her hands were moving. The line on his arm where tan faded into paleness, the muscles on his thighs, the smoothness of his chest. 'On the pill,' she managed, reaching for him.

'We can stop if you want.'

'No, please.' She pulled him in, felt him hard against her. The moment had shifted things a little, though. It was all still there, the need, the receptors on her skin alive for his touch, but the rhythm had changed, had come somehow out of sync. His touch wasn't quite in the right place, and ended too soon, or moved away from the exact right spot to leave her just short of the tipping point. And then it became the two of them scrabbling around in the sheets, the second-hand thrill of hearing his voice burst out, as if in pain. And the tension breaking as Bella skittered through from the sofa in answer to the call, jumping on the bed to thrust a cold nose against their faces.

They stayed together in the exhausted aftermath. Dave slept and she watched him sleep, the weight of his arm heavy across her. It wasn't that she hadn't enjoyed it. Maybe it always took some time to get it working for both of them. Though would they end up taking that time? She wasn't sure. So many things she wasn't sure about. Her hand moved, its familiar touch bringing a surprisingly satisfying end to the encounter, and finally she slept.

198

Twenty-one

She was woken by her phone ringing, and rolled to one side to grab at it. Dave was gone, in the kitchen with Bella by the sound of it. Eleanor's name was on the screen.

'Hello.' She hadn't got around to checking the time, had no idea if it would be appropriate to sound as if she'd just woken up.

'Late night?' Eleanor's tone made her think it was late enough. 'I thought I should check in, see how you were getting on.'

Charlie dragged her mind back to their last call. How many days ago had it been, three? Four, even? She remembered crying on the phone. She was going to have to stop that, all the crying on people. Look what it got her into. She pushed herself up so that she was sitting against her pillows. 'Yes, I'm all right, good actually. Sorry, I did mean to call, but it's been a bit busy.' She couldn't decide whether to tell Eleanor about Bella or not. She probably wouldn't approve, would think she should have waited to sort it out properly, like a grown-up. And telling her would also mean explaining about Dave, and she really didn't want to get into that. Not yet, anyway. As if on cue, Dave's face appeared around the curtain. She gestured to be quiet, pointed to the phone. He mimed drinking and she nodded.

'Is someone there?' Eleanor's extra-sensory perception made her jump. How had she picked up on that?

'No, just someone on the bank. Look, I've got loads to tell you, but can I call back in a bit? I need some coffee.'

'Yes, sure.' It struck her that Eleanor sounded tired and irritable. 'Poppy, no, leave that alone, put it DOWN.' Charlie held the phone away until the volume decreased. 'Look, I've got to go. Can you make it after bedtime?' And she was gone before Charlie could agree.

Charlie swung her legs over the edge of the bed, noticing that her clothes had been picked up and folded into a neat pile. She reached for her T-shirt and pulled it on. There was time for a shower before she did anything else.

As she stood under the water, letting it run for longer than she usually allowed herself, she thought about Dave, about the previous night. How much had it complicated things? How much did she want to take from it? And, if she did, what would he want to do? He'd seemed to be saying that he'd be heading off after going back down the locks. She ran it around in her head as she washed off the traces of their encounter. It would be neat, in a way, saying goodbye more or less where he'd met up with her. And she wanted to, maybe needed to, do the next stage of the journey by herself. Sneasham and Margareta. Was there any chance of finding an answer?

Dave was out on the bank, playing with Bella. Charlie felt as if she was seeing the towpath for the first time. The rain from the past few days had made the season take a jump forward, the greenery of the hedgerow switching into summer as if with the turn of a dial. Plants jostled for space, all the new growth green and thick and pushy. She could smell their vigour, pungent and spicy, dark green and bitter. Standing at the hatch with the coffee Dave had left for her, she tried to put names to what she could see. It was the time of year for frothy white blooms: cow-parsley, and what she thought was hawthorn in the hedge. Elderflower hanging over them, the smell part nectar, part cat's piss. Maybe she could make some cordial. Then there were nettles, of course, the lower leaves thick, the new growth tiny and pale. *Watch for those nettles, Charlie, they will sting you. Unless you grasp them firmly.* Britta's voice came out of nowhere, another forgotten moment pushing its way into her mind's eye. Her mother standing up with a sigh, a small smile flickering into life. *In Norway nettles don't grow as weeds. We have to plant them from seed, then we use them for tea, it's very healthy.*

It was odd, really, that there weren't any plants on the boat. The garden at home had been one place Britta had engaged with. Charlie could picture her at different times of the year, deadheading roses, planting out annuals, her hair always tied back with a scarf. The absence of anything green here was stark, now Charlie thought about it. Maybe Britta hadn't liked gardening as much as she'd claimed. This thought shook Charlie more than she expected. It would have meant a lot of acting, and for what purpose?

Thinking of plants she might herself buy – geraniums, herbs – Charlie turned to the worktop where she had the canal guide laid out. It was time to trace the route

201

ahead, to work out how many hours it would take, count up the locks and swing bridges. Knowing exactly what was coming made it feel like she was in control, that she could manage. She ran through the names of towns she'd be passing through: Rugeley, Hopwas, Fenny Stratford. The list reminded her of the train stations she'd passed on her way across to Sheffield all that time ago. How long was it that she'd been back? Two months, a flash into nowhere or a lifetime, she couldn't decide which. *Concentrate on what's happening now.* The guide took a leisurely approach, the section of water on each page in close-up. On this page, the train line was shown, running in parallel to the canal. It curved away as she turned the page only to reappear further along. It was as if it was checking in, keeping an eye. Who would be keeping an eye on her? Not Dave, though he might want to know how she was getting on. Eleanor. Britta.

She felt the boat rock as Dave came back on board, and seconds later Bella was pawing at her legs.

'Hey Bella, was the bank fun? Did you see any rabbits?'

'There may have been some rabbit smells.' Dave was behind her, stopping short. He wasn't hesitant, exactly, more giving her the space to make the first move. Charlie wasn't sure if she was glad about that or not. 'Looking up what you've got coming?'

There it was, *what you've got coming.* You, not we. That was what she wanted, though, wasn't it? She smiled without moving towards him. 'Yep. Just scoping out the tunnel.' Her first tunnel. She didn't want to admit how daunting the thought of it was.

202

'You'll be fine.' Did he seem a tiny bit disappointed? It was hard to say. 'Well, let's get back down the locks, then I'd better be off.'

'Dave.' She paused, not sure what she wanted to say, but he was there, waiting. 'Look, about last night—'

'It's OK.' He smiled, gave her shoulder a quick caress. 'You have things to do.'

'Yes, but thank you.' She touched his hand, kept it on her shoulder for a long moment. Then she stood up decisively. 'Let's get this boat on the road.'

Twenty-two

He left her at the junction, heading up the towpath on the route they'd come down just a couple of days earlier. As she watched him give one last wave before disappearing around the corner, Charlie felt a burst of emptiness. The boat felt empty, too light. It was a mistake, going on by herself. For a minute she hesitated, on the verge of calling him back. Just for the tunnel. Or the next lot of locks. It wouldn't do, though. She'd made the right decision. At least she had Bella with her. The terrier ran around her feet as she went inside to get a bottle of water. No point in waiting. She might as well get through the tunnel, and then she could have a proper rest without the thought of dark spaces invading her dreams. As she went into the kitchen, she spotted something new written on one corner of the blackboard-fronted cupboard. A mobile number and a message: *Let me know how you get on x.* She squatted to look at it more closely, the letters giving her a surprisingly strong jolt of pleasure. Without thinking too hard, she pulled out her phone and tapped a message. *If you don't hear from me, it's because I'm lost in the tunnel.* The answer came straight back. *Watch out for monsters! (You'll be fine x)*

204

Two miles underground, more or less. Just her and Bella and *Skíðblaðnir*, heading towards the dark. A little team of women. She went through the checklist in her mind, silently thanking Dave for making sure she was prepared. Headlight on, torch at the ready. Waterproof for the drips from the roof. It was nearly time to shut Bella into the boat, no matter how appealingly she used her eyes to ask to stay on the deck. Charlie imagined her slipping off, scrabbling at the side, squashed up against the walls in that narrow space. It made the bottom of her stomach disintegrate into a kind of vertigo.

She was so focused on where she was going that she didn't notice the figure loping along the towpath. Two minutes later and she'd have left him behind, unseen. It was Bella who spotted him first, wriggling flat on her stomach with her tail lashing back and forth. Charlie would have looked round to see what was causing the excitement, but there was a tricky section coming up. A bend, a swamp of reeds blocking the far side, moored boats to avoid.

'What the FUCK do you think you're doing?' The sound made her nearly lose hold of the tiller, and *Skíðblaðnir*'s nose began to head towards the first of the boats as Charlie spun round. Max. What was he doing, how had he found her? He was in his work clothes, suit jacket open and flapping as he strode along, leather shoes slipping on the muddy path.

Charlie turned back to check where she was. Too close. She shoved the throttle forwards for a burst of power whilst leaning her full weight on the tiller arm to kick the boat back out towards the channel. She missed the moored boat by a whisker, leaving it rocking. With a quick step forward, Charlie bundled Bella down into the boat and slammed the door shut. Then she was back up to correct her line again, and there was the tunnel, almost upon them. She sent the engine briefly into reverse, to slow down, and then neutral, so she could be heard above the sound of the engine.

'Bella was tied up in the garden, by herself, in the rain. With no one in the house. I'd like to see your girl-friend exaggerate her way out of that one.' She gave the engine a short rev, and then paused it. 'And before you say why didn't I talk to you about it, after the email you sent I didn't think there was any point.'

With that, she set the boat off again. Her legs were trembling, her hand shaking as it grasped the wooden handle, but at least she'd had her say. Behind, she heard Max shout something, but the engine noise drowned out the sense of the words. She glanced back briefly to see someone coming out of a moored boat, apparently asking what the hell was going on. Then the impact of the bow bumping up against the tunnel's entrance shuddered through the boat and she turned back. She needed to concentrate now.

Skíðblaðnir was vanishing chunk by chunk into the tunnel, her colours changing as she went from the light to the darkness. The tunnel was reaching out to her, enfolding her, but whether in a helpful or daunting way, she couldn't quite decide. She was committed, anyway. The brickwork came up around her, like blinkers, leav-ing the world behind. And then she was underground.

Inside, the atmosphere was heavy and cold. Did the

air absorb the damp of the brick walls, giving it a different composition to the air outside? Or was it just that it sat here, sluggish and dense, never quite being refreshed by incoming boats? She was pushing into it as an explorer might make their way through thick jungle foliage, the vines and creepers falling back down as she passed, hiding her from view. For a brief moment she found it hard to draw in a full breath. Her lungs twitched with a sense of desperation, as if she was going under the water as well as under the ground. There should be a candle on the distant front edge, flickering steadily as a marker of safety, a canary perched way ahead.

She could still hold on to an awareness of the world behind her. The half-moon of the tunnel entrance was reflected in the water, creating an oval of light, a portal that she could not now access. It retreated behind her at a speed that was surely greater than that at which she was travelling. She had to stop holding her breath. For a second, she allowed herself to think of the weight of earth above her, a mound enclosing her as completely as a body in an ancient barrow. The throb of the engine filled the space, the sound waves bouncing from the curved walls, cutting her off from anything beyond her vision. On impulse, she turned the key and quietened the racket. *Skíðblaðnir* continued forwards in the sudden quiet, as yet unaware that the force pushing her had stopped. The remembered thump of the engine still reverberated, a silent bass accompaniment to the dripping of water from above, the light swish of the hull below. Charlie could almost hear the sound of footsteps above her, as if Max was up there, his weight making the earth ceiling creak. The boat moved at walking pace so, if he did follow them, they'd arrive at the tunnel exit at the same time. Briefly she pictured him forcing his way through scrub, vaulting gates, squeezing between strands of barbed wire. It wasn't going to happen. There was no footpath for him to follow, for a start, no markers to indicate where the canal was heading far below. And he wasn't dressed for a cross-country walk.

The scrape of metal against stone brought her back to the moment. Still she paused, not wanting to lose the ability to hear. She couldn't stay there, though, suspended in the dark. Not least because another boat might come at any time. With a slow hand, she turned the key and the engine jumped to life again, demanding movement, and Charlie felt the darkness begin to move past. She should put the headlight on. It would give her a sense of reality, never mind give notice of her presence to a boat coming the opposite way. A crump of metal. The slow sinking of her boat, her plans. With a sudden flash of panic, she turned the engine off once more, straining for the sound of another engine. How close would it have to be for her to hear it? But what if it was silent, creeping up behind her in ambush? Her mind flashed out a complete image, perfect in every detail. Figures emerging from dark boats at the tunnel's opening, untying ropes, pushing off to sneak in under cover of the noise *Skíðblaðnir* was making. Closing in, silent figures in wetsuits swarming up from the black water. *Watch out for monsters.*

'Get a grip.' Her voice was small, but it pushed her into snapping on the headlight, and a glow of yellow

208

was thrown against the red of the walls. It brought rationality along with colour, and she shouted the words out as she set the engine going again. The only way she was going to get out was by going forwards.

Even so, the journey felt endless. The bricks alongside her slid past. They didn't care. She was one of many. Behind her, the water was churning in a vacuum. At times it felt as if she was stationary, the tunnel walls a trick, moving onwards in an endless loop. Blood throbbed through her ears in time with the engine noise. *Skíðblaðnir* slid onwards, oblivious, the long line of her roof oddly comforting. The two of them against the world, the boat a weight of steel at her command. As if aware that she was being left out, Bella scrabbled against the door. Charlie called out to her, promising it wouldn't be long. Underneath the water, the blades of the propeller were a bonus weapon in a computer game, protecting her from foes behind. The idea made her laugh out loud, the sound becoming absorbed by the air behind her as if it had never been.

A sudden trickle of water splashed cold on the back of her neck, making her jump. For a second, it was the sea above the tunnel's roof, about to pour down and drown her. At least that wasn't the problem. She saw herself from a distance, *Skíðblaðnir* nothing but a tiny shape moving along the narrow strip of the canal, herself a miniature figure on the back deck, a stick person holding an invisible tiller. With a rush, she came back to the tunnel, the wooden end of the tiller arm smooth under her palm, the water churning along the sides of the boat.

209

When it came, the pinhole of light at the far end seemed like an optical illusion, conjured up from too much looking. Charlie flicked the headlight off to check, leaving the tunnel dark around her. For a second, she couldn't even see the flat line of *Skíðblaðnir*'s roof, right there in front of her. As the reminder of the outside world ahead of her grew, from a speck to a blob to an oval matching the one she'd left behind, it was as if the straight edges of the tunnel began to distort. Would Max be waiting for her, ready to carry on arguing? Before today, the boat had felt like a hiding place, somewhere she couldn't be traced. But that was an illusion. He wouldn't be there, because now he knew where he could find her. Because how could you hide on a strip of water, with no escape routes, no alternatives?

The tunnel was widening as the light grew stronger. Charlie reached for the throttle but, instead of speeding up to reach the approaching light, she pulled back into neutral. The boat hung in space, mirroring her reluctance. It was as if the dark length of tunnel behind her pulsed, but she couldn't tell if it was trying to draw her back in or spit her out. There was only one way, really. With a final burst of acceleration, *Skíðblaðnir* bucked forwards.

The sunlight was golden, the world reset in her absence. An impossible collage of light and colour flared across her eyeballs, leaving her in a moment of blindness. And then the anticlimax. She'd made it through the tunnel, by herself, but what was the use of that when there was no one to share the news with? Instead of the mass of the hill sitting above her, each boat-length she moved brought a weight of negative thinking. She'd never find Margareta, never work out what her mother had been thinking. Bella, released back onto the deck, sensed her mood and kept close to her legs. That small pressure, of warmth and fur, kept Charlie going, far beyond the limits of tiredness. It wasn't rational: there were only two ways she could go, after all, forward or back. If Max really wanted to find her, all he had to do was keep walking along the canal. She didn't think he would, not really, but she wasn't going to risk making it easy for him.

The conversation with Eleanor, when she finally got through, was brief and unsatisfactory. She couldn't explain why her plan to follow the clues on the boat made sense, and Eleanor seemed to be less interested in the possibilities of the discovery than in picking holes in her reasoning.

'It just seems like a waste of time. And what are the chances of that woman still living there?'

'She's called Margareta,' Charlie told her. 'And you never know.' She had the cutting in front of her, and she tilted the sheet in case that made it any easier to decode. 'I just think it's interesting. Look, I'm going to take a photo of it and send it to you.' She switched the phone onto loudspeaker so that she could do it as they talked. 'Did you ask about any relatives, by the way?'

There was a pause at the other end. Finally Eleanor spoke. 'It's a bit weird, actually.'

'Weird in what way?' Charlie waited for the answer. 'Eleanor? What's weird?'

211

She heard a sigh. 'Dad wouldn't talk about it, and he claimed to have mislaid all the paperwork, birth certificates and whatnot. So I went to the library to see if I could find anything on Ancestry.'

'On what?'

'Ancestry. It's a website you can use in the library . . . Look, it doesn't matter. I just couldn't find her on it, that's all.'

'What, like a birth record?'

'It was probably my fault. I'll try again when Poppy's at school. I'll have missed her in all the Nilssons, it'll be like looking for a Smith here.'

'OK, let me know. What's happening about the move?'

Eleanor sighed again. 'It all fell through. We were literally about to sign the contract and something happened at their end, some problem with the solicitor they'd been using. It'll be all right, I'm sure we'll find somewhere else before long. Look, I should go.' She didn't end the call though. Charlie got the impression that she wanted it to go on, that it was something of a welcome distraction from whatever she had to go back to. 'You didn't finish telling me about Max. You've got Bella back then, that's good.' She was trying her best, even though she didn't really understand why anyone would want to have a dog about. 'Did you agree about the house?'

Charlie hedged, saying something about it being in progress. Going into the whole thing would take far too long, and then she'd have to explain Dave, the raid on the garden. She could too easily imagine what Eleanor would have to say about that.

212

She pulled herself back to the phone call. Eleanor was saying to let her know how things were going. 'And can you please send a message to Martha? She's checking every couple of minutes, and I had to prise the phone out of her hand before school this morning.'

When she'd gone, Charlie checked her messages. There were four from Martha, starting out cheerful and ending with one made up entirely of sad faces. Charlie quickly tapped a reply.

Sorry, no signal!! I'm going on an adventure, will let you know more soon! Hope school was fun!!

It was pretty much the truth. She'd make an effort to keep it up. And send her a picture from the next place she stopped. In the meantime, she really needed to get a move on. If she made good time over the next few days, she'd reach Sneasham. Never mind what Eleanor said. She had a feeling that this was a necessary visit.

The days settled down into a steady rhythm, with towns and villages, roads, bridges and valleys slipping by. Charlie had the sense that she hadn't been there at all, not really. Nothing stuck in the passing, no more trace of her being left than there might have been of her mother. How close had Britta been to following this route? She seemed to be there as the world contracted to what was inside the boat, or that which was seen from her deck or porthole. Locks lifted or sank, junctions turned. Charlie could see from the map that known places were nearby – Wolverhampton, Birmingham, Coventry. They were just words on a map, though, with nothing to do with her or her boat. Time had little

213

meaning either. A day might feel like a month, the only marker the next bridge, the next mooring.

The sense of distance, of separation, was amplified by an incident on the second day. She'd taken Bella out for a last walk before turning in for the night. They'd played on the bank, Bella charging tirelessly after a chunk of wood. She insisted on carrying it back to the boat and, when they got there, collapsing with it on the bank. Charlie let her chew for a while, soaking up the silence, the isolation. The sky was holding the blue of the day at a hover, as if someone had hit pause. There was a sliver of moon, the tiniest, most delicate fragment hanging in the gap between the trees on either side of the canal. As Charlie stood there watching it, colours had built up in the corresponding patch of sky in the other direction, so many shades it was hard to differentiate them. Purple fading into pink and yellow and a clear light that was almost beyond colour, before merging back into what remained of the blue. It didn't change whilst she looked at it, but only when she glanced away. It wasn't that it got dark exactly, more that it blurred so much as to become dark air. And around her, so fast that she didn't believe they were there to begin with, bats began to fly. Breathless, momentary. Moving without sound, a flit almost impossible to catch with her eyes.

She'd taken her phone out with her to snap a photograph of *Skíðblaðnir* at her mooring, something to send to Martha. The moment for doing that had passed but she still had it held loosely in her hand. And then Bella, tired of her stick, came up at a run, bouncing at her with both front paws. For a small dog, she could build some

214

serious momentum. Not expecting it, Charlie stepped back, almost losing her footing on the bank. As she twisted in an attempt to stay out of the water, she let go of her phone. It fell on the grass, but too close to the edge. Charlie dropped to her knees, making a grab for it. But at exactly the moment she got her freeze-framed hand to the spot where it had been, it slid down the edge and into the water with the quietest of splashes. She'd stared, unable to believe the timing, before making a final lunge just as the floating case had begun to sink.

At least she still had it, even if it was turned off and buried in rice. Which meant no calls or texts or checking emails. And her fingers crossed that the drying process would actually work. She could try now, brush the dust from its screen and try the button to bring it back to life. Make the move too early, though, and the circuits would fizzle into burnt uselessness. A bit of patience wouldn't hurt. In a way it was a relief. If she couldn't check for messages, they didn't exist. If only all her problems could be dealt with so easily.

Twenty-three

Sneasham wasn't much more than a big village, though the wharf buildings near the moorings suggested that the canal had once been busier, and more important, than it was now. Charlie had decided that the best place to start her search for Margareta would be the library, assuming there was one. She was lucky. Going down the main street, with Bella bobbing around on the end of her lead at all the new smells, she went past a Post Office, a hardware shop and a beautician's before seeing the blue and white sign. The library itself, tucked down a side street, was not much more than two rooms, but it was busy. A children's story group was in full swing in one corner, and there was a cluster of computers in another, most of them being used by a chatty group of older people.

Charlie waited at the desk, half tuning in to the librarian's discussion with the young man at the front of the queue as they tried to identify a book from a misremembered name. Then there was a young mother with two lively toddlers, checking out a pile of DVDs and picture books. The librarian knew the children by name, coming out from behind her desk to ask questions about the

216

books they were bringing back. Charlie smiled as they jumped about in front of her, acting out their favourite lines. She looked behind her to make sure Bella was OK. There was a hook to loop her lead around and a water bowl just outside the door, and she could see her from where she was standing, but leaving her alone still made her edgy. Bella was sitting as close to the door as her lead would allow, her gaze fixed on where Charlie had gone. The librarian cleared her throat and Charlie realized that the toddlers had moved on.

'Oh, I'm sorry.' Charlie stepped forwards. 'I'm trying to find some information about the canal, people involved in the restoration projects back in the sixties?'

'OK.' The librarian was about Charlie's age, with purple hair and a very pregnant stomach. 'Would information about the canal in general be of any use? Because we've got a local history section. I'm not sure there's much about restoration though.'

'I'm not really sure quite what it is I'm looking for yet,' Charlie said. She screwed up her face, trying to decide how to explain. 'I think my mum had some connection here, or at least visited, and the only thing I've found so far is a friend or family member who had something to do with the canals.'

'There's the census? You can view them online . . . But you said the sixties?' Charlie nodded and she grimaced. 'That's a bit late for the accessible records. And did they live on a boat? Because then they wouldn't show up anyway.'

'I really don't know that much at all,' Charlie told her. She pulled the newspaper cutting out. 'This is it, really.

217

I'm guessing it's from around here, but the woman I'm interested in might have just been passing through.'

The librarian held the paper up to read the caption, then gave a wide smile. 'If it's Margareta you're looking for, then I can probably help you.'

'You're joking?' Charlie blinked. It surely wasn't going to be that easy.

The librarian laughed. 'It's hard to mistake a name like that. Look . . .' She checked the time. 'I've got a reading group now, and then it's the U3A computer group, but if you want to come back at about four, we can have a proper chat.' She held out a hand. 'I'm Sally, by the way.'

The timing was perfect, giving them the opportunity to wander through the rest of the village and explore a footpath off across some fields. There was no one else in sight, and the walk was almost too ridiculously perfect. Charlie watched Bella sniff and charge at hidden possibilities in the hedges or fall over her feet as she raced for a tossed stick. There were cows standing in the shade, tails flicking, and the grass was dotted with buttercups. Charlie wondered what it would be like to live there, to come out every day on the same walk and never get tired of it. Maybe it was possible for some people. Maybe it just meant finding the right place. The footpath curved in a generous arc to rejoin the canal, and they ambled back to *Skíðblaðnir* with the sun dappling through the trees, the breeze shifting the water of the canal just enough to form and re-form an endless camouflage pattern of browns and greens.

218

Leaving Bella on the boat with a peanut butter-filled bone to keep her company, Charlie made her way back to the library. Sally was waiting outside, a leather jacket open around her belly. She waved as Charlie walked up, coming to meet her along the pavement. It was like meeting up with a friend. Charlie couldn't remember the last time that had happened.

'Let's go for a coffee,' Sally said, pointing towards the main street. 'Partly because I really need one – have you ever met a U3A group with a grievance? – and partly because my mum's just opened a café and she needs the custom.' She laughed. 'Though her cakes are pretty damn good.'

'What exactly is the U3A?' Charlie asked, having to jog slightly to keep up.

'University of the Third Age.' Sally laughed at the expression on her face. 'Like when you've retired but want something to do. They run a bunch of stuff here: language classes, art, wine-tasting, rambling. And there are talks. That's where I met Margareta, she came to tell them about canal restoration.' She pointed along the street. 'There's Mum's place.'

'Is this where you grew up?' Charlie tried to imagine living in the Derbyshire village all her life, never moving away.

'I left for uni.' Sally laughed again. 'It was good to try somewhere else. But then this turned up,' she patted her bump, 'and a vacancy came along in the library, so I came home for a bit.' She held up her hands in a shrug as they reached the café's door. 'What you gonna do? Though I thought I'd be getting free childcare and then Mum had this bright idea, so the baby'll just have to learn how to wash up really fast.'

She led the way in. The café was tiny, just one room with three round tables and a sofa in the window. There were plants everywhere, hanging in macramé holders and balanced on shelves. A cheese plant with leaves the size of side plates dominated one corner and drooped above the counter.

'I swear these have grown since I was here yesterday.' Sally pushed a spider plant aside and rang an old-fashioned bell. 'Mum, you there? Customers!' She turned back to Charlie. 'She's a miniature plant whisperer. That's why she opened this place, I reckon, more space for the plants.' She rang the bell again.

'I'll be right with you!' The voice came from the other side of a swing door. 'Just putting the kettle on.' Almost as she spoke, she was coming through, a short, round woman moving at double speed. 'Let's sit here. Tea? Coffee? Cup or mug? And you'd like some cake, wouldn't you?'

Charlie found herself in a chair, facing the rapid fire of questions. 'Tea, thank you. No sugar.' She couldn't keep up.

'I need coffee, Mum. And we'll both have scones.' Sally turned to Charlie and gave the briefest of winks.

'You don't need coffee, it's bad for the baby. I'll get you some of that ginger tea instead.' Sally's mother was already on her way back to the kitchen. 'And the scones aren't nice at the end of the day. I'll do you some teacakes.'

Sally chuckled, watching her go. 'You don't really need an opinion of your own,' she said.

'And this is at the end of the day? What's she like in the morning?' Charlie was feeling a bit winded.

'Let's just say she doesn't do lie-ins.' Sally was moving across to the sofa. 'Come on, while she's gone. We might as well be comfortable.' She sank down into the cushions with a happy sigh. 'Now, tell me why you want to see Margareta.'

There was something about Sally that made it feel like she'd known her for ever. And when her mother came back (*call me Jean, now*) it was as if she'd been adopted into some kind of wider family. It made it easy to tell them everything, which was just as well because they wanted to know it all. She ended up going right back to before Thailand, and what made her take the decision to leave, via a comprehensive overview of her own family's dynamics.

Jean was studying the photograph of Margareta and Britta. 'That's down by the bridge, isn't it? Where the stream goes under.' She turned to Charlie. 'We get a lot of boats. Some of them stay for years, and you get the ones who come back every so often.' She turned to Sally. 'Who was that girl you used to play with?'

'Tabitha? I wanted to run away with her, live on the boat with her and her mum for ever.' Sally was examining the photograph now. 'You mean down by Dixon's farm?' She nodded. 'I think you're right. And what about Charlie's mum, ring any bells?'

'I don't know. 1964. I was only five or so.' She took the picture back and held it right up to her face. 'She was Norwegian, you say?' Charlie nodded, and she studied it again. 'There's something about her face—' Her tone

221

was doubtful. 'Sneasham was small back then, everyone knew everyone. A girl started in my class at school who'd come from Manchester and that was exotic. I just think I'd remember if someone foreign lived here. Everyone knew who Margareta was, though she wasn't one for making friends. Maybe your mum was on a boat, just passing through?'

'I don't know.' Charlie took the photo back and stared at her mother's face again, as if this might tell her something. 'As far as I knew, she wasn't even in England until several years after this. I can't believe Margareta's still here. Do you think I'd be able to talk to her?'

'I don't see why not.' Jean got up and started getting the cups together. 'Sally can call her and find out when she's in.'

'Why me? Because she can't be mean to the pregnant lady? Except she won't be able to see I'm pregnant on the phone.'

'Because you've got her number at the library.' Jean was halfway to the kitchen.

'I'm not sure that's ethical,' Sally called after her. She turned to Charlie. 'What's she like?'

'I don't want to be any trouble,' Charlie said.

'Oh, you're all right, I just like to wind her up. The number's probably in the phone book. And it might be better having an introduction from someone she knows. Leave it with me.'

Twenty-four

Margareta lived in one of a cluster of almshouses, tucked away behind the remains of a country house. They weren't easy to find, even with the instructions Sally had written out for her. Finally, Charlie spotted the hidden entrance to a narrow road which disappeared behind a row of cottages. It followed the line of a high, old brick wall, the mortar crumbly between bricks of a beautiful, mellow terracotta tone. An information board showed grainy images of the old manor house that had once stood in the nearby grounds. In the pictures, ladies in wide hats sat on a terrace; oak trees bordered a sweeping driveway. The wall and the cottages were now all that remained. The houses, when Charlie finally reached them, were charming – tiny, red-brick doll-houses with exaggerated eaves and perfect bow windows.

The woman who opened the door was unexpectedly small, her blonde-grey hair cut bluntly at chin level. Her blue eyes were sharp, vivid, and she had an edge of energy to her that was unconstrained by age. Was she the woman in the photograph with Britta? Charlie was suddenly doubtful. She held out a hand.

223

'Hi, I'm—'

'Yes, yes, Sally has told me. Come in.'

It was a surprise to hear her accent, even though Charlie had been expecting it. The words were clipped, holding a cadence that had lingered in Britta's voice, though to a much lesser degree. An English husband and no contact with family from Norway had taken Britta's accent away, she supposed. Would she find out today why there had been such a breach? She followed the small, brisk figure into the house with her pulse racing.

'Are you sure you don't mind if I bring Bella in?' Jean had been adamant that it would be fine. *It's a lovely walk to get there, and you don't know how long you'll be, do you?* And it seemed that she'd been right. The old lady was looking down at the dog with a half-smile.

'As long as she has clean paws and doesn't poop on the floor. Yes, yes. The dog is fine.'

They went down a short passage and into a living room. With its low ceilings and rustic air, Charlie would have expected country florals and an open fire, the walls hung with botanical prints and horse brasses. Instead, despite the thick wooden beams and deep windows, here was a sense of space. Charlie stood and looked at the pale wooden floor, the delicate blue of the walls, the spare lines of the Scandinavian furniture. She could smell lavender, and the hint of freshly ironed cotton, a real smell, almost tangible. In one corner stood a brushed steel cylinder. It took her a minute to realize it was some kind of heater. A moment later, and she spotted the neatly stacked chunks of wood waiting next to it. There was nothing here even remotely folksy.

'Come, come, we will go to the kitchen.' Margareta hustled her into an airy room, this one larger, surely, than the original building had allowed for. Much of the roof was made of glass, and the room was full of light even though, outside, the weather had again become dull and wet. Charlie could hear the odd tapping as a drop fell from an overhanging tree. One whole side was made up of sliding glass doors, the view an uninterrupted sweep of gently rising fields leading to a low hill topped with a cluster of trees. A covered area of decking held a basket armchair standing next to a low wooden table. On the table's surface were binoculars and a pile of books.

Inside, it was warm but not stuffy. A pale blue range stood nearby, radiating comfort. Bella nosed forwards, pulling at her lead. On the worktop was a loaf of freshly baked bread. Charlie's stomach rumbled. She hadn't felt like eating that morning. Maybe it was waiting for lunch, to go with thick vegetable soup, homely and filling. Margareta was at the sink, filling a round orange kettle. She took it across to the range, lifting one of the lids before setting it down. The whole place was like a blueprint of a perfect home, sprung into being from a dream. It was like finding *her* home, the perfect fit, the ideal. An image flashed into her brain, ready formed. Herself, wrapped in its charms, a new daughter to this unexpected fairy godmother. Taking up where her mother had left off. Why, though? Why had they never been here to visit?

'I think you are here with questions about your mother.' Margareta's matter-of-fact tone cut across her daydream.

225

'Yes.' Charlie found herself linking her fingers together, squeezing them so that the bones tightened, hard against each other. For the first time she considered the possibility that Britta had left on bad terms, that Margareta might not welcome the connection. She suddenly felt she could deal with anything except that. 'She died, you see, just a couple of months ago. I'm sorry, I would have contacted you, but we'd never known—' Why was she apologizing? There wasn't any way you could tell everyone a person had ever known in their lives when they died. 'It's just that she bought a boat, you see, a little while before she died, and I found this on board.' She held out the photograph. 'I think she was on her way to see you,' she said, waiting for the old lady to take it. 'She'd talked to her boat neighbours about making a journey, and I found this in her room.'

'So, Britta got her boat in the end.' Margareta's gaze was distant, as if reliving many memories. Did it ever become less of a shock, to hear about people from your younger days who were no longer there? She came out of her reverie and examined Charlie's face. 'And here is her daughter. This is very nice to see.' Finally, she took the photograph, adjusting her glasses before examining the scene. It was strange to think of this small woman in charge of that big working boat, dressed in her overalls with oil staining her skin. Was she thinking of the changes time had made? The bright eyes came up, as if Margareta had heard her thoughts. 'The changes time makes. But here we are. Do you like the boat?'

'I do, yes.' Charlie assumed she meant *Skíðblaðnir*. 'The people I was moored next to remember you.

226

Bob. He got me started on the boat, showed me the ropes.'

'Bob.' Margareta's face was thoughtful, then she shook her head. 'So many people. And is he old like me?'

How did you answer that? She tried. 'He's, well, I think it was his father who knew you?'

Margareta thought, then gave a brisk nod. 'So. We will leave that behind. I am so glad you are here, Sylvia's daughter. I always hoped I would meet you.'

Sylvia? Charlie thought briefly of her father, of Eleanor's concerns over his memory. Had she got here only to find it was too late to talk? Margareta had seemed so sharp, though. She grappled for the right words. It was a natural slip, confusing names, but embarrassing to have to put her straight. 'Britta. My mum was Britta, remember?'

'Britta, Sylvia, a name makes no change. I would have told her that if I had been there.' She sounded irritated, cross at having made the mistake. 'But it is good for you to know. And you have met your sisters?'

It was getting worse. Maybe she should just say thank you, how lovely it was to meet, and make a quiet exit. Did Sally and her mother know that Margareta was getting confused? Surely they'd have said if they did, would have warned her to be careful. 'I've just got the one sister,' she said. 'Eleanor. She'd have loved to be here, but she's got small children.'

Margareta answered with a touch of impatience. 'Yes, two more. Eleanor and Charlotte. But you've come to ask about Sylvia.'

'I've come to ask about Britta,' she said, trying to hold

227

on to what she thought she knew. 'My mother was called Britta, and I'm Charlotte. And I only have one sister.'

Just then the kettle murmured before seeming to take a breath, letting it out in a loud and sustained whistle.

'We shall make coffee first,' Margareta stated. 'And then we will sit down and talk. And the dog does not need to be on a lead. She will be fine.'

They were back in the living room. Margareta was in the armchair, Bella somewhat unexpectedly sitting as close to her as she could. The old lady reached down to ruffle the terrier's ears as if she was used to having a dog by her feet. She was completely relaxed, as far as Charlie could judge, which was more than Charlie could say for herself.

'Now, explain how you knew where to find me.' Margareta's tone was firm, judicious. Charlie must make a case, and it had better be convincing, it said.

Charlie took a deep breath and laid out the main points, the photograph and Bob's suggestion, finding the newspaper cutting. She had placed that in its plastic folder on the side table by her chair when they came into the room. Now she picked it up and held it out.

Margareta took the offered sheet, but she was reading the wrong side, the one with the fete and the story of the grandmother. Charlie wanted to explain, but there was something in the silence that stopped her. She could feel her pulse beating in her throat. Everything beneath her, around her, was beginning to wobble, like a stage set knocked up out of remnants. Margareta spoke first.

'I am sorry, this was my mistake. And of course, you

228

are young, too young. But I have been waiting so long for the baby to come and find me. When Sally called me and said Britta's daughter was here, I just assumed—' For the first time, her voice trembled. Then she reached out to touch Charlie's hand. 'But you, also, have come to find out who Britta was. Perhaps if you tell me what you know?'

Charlie swallowed. It sounded as if she didn't know anything, but the bones of the story were at least a familiar tale, a story she could tell without too much thinking. 'She grew up in Norway, near a forest, but I don't know exactly where. I think she was an only child. The only thing I know for certain is that she came to England at some point and met my father.' That was it, that was all. It sounded threadbare, pathetic. How could she ever have believed that this was the whole history? 'Did you know her when she first came to England?'

'In a sense, yes.' Margareta paused, resting her finger-tips against her mouth. She seemed to be deciding what to say next. When she did speak, her voice had taken on the rhythm of a storyteller, the sound of it setting off a trigger somewhere deep in Charlie's subconscious. She had no time to follow the sense, though. 'There was a woman in the village, a strange woman, with one son and one daughter. Her name was Hilda Burrows, she was of a type that I think you don't see these days. She believed that she was right about everything, and expected her daughter, in particular, to conform.' She turned her head so that she was looking directly at Charlie. 'People say that the world is a different place now, but human nature has not changed so much.

Bullies will be bullies. The only thing that really changes is how they act it out.'

Charlie waited for her to continue, but Margareta was resting her hands on the arms of her chair, in preparation to stand. The delayed movement somehow emphasized her age, an awareness of what her body was unable to do. She paused, the weight of herself balanced in transit. Then, finally, she completed the movement with a momentum that carried her on at a brisk, decided pace towards a set of shelves at the side of the room. With her back to Charlie, she spoke again. 'I came to this country as a young woman, as a bohemian. We had ideals, you know, for the possibilities of a better world.' Charlie nodded, though she didn't think Margareta was waiting for an answer. The left-hand section of the shelves had a door closing the contents in, swinging out with no noise, no creak of hinges or catch of a lock. This wasn't a cupboard that would smell of the past. Margareta's hand went towards a large book, lying on its side on the top shelf. It came out slowly, its weight wanting to stay where it was. Margareta balanced it in both hands, her face turned down towards the blank cover. She picked up something else, a paper folder stuffed with loose snaps. Then, with an abrupt dismissal of the hesitation, she brought it all back to her chair. 'Come.' She gave an impatient gesture to summon Charlie towards her. 'It will be easier if you see.'

The book was an album, the cover dark blue and ridged in mock snakeskin. One corner had a gilt protective edging, the other curled up, revealing a soft crumble of grey, cardboard layers. Margareta leafed through the

230

stiff pages at speed – not, it seemed, to stop Charlie from seeing them but just to reach the point she was aiming for. The page she stopped at had six prints caught beneath the plastic film layer. They were all small and square, and age had given them an orange tint. Charlie examined them more closely. It was odd how that was the shade to endure, bathing each scene in a permanent glow of sunlight.

'I came to London in 1959,' Margareta was saying. Her finger touched on the image at the top of the page nearest to Charlie. They were bending their heads at the same angle, caught in the intimacy of the action. She wished Eleanor was there with her, to take charge, to ask the right questions. Margareta's finger tapped on the page, demanding her attention.

The print was of a young woman, sitting cross-legged on what seemed to be a wooden deck. She was partway through coiling a rope and was looking up at the camera in laughing protest. 'Was this you?' Charlie asked.

'Yes.' Charlie sensed rather than saw her nod. 'I was supposed to be in England for one year, attending classes at the School of Economics. A friend's boyfriend lived on the river, in an old barge, a wreck.' Her finger went to the next picture. Four young people this time, heads together, captured in the middle of a burst of laughter. 'This one, Freddy.' She touched on the figure at the end of the row. He was somewhat older than the others, dressed in a dark fisherman's jumper, the brim of a cap shading his expression. 'When Lisa went home that summer, I stayed. I was—' Charlie heard exasperation in the pause, a retrospective wonderment at the

231

choices one made in one's past. 'Less interested in economics than I had thought,' she finished up. She turned over more pages, stopping to go back before flicking through further. She didn't stop to explain the in-between sections. 'These weren't the boats that you find today, you understand, with their shiny paint and satellite dishes.' She shook her head. 'Freddy's boat was old, could not be moved. We took on water every time the tide rose. The hull was crumbling about us. He refused to see it, imagined that he would one day wave a magic wand and take to the sea.' Her finger dropped again, this time on a slightly under-exposed snap of a different boat. The small figure of the young Margareta was alone this time, though wearing what looked like the cap from the earlier picture. 'I had an opportunity to take on a working boat. The waterways were supposed to be at an end, you know. These boats had been used for maintenance; they were obsolete, superfluous. And so I gained *Guillemot* and told my parents I would not be coming back.'

Charlie glanced from the tiny figure on the yellowed page in front of her to the face of the old woman. *Guillemot*. The boat in the photograph. 'And was this still in London?'

'No, no.' Margareta turned another page. 'I took over the boat in Oxford.' She pointed to another grainy shot, though there was nothing visible to pinpoint any identifying features of the place. 'And, that year, I was making journeys to keep canals open. We wanted to show that they were viable, you understand, that they could not just be filled with concrete.'

232

The pages were turned again, this time stopping on a double spread where there were mostly gaps. Charlie could see the empty outlines of where the photographs had been, yellowing edges blurring into faded brown. The plastic film had lost its stickiness as well, rustling weakly as Margareta came to a stop.

'Do you recognize here?' Her finger directed Charlie to the one remaining image. Charlie examined the gathered faces. It was still on the canal, but this time facing away from the water. Behind the figures were brick walls, a clock tower just visible in the top corner.

'Sorry, no.' She shook her head.

'You will have passed it on your way.' Margareta's tone seemed to hold a hint of reproach. 'I spent my first winter here. Everybody was telling me how lucky I was to miss the winter of '62.' She gave a dry laugh. 'Although they were forgetting that I grew up in Oslo, of course. These winters did not seem special to me. But there was still enough ice to keep me in one place, and that is when I met Sylvia.'

233

Twenty-five

The photograph album slipped away as Margareta told the next part of the story. A young girl, tiring of the constrictions of her life. A chance meeting on a snow-stranded bus followed by a shy first visit to the canal. Margareta, cold and lonely on her half-converted boat and ready to take on the role of inspiration to this eager acolyte. Margareta spoke in an even tone, relating facts, a judicial account. At least, that was how it seemed. Sylvia escaped to the boat as often as she could, ready always to absorb more of everything. More about the possibilities ahead, of the end of war, the end of capitalism. Margareta wanted her to know there was a wider world out there. And she was ready to talk about her childhood. The cold reminded her of it, yes, but it was also the distance. She was feeling nostalgic, *ridiculous, you know. But Sylvia wanted to hear, and in the retelling it became epic, memorable.*

The story came to a stop. Margareta was sitting perfectly still, her gaze fixed on the open album. Her forehead was contracted, as if she was mentally untangling a tricky proposition. Slowly, she began to turn the pages again, looking for something in particular. It seemed to elude her, and she went back to the start, scrutinizing each page until the last one was reached. Then she laid the album by her feet and made her way back to the cupboard, murmuring to herself as she searched for something.

Charlie hesitated, but finally gave in to the temptation. She dropped to her knees, pulling the album closer and leafing on to the pages she had yet to see. There were landscapes, with views of the canal hidden by snow. A snapshot picture of children wrapped up in woollen hats and scarves but wearing shorts, their bare legs purple in the cold. They were pushing a huge snowball along the towpath, leaning in with a colossal communal effort of construction. Next came a series of pictures tracking the transformation of *Guillemot*'s interior. Wooden panels began to cover the metal walls, rolls of insulating wool visible in the corner of the boat. A pot-bellied stove was installed, and a small cooker to replace the camping stove of the earlier stages. There was a bathroom, crude but recognizable, and finally one photograph of a bedroom, with two girls curled up on a bed. Charlie froze. It wasn't just the picture. She could hear a voice, reading them a story. *Britta is nine and Anna is the same age as me. I like them both just the same. Well, perhaps I like Anna a tiny, tiny bit more.* It was the story from the book on *Skíðblaðnir*. She looked at the picture again, at the thick, shiny eiderdown laid out across the bed. Smelling of dust and damp. *Eye-der-down.* 'It was you, wasn't it? Reading the story?' Charlie looked up at Margareta's face. 'We came to the boat. I'd forgotten. You made us cake, with cinnamon.' And then she began to cry.

*

235

Margareta refused to say anything about it until they had another cup of tea. This they drank in the kitchen, sitting side by side at the table. The album had been left in the living room, but Margareta had brought the packet of photographs with her. The cardboard folder rested between them, fat, waiting. Margareta still seemed detached, but Charlie sensed a certain relaxation, a growing solicitude, even. Finally, the warmth of the drink beginning to ground her, Charlie spoke.

'I'm not wrong, am I? I went to your boat, when I was a little girl.' She waited, her hands rigid on her mug, for Margareta's reply.

'I didn't think you would remember,' she said at last. 'You were such a very small girl at the time.'

'The books are on the boat,' Charlie told her, but without looking at her face. 'Pippi Longstocking, the Bullerby ones. It was when I saw them that I remembered. It was you, wasn't it, reading them to us?'

'Yes.' Margareta didn't elaborate, but after a moment asked, 'They are in this boat of Britta's?' She closed her eyes, giving a tiny nod as Charlie agreed. 'I had them on my boat, I can't remember why now. They were books I had read as a small girl, in Norwegian, of course. Sylvia liked to read them when she came to spend time with me. She was still a child.'

'Sylvia is Britta, isn't she?' The question didn't really need an answer, but still she looked to Margareta for confirmation.

Margareta nodded. 'You will want to know how Sylvia, that child of Hilda, came to be Britta.'

This time, she emptied all of the photographs out

236

onto the table, shuffling them round into new configurations as if she was trying to work out a pattern. Charlie didn't try to follow her movements. Instead she sat, half aware of Bella's movements around the room, tracking crumbs on the floor. The light was beginning to ebb from the sky, and she could make out the faintest shading of reflected sunset along the horizon. It must be beautiful from the other side of the house.

'Now, you can follow the progress of these.' Margareta's voice brought her back to the table. She moved the top left photo up slightly as she spoke. 'I put them away,' she went on, 'which felt like a coward's answer at the time. Now I think it was a good thing. This was the summer of 1964.'

Britta smiled at the camera, a beam of confidence and a certain bravura. Sylvia, Charlie thought. She looked older than in the photograph Charlie had found on the boat. Her hair was pulled up into a high ponytail, and she was dressed in cropped trousers and a sleeveless white blouse. Even with the tiny size of the print, Charlie could see heavy mascara, the pale layer of powder on her face.

'I found it fascinating, watching this child blossom,' Margareta said, moving the print back into its line. 'Sometimes I wonder if I should have left things alone, encouraged her to stay within her sphere, but all I provided was the soil, you see, the possibility of another life. It was Sylvia herself who took the steps to inhabit that place. And then she would go home and change back to the little girl that her mother expected. I would tell her, leave, create your own life, but she carried on hiding behind the person she had been.'

237

Charlie took in the girl's radiant face.

'She wasn't ready, you see. Another year and she would have been out, pfft.' Margareta made a flicking motion with her fingers and then shifted the next photo out of the line. This was of Margareta herself, standing on a beach with a young boy and a dog. 'My brother, Lars.' She rested a fingertip on the boy before moving it along. 'And our dog, Svipp.' She watched Charlie's face, waiting.

'Svipp,' Charlie repeated. Another tiny window opened in her memory. 'One of the children had a dog, didn't they, in the book?' What was his name? It buzzed faintly at the back of her mind but wouldn't quite come out. 'Ollie? Olaf?'

'Olle.' Margareta nodded approvingly. 'I went home that summer, to visit my grandmother. I left the keys of the boat with Sylvia, so that she had somewhere to go. She liked to read, you see, but her mother thought it a waste of her time. But the keys also, of course, gave her opportunity. And her mother was not always well.' She paused for a long time, and Charlie sneaked a glance at the next photograph. There was a group of people in it, she could make out that much. Margareta picked the photo up, holding it close, as if searching for clues. 'So many years.'

Finally, she passed it across. Charlie looked at the faces, young people standing in a tight group, laughing towards the camera. They were untouched, somehow, even with their confident bravura. The boy in the middle had a quiff, and she could just make out the shine of a leather jacket. Sylvia stood next to him, her face

238

tilted towards him as if he was the only person there. 'Who are they?' she asked.

'I'm . . . not sure.' Margareta took it back, giving it one more searching glance before placing it down. 'I found this much later, when it was too late to ask. But I imagine it had something to do with the events of the summer. The little Sylvia found more than books to amuse herself.' She turned away from the table as she carried on speaking, separating herself from the gallery. 'When I came back from Norway, there was no sign of Sylvia. The keys had been taped in an envelope to my door and there was a note inside informing me that Sylvia would not be coming any more, a request not to contact her.' She caught and held Charlie's gaze. 'I did try, of course I did.' Was she trying to convince Charlie or herself? 'But Sylvia was kept to the house, a house with no telephone and the mother guarding the door.' She sighed, shaking her head. 'When people talk about the good old days, they should remember these things.'

'She was pregnant?' Another question that didn't really need an answer. Charlie thought she knew the ending of this part of the story, or at least some of it. 'What happened to the baby?'

'She was adopted. It was what happened at that time,' Margareta said. 'If I had been there, if I had known, I would have found a way to talk to her, I would have told her she had a choice.' She tapped the newspaper article. 'But by the time I returned, she was already gone. Somebody showed me this. I think they hoped I would add to the gossip.' She shook her head. 'There was enough of that already, and everyone wanted to talk about it. Her

239

labour came early, they said, but before a message could be sent for the doctor, Hilda collapsed and Sylvia gave birth by herself, unable to call for help, for herself or her mother. That poor child.' They sat in silence. 'It was brave of her, to go away, to reinvent herself.'

'How did she find you again, when she brought us to the boat?' Charlie was remembering the sense she'd had that she could disappear on her boat, now, with all of the mobiles and location trackers there were. How much easier it would have been back then, when you had to work at staying in touch.

'I had friends here. I remained in contact even as I moved,' Margareta said. 'I wanted Sylvia to know where I was, if she ever needed me. I felt responsible.'

Charlie didn't need to ask the question any more. She already knew the answer. 'And when she came back, she was Britta?'

'Yes.'

240

Twenty-six

Charlie didn't notice that Margareta had gone out of the room. She was barely aware of where she was. The facts revolved around her head, trying to settle, to make sense, but just as she had them in order, they'd float off again. After a time, she remembered the photographs and, much as Margareta had done, she began to shuffle them into different configurations.

Her mother as a teenager, trying to escape along the time-honoured route of covert rebellion, the widening boundaries of her life opening out worlds before her. Instead she'd ended up escaping from notoriety, damaged and battered. Sixteen, alone, abandoned. Charlie gazed at her fingers, spread over the photographs as if they were teasing out the ramifications of becoming a new person. And that brought her to Hugo.

The story she knew was of late-blossoming romance, though Britta must still have been in the first half of her twenties at the time. Her own voice as a young girl flashed through her memory. *Grown-ups are always married, aren't they?* And Eleanor's reply, laying down the law, setting a precedent that part of Charlie's mind had absorbed and retained, any later understanding surrounding it but leaving the sentiment whole and untouched. *You have to get married by the time you're twenty-five. It's the rule.* That was Britta's age when she married, if the age she had claimed was in fact the truth. The only photograph she'd ever seen from that time showed Britta in a trouser suit, her floppy hat concealing her face. Their father had been in his late thirties, an anonymous figure looking away from the lens. Who had been there behind the camera? And did he know the woman he married as Britta or Sylvia?

'You should drink this.'

Margareta's voice made Charlie jump. She looked round to see her holding a small glass filled with clear liquid. Automatically, she rejected the offer. 'I'm fine, honestly. I just need to—'

'No, I insist. You have had a shock.' The glass was placed in front of her and she caught the sharp edge of raw alcohol, a touch of aniseed. Aquavit, the only drink her mother claimed to like. As if she were a child being told to finish her meal, Charlie lifted the glass and took a sip. The spirit burned down to her stomach, leaving a trail of energy. Margareta was right, she had needed it.

'Why did we come to see you that time?' Charlie swivelled the glass on the tabletop, keeping her gaze fixed on the slightly wet circles it was making. 'Was it just a visit?'

'Not really.' Margareta paused, and Charlie could feel her assessing the situation, assessing Charlie's ability to take in more information. Charlie lifted the glass to swallow down the rest of the aquavit in one.

'I'm fine,' she said, meeting Margareta's eyes. 'And I'd rather know, honestly.'

Margareta nodded. 'You are right, it is always better to know.' She lowered herself into a chair on the other side of the table. 'Britta arrived one night with you and your sister. You were small children, perhaps five and eight? I hadn't heard from her in many years, you understand, but I had an address for her, sent cards at times to let her know where I was. She didn't want to talk, presented herself with her new name without explanation.' There was a pause and a wry smile. 'Perhaps I was flattered, that she wished to become Norwegian. I had no children, no family in this country.' There was a longer pause, then a sigh. 'I should have pushed harder, but if she didn't want to talk . . .' Her voice faded away briefly. 'I thought she would tell me more when she was ready. She said she had left her marriage. There had been an upset, she was holding herself tightly. But when your father came—'

'He came to the boat?' Charlie stared for a moment before squeezing her eyes closed. She must be able to remember something, have some imprint of these happenings. But there was nothing, just that brief image of the bed, the story.

'I didn't meet him. Britta took him along the bank and I read stories to you and your sister. I tried to talk when she came back, I told her she could stay with me, that she had choices, but she would say nothing. She gathered the two of you and said you were going home. And that was the last time I saw her.'

'And the books?' Charlie grabbed onto the one bit of

243

the story that could be comprehended. It felt important to know their journey, to have at least one piece of information straight.

'I gave them to her to take for you. It was a small thing.'

And Britta had put the books away, hidden them rather than letting Charlie and Eleanor read them. Saved for the other baby, perhaps. For the first time, Charlie felt the impact of that statement. Another baby, a sister. Not a baby any more, though. If she'd been born in the mid-sixties, how old would she be? Charlie counted the decades on her fingers. Fifty, at least. That couldn't be right. How could she have a sister that old? Thoughts ricocheted, none of them taking root for long enough to be examined properly. Eleanor being bossed around, family dynamics shifting like tectonic plates on the move. For a second, Charlie felt a sharp regret at having been left out of something, of not being enough. Had Britta spent her whole life wishing that she had that different child? But then she thought of the boat licence, the gift made to Charlotte Nilsson. She hadn't wanted to keep her out entirely. She'd bequeathed her a boat, and a name that had never existed. And another sister.

244

Twenty-seven

She sent Eleanor a message as she walked back to the boat, to say she'd be arriving the next day. It was too much to pass on by telephone. She needed to be able to see her sister's face, and Eleanor would need to sit and process the news, just as she had. Or as she was still doing.

Bella ran ahead, pleased to be on the move. Every so often, she'd circle back with a new find: a stick, an empty plastic water bottle. Charlie threw them along for her to chase, but she wasn't really seeing her. This was a towpath her mother would have walked along many times. Her mother, who wasn't called Britta, who wasn't Norwegian, who had another daughter. In the ebb of dusk, the colours around her were fading. She was walking into a sepia world, stepping back into the past. Around every turn she half expected to see an old working boat, or a girl with a ponytail hurrying. But would she be hurrying towards something, or hurrying away? A figure loomed, making her freeze. For a second it was a boy in a leather jacket, quiff tumbling on his forehead. Then the shadow solidified into a fisherman, heading home after a day of sitting and watching the water.

245

Her phone pinged to tell her a reply had come back. Eleanor didn't ask for any details: *Make it the afternoon, and I'll pick you up from the station. Before three best x*

'What's happening, then?' Eleanor gave her a brief hug as she came out from the station before herding her to the car.

'I just thought it would be a good moment to catch up.' Charlie had decided on the journey to leave telling Eleanor until they could be sure of some quiet.

'Well, you're just in time for the school run,' Eleanor told her. She looked down at Bella, who was snuffling in the gutter after the lost smell of a squirrel. 'I suppose the hound can come as well.'

Charlie waited by the car when they got to the school, watching as the knots of mums formed and dispersed outside the gates. She felt dislocated, as if she was jet-lagged. She'd been gone for, what, a month? Six weeks? Not all of the time had been spent moving on the canal, but the speed with which the train had brought her back, a brief couple of hours, was disconcerting. Eleanor had quickly become involved in a three-way discussion with some other mums which seemed to be veering from high indignation to near-hysteria, something all of the participants managed whilst at the same time greeting their assorted children, fielding questions and forms, and then watching as they all rushed off to play on the square of grass.

Poppy appeared first, swinging her book bag with concentrated energy. She stood in front of her mother, a

246

soldier at attention commanding notice, holding the bag out at ninety degrees to her body until it was taken from her. Then she turned to another little girl, giving her instructions before they both ran away and started a complex series of steps along the painted hopscotch grid on the tarmac playground. More children flooded out, their average size going up with each wave. They carried their bags and lunchboxes like a horde of miniature Sherpas. Some had instruments as well, violins, guitars, one small boy lugging a cello bigger than himself.

There was no sign of Martha, even when the older children began to appear. Charlie followed their progress with interest. A number of the girls seemed much older than her niece, with long hair pulled up into still-smooth ponytails, their pleated skirts and neat shoes almost corporate in their conformity. It was a relief to spot one with her shirt half out of her waistband, curly hair exploding from an elastic band. The boys as well: barbered cuts and branded, pricey backpacks. One in particular caught her eye, sauntering at the head of a group, his hair shaved close around his neck with the longer top section gelled back. He had his collar up, just needing some aviator shades to complete the look. The explosion of released energy that had come with the younger children was missing here. And still no Martha.

Eventually, Eleanor's companions gathered in their children and began to make their way out. Charlie watched her sister call to Poppy, then check the time. She didn't seem worried. A normal event, expected. A music class or some hidden classroom happening. Then Eleanor came across to call over the fence.

247

'Can you keep an eye on Poppy? I'd best go and see where Martha's got to.' She gestured to where Poppy was squatting down, alone now but completely involved in scooping loose stones into a tiny range. 'She won't even notice I'm gone.' She turned and disappeared through the main doors.

Charlie went over the grass verge, letting Bella stop to consider all of the new smells. Poppy ignored her for a time, before turning with her lower lip stuck out.

'You can't have dogs in cars.' It was a statement, a matter of obvious fact.

'Bella must be very special then,' Charlie answered. 'Because she came here in the car.'

'I'm not going in the car with her.' Poppy had her arms folded, her jaw set. Charlie was thinking how best to respond when she saw Martha coming around the corner of the school building.

She was walking slowly, her rucksack hanging from one shoulder and her coat dragging along the ground. Eleanor came hurrying out behind her, taking her bag and coat whilst firing off questions. Martha answered in monosyllables, pulling away from her mother with a dismissive shake. Her expression lifted a little when she spotted Charlie, but there was no enthusiastic run, none of the delight Charlie had anticipated. Was it because of the texts? Or was something else going on? Charlie thought of the swaggering boy, the cliques of the girls. Was Martha having trouble with them? A wave of protective rage flared.

Poppy came scudding up to the car ahead of the others, coming to an abrupt stop when she spotted Bella.

'I said no dogs in cars!' she stated, as Eleanor and Martha reached them.

'It's fine,' Eleanor told her. 'Bella will be sitting by Aunty Charlie's feet.'

Charlie made some placatory noises, bending to fondle Bella's ears and reassure the now screaming Poppy that she was friendly, that she wouldn't rampage around the car in a canine frenzy. Mostly she was watching Martha, and the look of misery that had descended as soon as her sister started making a fuss.

'How about I walk home, with Martha and Bella?' she suggested. It wasn't that far, and she really didn't want to listen to Poppy any more. And Martha might talk if they were on their own. There was some upheaval as Poppy was told no, this didn't mean she could sit in the front seat, and Charlie gave an assurance that she knew which way to go, and Martha shrugged off an instruction from her mother not to dawdle because it was Brownies. Then finally they were alone.

They walked in silence for a time. Bella zigzagged ahead of them in an effort to identify each and every smell she could find. Charlie wanted to let Martha make the first move, but she remained silent, hunched into herself. After a comment about the weather and another about a giant monkey-puzzle tree in front of a tiny bungalow, she decided to be more direct.

'Is everything OK?' she asked at last. There was no reply other than a tiny hitch of the shoulder nearest to her. Charlie paused a second. She needed a different approach. She tried to remember what it had been like at that age, how little she'd wanted to respond when

249

people asked her about her day. Instead, she went for an apology. 'Look, I'm really sorry I haven't texted lately. I went and dropped my phone in the canal.' The shrug came again. 'I had it buried in rice for days, wasn't sure if it would ever work again.'

There was another silence, then Martha's voice came from behind the curtain of hair shielding her face. 'You managed to phone Mum. I heard her talking to you.'

'I know.' She'd actually thought about sending a message then, but the impulse had been submerged under everything else. Not that she could use that as an excuse. A reason, though. If anything would bring Martha round, it would be the sense of being let into things, of being given the chance to understand. Was that what was wrong, that she could sense things happening and was resenting the fact of being treated like a child, like Poppy? Charlie made the decision. 'I don't know if your mum's said, but I've been finding things out about your grandma, where she used to live. It's been taking up a lot of my brain space.' She thought of the other reason she'd turned her phone off as soon as the calls had been made. She didn't want to see any emails that had built up whilst her phone was in pieces. 'And I've had my phone off otherwise. You know when you're expecting something but don't actually want to get it? When someone's being mean?' She saw Martha's head give a little nod. 'Well, I kind of pretended my phone wasn't working even after it was, so that I didn't have to check for that. And it meant I missed out on some stuff I wanted, like messages from you. And I'm really sorry about that.'

After a few moments of silence, Martha pushed her

hair back behind her ears. Without looking at Charlie she asked, in a small voice, 'Can I hold Bella's lead?'

Their pace picked up after this. Martha wasn't quite ready for eye contact, but there was a relaxation, even a smile when Bella jumped in surprise at a plastic bag blowing out in the wind from its anchor in a hedge. They were coming up to the gates of a park. Charlie stopped, looking through at the stretch of grass on the far side of the iron fence, with clumps of trees and a dip down to a stream beyond. It wasn't the fastest way back to Eleanor's house, but it wouldn't take them much longer.

'Shall we let Bella have a run around?' She waited for Martha's nod, and let her take Bella in and bend to unclip the lead. Bella didn't run straight off, instead pausing expectantly.

'Go on,' Martha told her. 'What does she want?'

'A biscuit,' Charlie told her, feeling in her pocket. 'Here you go, she'd like you to give it to her.' That was the finishing link. Martha held the biscuit out, exclaiming at Bella's wet nose, then laughed as the dog bounded in front of them. Charlie picked up a handy stick, weaving it through the air just out of Bella's reach, making her dance on her back paws. Then she threw it as far as she could, and they stood together watching her streak after it.

Martha's chatter began to return as they wandered along. She had questions about the boat, though avoided asking when she could come and see it. There was something in her tone, as if she was expecting to be slapped down. Could it be from not getting a couple of text messages? Surely not. Charlie tried out a couple of openings, general questions about school, about friends. Martha

251

answered without any obvious sense of reluctance, though there was still a certain amount of restraint in her tone. It was quiet, no one in sight, and Charlie led the way towards a sandy shallow, warm in the afternoon sun.

'Shall we sit down for a bit? Bella likes the water – look, there she goes.' Bella had already launched straight in, chasing the splashes she was making in a skitter of concentration. They perched side by side on the remains of a fallen tree. 'How are things at home?' Charlie asked after a while. 'Is it a bit annoying having to share with Poppy?' There was a tense pause. Charlie shifted so that she could see Martha's face. The girl was rigid, her face a blank. What was going on? Charlie felt curls of anxiety unreeling in her chest. She shuffled a bit closer, so that their shoulders touched. Martha remained where she was, not pushing Charlie away but also not seeming to welcome the contact. Then she gave a sudden, wrenching sob and buried her face against Charlie's shirt.

'What's up, sweetie?' Charlie said the words automatically, but the only response was a tightening clutch of hands and more sobbing. Charlie wrapped her arms tighter, murmuring a comforting string of sounds. Bella, tiring of the stream, came puddling up, water dripping from her coat. With a quirk of her head to one side, she stopped to give a vigorous shake, spraying them both. It was enough to break the tension, and Martha sat back up, half laughing through her tears. Charlie let her recover for a moment and was about to ask her what was wrong when Martha began by herself. It was partly that there was nowhere to be quiet, and Poppy kept taking

252

all of her things. She gave a slightly confused account of a disastrous afternoon with a friend around, about Grandad shouting at her.

This last was said in a quieter voice, a whisper, almost. 'We weren't doing anything, just playing. And Poppy kept trying to join in so we were hiding from her. And he came and shouted at us because we were giving him a headache and getting underfoot. And that made us giggle, and he held on to me and shouted again, and he was spitting in my face. It was horrible. And now my friends are saying I live with a mad man and won't play with me.' She ended with a sigh, as if a weight was lifting from her.

'Have you told your mum?' Charlie asked. She was shaken at the intensity of Martha's emotion. It was true she could recall a couple of times when her father had scared her as a child, but in the past, when he was vigorous and tall and always coming home tired, *so don't be a nuisance, girls, your father needs some peace.* But he'd mellowed with age, hadn't he? Or was it just that she'd become taller, had been able to get away more easily?

'Yes, but she said to be a good girl and it would be all right in the new house. But I don't want to go to a new house. Mummy told Daddy that she'd be able to go back to work, because I was growing up and Grandad would be able to keep an eye on us after school.' She took a hiccuping breath. 'I don't think Daddy wants to move either. He said it was a bloody nuisance.' She took a quick glance up at Charlie as she repeated the words, giggling a little as Charlie crossed her eyes in mock horror.

'I'm sure we can work something out.' Charlie was

253

wondering what on earth her sister was thinking. Even at his best and living in a separate annexe, she wouldn't consider Hugo an ideal childminder. 'I'll have a chat with your mum and find out what's going on, OK?'

'Don't tell her I said anything!' Martha had shot back to upright, staring at her with wide eyes.

'I won't, unless you say I can.' Charlie thought quickly. 'And you can come to the boat with me, like I said, and then you can tell your friends about it. I bet they've never steered a boat or opened a lock.'

The distraction seemed to work, and they carried on towards the house, hand in hand.

254

Twenty-eight

She didn't see Hugo until after tea, when Eleanor took the girls to Brownies and Rainbows. As they left, she could feel the silence of the house around her. That should have been welcome, after the chaos of the evening. As Eleanor had said, the place was already too small for them, let alone with one room given over to Hugo. Every surface was littered with stuff belonging to the girls: artwork, homework timetables, hairbands. There were coats hanging over the end of the banister, shoes piled by the door. Toys and books and piles of small clothes had been left on every step of the staircase, waiting to be taken up. It could have been cosy, a sign of a warm family life, but that wasn't how it felt. Maybe it was the presence of the old man, crouched up there behind the closed door. Or maybe she'd got too used to the quiet of the boat.

On her way up, she picked up some of the clothes. She wasn't sure where they were supposed to go, but Eleanor's bedroom door was open. She'd leave them on the bed. Even in here, the girls had colonized all of the space. Was that how it went? This really was a house of girls, all pink book covers and pink dolls. She and

Eleanor hadn't been like this, even with the same gender ratio. Another time, a different way of doing things. What did Jon feel about it all? She realized that at no point since her return had she thought to ask about him. Looking around, there was no sign of him here either. He'd leave more of a trace as an overnight visitor to a Travelodge. Charlie dumped her armful and backed out, aware of somehow intruding into a place she wasn't supposed to be.

Back out on the landing, she had the feeling that she was alone in the house. She paused when she got to Hugo's door, still covered in Flower Fairy stickers. What if he wasn't there? It almost wouldn't surprise her. She tapped and went in.

In contrast to the rest of the house, it felt empty. She stood in the doorway, taking in the stripped-out feel of the place. There were only the necessities here: bed, wardrobe, a small desk in front of the window. He'd brought no oddments or personal touches, and the overall effect was institutional. It smelled odd as well, of old breath and no ventilation.

Hugo was half hidden by the wings of his armchair. He was smaller than she remembered, insubstantial. A frail, bent shell taking little notice of the world around him. Eleanor hadn't said anything to prepare her for this, but maybe she hadn't noticed. It was different, coming from outside rather than spotting each day's minute changes.

'How are you?' Charlie came into the room and crossed to the desk, pulling the chair out to sit down. In a way, the alteration in him made it easier to be there.

Everything else she knew had changed, so why would this be any different?

'Well, thank you, if somewhat constrained by the environment.' He didn't move, but she looked around, at wallpaper covered in cheerful polka dots, a pastel lampshade in the centre of the ceiling with colourful ballerina cut-outs hanging down around its edge, swaying gently in the aftermath of Charlie's passage through. Then her gaze went back to her father. He was tidily dressed in his usual style: muted V-neck jumper over a soft cotton check shirt. A silk cravat tucked into the shirt's neck, an affectation he'd had for so long she barely noticed it. His skin was mottled, brown age spots concertinaed in the wrinkles crossing the bald skin on the top of his head. The hair he had left was soft and fine, and still with a hint of its original gingery brown. His head poked forward on his neck, tortoise-like. Ready to snap or withdraw completely. He seemed entirely uninterested in her coming.

'I've been in Sneasham this week.' She watched for a response, but there was nothing. It was as if he hadn't heard her. 'And I met some people Mum knew. Do you remember Margareta?'

There was the briefest pause and a slither of dark as his eyes flashed towards her. Or maybe she imagined that. 'I can't say I remember the name.'

'She had a boat,' Charlie pressed.

His eyelids hooded even further down as he replied. 'It would be from before we met. I was never in that part of the world.'

'You met Britta in London, didn't you? I've been

257

wondering where she came from, what brought her to England. I'm thinking of going to Norway, trying to find her birthplace, you know.' His eyes flickered again but he said nothing. It was like one of the games of chess he'd tried to interest her in at different points of her childhood. Except this time, she would hold on to her pieces for longer, place them where she wanted rather than be forced into the open spaces. The balance between them had shifted. 'I thought maybe you could let me have her birth certificate?'

'Yes, yes.' She had to admire his composure. But then he'd had decades to hone it. 'I said I would find it. Now I'm tired. There's so little opportunity for quiet rest here.'

'Yes. Poor Martha,' Charlie said, in a gentle tone as if following her cue from him. 'It's so kind of her to give up her space whilst you're here. Do you know when the move will happen?'

'Nobody tells me anything,' he said, closing his eyes to show that the audience was at an end.

She was left feeling wrong-footed, uncertain of what exactly she wanted to ask.

'So, what's all this about then?' Eleanor was unscrewing the lid from a bottle of red wine. 'Can you get the casserole out of the oven?' She waited for Charlie to bring it over, slumping in her chair and twisting the stem of a glass between her fingers.

'I've been finding stuff out.' Charlie came back, the handles of the heavy pan burning her fingers despite the oven gloves.

'And?'

'Let me do this first.' Charlie began to spoon out the fragrant meat. Eleanor had always been a good cook, even when they were small. 'Is Jon not going to be here?' Partly she asked to make sure they wouldn't be interrupted, but also because of that sense of his absence.

'Probably not. I barely see him.' Eleanor forked some food in as if she hadn't eaten for days. 'They keep him for long hours in this new job. He's indispensable, apparently. That's what he claims anyway.'

Charlie chewed for a moment, thinking there was something off with Eleanor's tone. Was she suggesting Jon was having an affair? The look on Eleanor's face put her off pressing the issue further. Besides, this was hardly the time to be thinking of her sister's marital arrangements. And the last thing she wanted was to threaten this new sense of camaraderie between them, the easy acceptance which seemed to have at least quadrupled whilst she'd been away on the boat. She did need to mention what Martha had told her, though, before they got too caught up in the past. 'This is delicious,' she said as an opener. Eleanor raised her glass in acknowledgement and Charlie carried on, choosing her words carefully. 'Martha was saying you're thinking of going back to work once you've moved?'

Eleanor gave a sigh. 'I thought she might have overheard.' She lifted the bottle as if to pour herself more wine, then put it back down. 'Maybe not, PTA meeting in the morning.' With a groan, she rolled her eyes. 'Just look at me! Organizing bloody fetes and arguing about who gets to collect toilet roll tubes.' She held up a finger.

'I'm sorry, I meant cardboard tubes, which have no connection at all with bottoms and poo.'

'But what do you want to do?' Charlie rested her elbows on the table. She was genuinely interested. Eleanor had been training to be an accountant before Martha came along, but that had been a pragmatic choice. There had to be something else, a hidden dream plan. Apparently she wasn't going to hear it now, though.

'I don't know.' Eleanor rested her head on the table, and Charlie wondered if she'd been drinking before they'd sat down for the meal. 'But that argument—' She sat up, pressing her fingers to her temples. 'Jon was pissing me off, saying all I did was drive the kids around and drink coffee. I said he could bloody do it, and he asked what exactly I was qualified to do. So I threw a plate of dinner at him and said Dad could look after the kids while I went back to re-train.' She gave Charlie a straight look. 'Is that why Martha has been playing up?'

'Well, she did mention it,' Charlie confirmed. 'But it was more Dad she was upset about.'

'Her dad or ours?'

'Ours.'

'I can see that. Oh, Charlie, he's been a nightmare.' She gave the wine another considering glance but got up to put the kettle on instead. 'And I'd never let him be in charge of the girls.' Her voice shifted tone. 'Not that he'd want to. He's not from that sort of world. I mean, it's not like he had much to do with us, is it? But seriously.' She stopped by Charlie's chair, twirling a strand of her hair around a finger. 'Look, can we leave it? Tell me what you've been uncovering. Dark acts on the canals of the Midlands? Was Mum planning a heist with a boat getaway?'

Charlie smiled at the thought of using a canal boat to escape from the scene of a crime. Then she remembered imagining Britta using the boat to drop off the map, boats being a means to escape.

'Not that sort of getaway,' she said. 'But in a way . . .'

Eleanor stared when she'd finished telling her the story of the photograph and Margareta. When she finally spoke, she was shaking her head. 'I don't buy it.' She gave a smile, the sort that was trying to be kind and diplomatic. 'You think Dad would have covered up that sort of story? He wouldn't have the imagination. And Mum being some kind of wild child having babies out of wedlock? She was too boring for that. She was too, I don't know, too bloody Norwegian.'

'But she wasn't Norwegian,' Charlie said, holding on to her temper. It did sound less convincing coming from her than it had from Margareta. 'That's the whole point.'

'How could she not be Norwegian?' Eleanor's voice rose. 'We'd have noticed, surely. She couldn't have kept it up that long!'

'She did, though. It was, I don't know, her way of coping.' Charlie reached out for Eleanor's hand. 'Think about it. She was sixteen. She had a baby, at home, with no medical help. Then she watched her mother die from a seizure and was stuck in the house with the body for several days. It's in the paper, she had some kind of local notoriety. The baby was taken away, and she ran away

261

herself and became someone else.' She waited in vain for her sister to respond. 'Explains a lot, doesn't it?'

'And this whole thing about her trying to leave Dad, running away to a boat. Who was this woman, how do you know she wasn't making it all up?'

'She gave me another photograph.' Charlie put her free hand into her bag to find it. 'Look, it's us, Ellie, like I remembered when I found those books. Mum took us to her boat when we were little. She was trying to leave Dad. We were there for a couple of days before he came and talked her into going back.' She waited again for a response. 'Come on, you were older than me. You have to remember something!'

'No.' The monosyllable was aimed at cutting off any discussion. The silence after it, though, echoed with uncertainty. 'And why would she have kept the baby a secret?'

'She was young, it was another world.' Charlie was starting to feel like the older sister, arguing the sensible side of the situation. 'She was left to deal with everything that happened by herself. She didn't have anyone.'

'Lucky her.' Eleanor said the words in a jokey tone but her voice wavered. 'And you think Dad knows about it all?'

'How can he not?' Charlie felt her voice begin to rise. She swallowed, carrying on in a quieter tone. 'We just need to check the paperwork. We need to know what else there is, if there is anything else, even. I want to know.'

'All right.' Eleanor dropped her head on to the table again. 'We'll do it as soon as the girls have gone to school

262

tomorrow. My dining room's full of bloody boxes. You can try and find the right one, and when it turns out you've built up a whole tale of nothing, you can come and look after the kids while I go and train as a—'

'As a what?' Charlie asked into the sudden silence.

'As a bloody something!' Eleanor turned, tears streaming down her face. Charlie wrapped her into a hug. They stood together, rocking, as Eleanor cried, the same heaving, painful sobs as Martha had cried earlier in the day. 'As a bloody something,' she repeated.

Twenty-nine

Eleanor's dining room had never, as far as Charlie knew, been used for eating. It was the room that had never been redecorated, the space for dumping whatever didn't need to be to hand. There was a set of Meccano-like shelves, which must have been destined originally for the garage, holding paperwork and boxes and bike helmets and DIY equipment. A doll-house sagged at one end, the roof hanging off, waiting for repair. There was a table just visible in one corner, buried by a tottering heap of stacked cardboard cartons. Charlie recognized them from the sorting of the house and wondered why they hadn't been sent with everything else into storage.

'We ran out of space.' Eleanor was obviously thinking the same thing. 'And I thought we might as well bring this lot here rather than pay for a bigger storage room. I warn you, it's mostly rubbish. I've no idea why they thought they had to keep it all.'

They started with a box each, pulling open the flaps and digging through the contents before moving it across to the other side of the room. It was like one of those games where you had to move a tile and another tile before finally shifting the one you wanted to get into

264

position. There were piles of old tax forms, brochures for double-glazing, payslips, astronomy society newsletters. They worked in silence, decades-old dirt smudging their fingers, making them sneeze. Eleanor had wriggled her way back into the tiny space she'd left between checked and unchecked boxes. She had an intent look on her face, one that Charlie recognized but hadn't seen for years. A response to a challenge, a desire to win.

'I was thinking about it after I went to bed,' Eleanor said eventually. 'About what you were saying, Mum taking us away.'

'Do you remember going to the boat?' The boxes were already dusty, as if they'd been stored for months rather than weeks, and Charlie rubbed her palms up and down her trousers to get rid of it.

'I think so. There was an old lady with short hair?'

'She can't have been that old, but yes, I guess when you were eight or whatever.' Charlie replaced the lid on a box and reached for the next one.

Eleanor turned to face Charlie, sitting back on her heels. 'I was working out dates,' she said. 'If Mum, for the sake of argument, had a child in 1965, then that child would have turned eighteen in 1983, when Mum was pregnant with me.' She waited for Charlie to nod, to make sure she was keeping up. 'That's when the child would have been able to contact her. But she'd dropped off the map, changed her name, her whole identity, right? According to this story, Mum tried to leave sometime in the early nineties. What if it took the child that long to decide she wanted to track down her birth mother, and then actually manage to find her?'

265

Charlie sat back as well to consider the thought. Eleanor's mind worked in a way she couldn't track. 'So what are you saying?' she asked in the end.

'That the child turned up, which triggered Mum leaving.'

'That's a bit of a leap.' It was Charlie's turn to have doubts. 'We don't know that she ever did try and find her.'

'I think we do.' Eleanor's face was white, her concentration fixed on a card she was holding. It had a teddy on the front, a big smile on its face and a bunch of coloured balloons grasped in one paw. Over its head, the card said *Happy 1st Birthday!* She read what was inside and then handed it over to Charlie.

> *Dear Anna,*
>
> *I hope you are well and having a nice birthday! I think of you every day.*
>   *Love, Mummy*

The words were heartbreakingly careful, written in a large clear print. Eleanor was already working her way through more birthday cards, a whole sheaf of them, passing each one across as she finished. Charlie carried on reading.

> *I don't know if I should call you that. Elizabeth. I hope life has been kind to you, Elizabeth. I want you to know that I never wanted to leave you. I tried my best. My little girl.*

The messages became longer as the pictures on the cards changed, both becoming more suitable for an older child.

266

The writing changed also, from the block letters to the handwriting Charlie recognized. It was less careful in other ways as well, with a sense of the words pouring out, complete with corrections and smudges.

My little Anna. I can call you Anna, can't I? It's strange to think you're thirteen now. You were the sweetest baby, always so quiet, keeping your eyes fixed on me. I would have kept you for ever. It is so hard now to remember why I didn't. They do now, these girls. I see them and I read about them and I wonder when I could have made a different choice. At what point should I have taken you away with me? But it was better this way, they all said it was better this way.

On and on they read. None of the cards were dated, but they developed into the record of a relationship, the writer sharing more details, referring back to previous exchanges, reminding the reader of events in the past. There were no replies though. The thought came into Charlie's mind, taking a little time to become a realization.

'They were never sent, were they?' She sensed Eleanor nod. 'Why didn't she send them?'

'That's what I've been asking myself,' Eleanor replied, sitting up on her heels, fingers still riffling through the pages. 'I can't believe this. How could they not have told us?'

'She lied to me.' The sound of Hugo's voice, coming from the open door, made them both jump. There was a roughness to his tone, and the words spilled out jerkily, in broken sentences. 'I didn't know, she didn't tell me.'

267

'Didn't tell you what? About the baby?' Eleanor's tone was sharp.

'About anything!' His voice broke, just a tiny, almost inaudible crack. He picked up on the sound himself and straightened, his Adam's apple working in an automatic attempt to control any suggestion of weakness. 'The act she put on, to make me marry her, and all the time she was lying.' He wavered, a small movement to and fro. Despite herself, Charlie went over to stand next to him, in case he fell. He made no sign of seeing her approach. 'I wanted to make her happy, but there was always something wrong. She said it was me, that I was too old.' He waved a hand towards the cards. 'She didn't tell me it was because of a child.'

Eleanor continued in that cold tone, an interrogator staying calm and impartial. 'Did you know about her real name?'

'Not at first.' His voice was barely audible. 'She didn't tell me until the letter came from the child, wanting to meet her. As if it was necessary. I said no, she should be concentrating on us, on her real family.'

'When was this?' Eleanor's voice was a cross-examination, flat, clinical.

'I don't remember.' He ran a hand over his face. 'When she went to see that woman on the boat.' Eleanor flicked her eyes towards Charlie and they both nodded. 'She couldn't leave me. She had nothing, no money, nowhere to live. I told her I'd take her to court if she tried to take you girls away, and she knew I'd win. Why would they give children to a woman who'd abandoned one already?' He wasn't looking at them any more. He was caught up in another world. Then he refocused on Eleanor's expressionless face. 'It was for your own good. An illegitimate child, coming into our home? You were both so young, it wouldn't have been fair. I couldn't let it happen. It was better for her to come back. Everything went back to normal.' He turned to face Charlie, anger crossing his face. 'And then you had to go and stir it all up again.'

Charlie was stunned. 'Me? What did I do?'

Spittle was forming at the corners of his mouth. 'She couldn't let it go, that you were leaving Max, "putting yourself first" or whatever nonsense you'd called it. Kept saying that she should have done the same. And then she got that money. But it was too late, she said.'

'Too late for what?' Part of her brain was checking the mention of money, wanting to ask where it had come from, but she didn't want to slow the flood down with questions that could be asked later.

'To have a life.' Hugo's voice rose. 'That's what she said. She pretended not to be doing anything, but I knew what was going on. I knew about the boat. I knew she was leaving. I was watching out for her lies this time.'

'What did you do?' Charlie managed to keep her voice quiet, though the effort made her tighten every muscle in her body. She was trying to decode the expression on his face, a look almost of fear. He didn't seem to hear her, and for a minute appeared to have disassociated himself from the scene. Charlie spoke again, sharply, in the tone a nurse might use on an unresponsive patient. 'Dad! You need to tell us!'

He turned to her at last, slowly, his eyes bleary, the

269

skin drooping away in defeated folds. 'Your mother didn't want to meet the child,' he said, pulling himself up to almost his original height. 'It was her choice, not to meet her. I kept the letter for my records.' With shaking hands, he reached into his pocket and pulled out his wallet, an old, leather pouch he'd had as long as Charlie could remember. She could see the same fascinated attention to his movements in Eleanor's face as she could feel in her own. Finally, he worked an envelope, folded in half on itself, from its hiding place and held it out to Charlie. He turned away as soon as she took it but stopped when he reached the door. He kept his back to them, and his voice was hard to hear. 'The second letter arrived the day before your mother was taken ill.'

It was only when she heard the door to his room close that Charlie was able to move. She went across to where Eleanor still sat on the floor. They had their shoulders together as Charlie opened the envelope.

The first letter was on a small sheet of writing paper, the kind that had had a separate lined sheet inserted under the top page as a guide to write along. The page had settled into its folds, the first made to fit into the envelope, the second to fit into Hugo's wallet. Charlie eased it open.

Hello.

I'm sorry, but I don't really know how to begin this letter. My name now is Elizabeth Brent, but I was born Anna Nilsson. I'm wondering if you might be able to help me find my mother, Sylvia Burrows, also known as Britta Nilsson?

I would be so grateful for any help; a reply sent to the above address will reach me.

Yours sincerely,

Elizabeth

'It's dated 1991,' Eleanor said at last, as Charlie was reading the second letter. 'The year Mum took us to Margareta's. And he's had it there all this time.' She shook her head. 'I wonder if he thought about it every time he had his wallet out? And whether Mum knew it was there?'

'She might not have sent all those cards,' Charlie said, holding out the second sheet to her sister. 'But it looks as though she did get in touch in the end.'

Though she'd only read the words once, they flashed up in her mind as she watched her sister read them, as clear as if she'd learned them by heart. *Of course I want to hear from you . . . I understand . . . Family dynamics can be awful, I know . . . A boat? That sounds so exciting . . . Things are so expensive these days . . .* A sister, a real person. With an address and a family of her own. And she didn't know that her newly found mother was dead. The implications billowing around her, Charlie tried to keep hold of the important fact. Elizabeth was a person, she was real. She knew that her mother wanted to know her.

271

Thirty

It was late when Jon came home, though Charlie wasn't asleep. The sofa wasn't quite long enough, and there was a ridge in the middle of her back. All around her she could feel unease and restlessness. She couldn't believe that everyone else was asleep, though the house was quiet. But the living room was too light, the orange glare from the street lamps outside bright enough that she'd draped a T-shirt over her face to keep it out. It was almost a relief when she heard the sound of a car pulling up, a key in the lock. Bella's ears twitched, and she sat up from her position on Charlie's feet, waiting for the door to open.

Charlie heard Jon come in, drop a bag to the floor and go into the kitchen. A tap ran, a cupboard door was opened, all with the soft movements of someone not wanting to disturb anyone. There was silence then, for long enough that she almost dropped off, until the door behind her swung open and the light went on.

'Jesus, Charlie.' He stopped, a can of beer in his hand. He was wearing suit trousers, his shirt hanging half out and his tie loosened. He made no attempt to turn the light off. 'Was I supposed to know you were here?'

Charlie was still blinking at the brightness. 'Hey Jon, good to see you too.' She reached over to turn a side-light on. 'Lights down, maybe?'

'Oh, yeah.' He flicked the switch off and came into the room. 'Did you want a beer?'

'No, I'm good.' Giving up on any thought of sleep, she swung her legs down. 'I might get a cup of tea, though.'

When she got back, Jon was sitting in the armchair with the television on, the sound muted. They sat for a little while without talking, the footballers on the screen racing about and then coming into close-up to shout silently at the referee.

'How's the boat?' Jon asked at last. He was slumped in the chair, possibly with exhaustion, but Charlie was picking up a crackle of energy as well. She found herself studying him for clues, for a smear of lipstick on his collar, the presence of incriminating perfume.

'Yeah, all good,' she said in reply to his query. She wasn't sure how much Eleanor had told him, if anything, about Britta and what they'd been finding out. She didn't want to get into it now, anyway. 'Just up to check how you lot are getting on. It was a shame about the house falling through.' Jon grunted in reply, finishing the last of the beer and crumpling the can. She persevered. 'You must be looking forward to the extra space when you do move.'

He glanced across at her, his expression unreadable. The tone of his voice wasn't hard to decipher though. 'Right, yeah. Grass to cut at weekends and your dad to point out what I'm doing wrong. Can't wait.'

'You can always stay late at work.' She wasn't even

273

thinking of what to say, just batting back the next comment.

'She's got you on to it, has she?' He was still for a moment, hands gripping the arms of the chair. '*Ask him why he's always late, tell him he needs to pull his weight.*' His mimicry vibrated with some sort of emotion, though Charlie wasn't sure if it was anger, or something less straightforward. 'You can tell her that if she's got something to say to me, she can say it herself. If she can make time in her very busy life.'

'Hey, nothing to do with me.' Charlie held both hands up. 'She hasn't said anything. Though—' She paused, feeling for the right words. 'It does feel like you two aren't quite in the same place at the moment.'

'Same place?' This time, the laugh was outright bitter. 'We're not even on the same planet.' He lurched to his feet and, briefly, Charlie tensed herself to duck. He noticed, and laughed again. 'No need for that. You know me, does what he's told, keeps his mouth shut and his hands to himself.' He went behind the sofa to the little sideboard. 'You want one?'

Charlie twisted round and saw that he was holding up a bottle of whiskey. Why not? It might even help her sleep, once this slightly surreal encounter was over. 'Go on then, just a small one.'

He came back with generous doubles, the bottle tucked under one arm. 'What do you want to know, then?' he asked, as he handed her the drink and sat back down.

Charlie took a sip, letting the spirit burn its way down her throat. It wasn't especially nice whiskey, but she was more than ready for it. 'I don't want to know

274

anything.' She paused. That wasn't actually true. She wanted to know that he and Eleanor were happy, that at least one part of her world was steady and stable. She wanted him to tell her that Martha and Poppy could live in some kind of perfect world where no one argued. The thought came out of nowhere and left her breathless. 'OK, I want to know something.' She took a bigger sip of the whiskey. 'Are you having an affair?'

'An affair? Me?' Jon coughed as his whiskey went down the wrong way. 'Is that what you think's happening?'

'It crossed my mind.' She was watching him carefully, ready for any hint of bluff. He seemed genuinely taken aback by the idea, and she didn't think he was a good enough actor to be pretending.

'Is that what your sister thinks?' His expression was momentarily angry. But after holding her gaze for a long combative moment, he slumped. Charlie watched as he rotated the glass in his hands, his attention apparently on what was left of the whiskey. He didn't look back up at her as he carried on talking. 'I've thought about it. There was someone at work, made it obvious she was interested. And it was nice, you know.' There was a pause, and when he spoke again, his voice was barely audible. 'I was finally in a job I was good at, doing something which might make a difference. Sharing it with someone.' He looked up at her now. 'I liked it. Being noticed, knowing she was interested in what I had to say, how I was feeling. I liked her. But you know what?' Suddenly he was too close to her, the force of his emotion pressing her into the cushions on the back of the sofa. 'This is what I want.' He waved an arm around the room, taking

275

in the toys stacked in the corner, the photos of the girls lining the mantelpiece. 'My girls, my family.' His voice broke, but he wasn't finished. 'But we're just on this merry-go-round of taking them to this, taking them to that, and it doesn't matter what I want to do, whether I'd like to spend some time with them doing something as a family. The routine can't be missed.' He was crying now. 'I don't want them not to do things, it's not that. It's just I'm starting to not know who they are, and that scares me. And you and Eleanor have something going on, I can see that, but she doesn't ever talk to me. So I stay late at work and that's wrong too, and I don't know what to do any more. And now there's your dad, and chasing a new house and . . .' He wound down, staring off into the middle distance.

Charlie let the silence hang for a while. The house breathed around them, and she pictured the sleeping inhabitants above. The two girls would be sprawled across their beds, surrounded by toys and books and discarded clothes. In the next room, Hugo. How did he sleep? Lying straight on the mattress, arms by his sides, his face collapsing in his unconsciousness. There was a vulnerability to the image that unsettled her, eating into the other picture, of him stopping his wife from meeting her first child, keeping the letter from that child folded into his wallet. Was Eleanor asleep? Or was she lying there, aware that her husband was home, wondering what he was talking about with her sister for so long?

'You need to talk to Eleanor.' The plan to live with Hugo had to change. She could see it, the whole complex coil of disaster unspooling to leave everyone damaged.

Especially with Eleanor's martyr approach. 'Look, I'm going to be here for a couple more days. Leave the girls with me and take her out. I know, I know.' She forestalled his objections. 'It's not going to fix everything, but it's a start.' She hesitated, wondering if she should share her concerns about the house plans in particular. Better not. She didn't want Jon charging in with *well, Charlie said*. She remembered his earlier comment, about there being secrets he wasn't part of. Should she smooth that over at least? 'There have been things going on, about Mum. It honestly wasn't anything Eleanor could share, though. She didn't even know most of it. That's why I've come up, actually.'

It was hard to tell what Jon made of it all, but she did extract a promise that he'd sort something special for him and Eleanor at the weekend. He left Charlie further from sleep than ever, turning over the conversation, the outcomes, what she could do, what she definitely shouldn't do. And there were no answers, nothing that could give her a clear direction, let alone anyone else.

'We'll have to stay up here for a bit longer in any case,' she told Bella, giving her head a rub. Bella made a half-hearted nudge back and curled in more tightly. She was right. It was time to sleep. But how, when she couldn't stop thinking? She lay down, too strung out to rest, although at the same time too tired to reach across for the T-shirt to put back over her face. The orange-tinted shadows of the room made her eyelids twitch. What could she think about? Not her mother, not Elizabeth. Nor did she want to dwell on what was going to happen to Hugo, to Eleanor, to Jon. The flicker of a

277

memory of Dave skittered through, chased by another one about Max and their house. Money. She'd need to think about that soon. She and Eleanor had to decide what to do with Britta's nest egg. And how to divide what was there and the boat. They'd balance each other out, perhaps, and Charlie could keep *Skíðblaðnir* as her share. But even a boat needed some income to maintain it, and how would she manage if Max carried on refusing to compromise? Perhaps it would be better to give in to what he wanted. Bella gave a little snore and Charlie felt the weight of her warmth. That was the main thing, having her there. The weight of indecision lifted a little, and Charlie forced her mind back towards *Skíðblaðnir*, quietly rocking at the mooring.

She visualized her mind leaving her body to fly over the Pennines towards Macclesfield and the start of the canal. Bob asleep, waiting for Libby to come back from work. The other boats steady in their silent ranks. Charlie let herself turn to follow the water along, past the bridges and locks, down to the junction. So fast to traverse by mind, all of the stopping and winding and filling and moving smoothed into one easy flow. She turned to the left, leaving out the turmoil of Max and Dave and the long hill of locks. To the left, though, the tunnel. It was as if she had lost any control she'd had over her movements as she paused at the mouth before swooping up and over, almost touching the treetops. She was going too fast, wouldn't be able to stop. The canal was there again, coming up in front of her, and she braced herself for impact. But the water skimmed beneath her and she was swept along, villages and roads

278

and boats swooping past. And now she was on a boat, not *Skíðblaðnir* but another one, which was too big for the channel and it was going too fast and the water was coming over one side and the boat was sinking and she was on the bank, holding on to a rope and leaning, leaning. And the far edge of the boat began to come up, water streaming from it, and she had to put all of her weight back against the pull of the rope until finally the bulk lifted and settled and was still. And then she was inside, this time in her bed on *Skíðblaðnir*, and she didn't have to open her eyes to know that everything was safe.

Thirty-one

Charlie woke up the next morning feeling slightly sick. Too much whiskey, definitely. She vaguely remembered stirring as someone had left that morning, which must have been Jon. He'd said something about an early start, a couple of days away, before he'd left the night before. Sooner him than her. In the kitchen, Eleanor was fussing over bags and sandwiches. As Charlie ran herself a glass of water, it became apparent that both of the girls' classes were going on trips today.

'Which is a nightmare.' Eleanor was raking through the contents of a drawer. 'Martha, have you seen the other sun cream? No, it's all right, I've got it.' She zipped one bag shut. 'Which they never do on the same day, but Poppy's one was cancelled last week. And now one of the parent helpers has had to drop out so I've got to go instead.'

'Why don't you come with my class, Aunty Charlie?' Martha was prodding at a puddle of soggy flakes in the bottom of her bowl.

'She can't,' Eleanor said, reaching over the table for a plastic water bottle. 'Someone has to take Grandad to the hospital.'

Charlie and Martha exchanged looks, Martha giggling at the expression on Charlie's face. 'It's probably just as well,' she told her. 'It's going to be the most boring trip ever.'

'Where are you going?' Charlie asked, dipping a hand into the box of cereal. She'd get to the question of the hospital visit later.

'She's going to a very interesting museum,' Eleanor snipped in. 'And don't do that, it's disgusting.' She snatched the box from the table, huffing as she rolled up the inside bag and put it all in the cupboard. 'And don't feed the dog from the table.' Charlie lowered the discarded crust back down onto the table and glanced over at Martha again. Martha gave an exaggerated shrug, which Eleanor caught sight of over her shoulder. 'Come on, finish up.' She started moving Martha's bowl away. 'We need to go.'

'But it's ages until it's time to leave.' Martha picked out a single flake and nibbled it with a look of disgust. 'And I want some toast.'

'Well, you can't have any toast. I need to be there early.' She was already bending to fasten Poppy's sandals. 'Charlie, you need to sort out Dad's breakfast. I've left the details of his appointment on the side. You'll have to get a taxi.'

Eleanor had definitely been crying. Charlie turned to Martha. 'Come on, you've finished with that,' she said. 'Do what your mum wants, OK? If you get your shoes on, I'll give you some money to buy something at the gift shop.' She caught sight of Poppy's face and could almost see her thought processes working. Any second, she'd be kicking off her sandals to make sure of her share of pocket money. 'And you as well.'

Poppy gave a nod, and Eleanor's lips twitched. Charlie went to find her bag, hoping she actually had some cash. Because otherwise she was going to be in trouble.

Hugo's appointment was at the memory clinic. He hadn't wanted breakfast before they left and he didn't want to talk on the way. He'd shown no preference one way or the other for having Charlie along, and he hadn't asked where Eleanor was. Just another family day out, Charlie thought, as she leafed through a motoring magazine while they waited. The other option for reading material was about dental work. Hugo sat next to her, upright in the plastic chair. There was a patch of stubble left unshaved on his jawline, and his shirt was rumpled. She felt a pang of responsibility, that she hadn't done enough beforehand to make him presentable. He was smaller than he should be, diminished. It was hard to reconcile him to the overpowering figure of her childhood, the man who'd kept a mother from her baby. Except he hadn't, not really. He'd been complicit in keeping her from that child once she'd grown up. Was that the same thing? Was it even the truth?

Then the nurse was calling them in and when Charlie held back, thinking that Hugo might not want her in there, the nurse waved for her to follow, saying she might be needed to fill in any gaps they might find.

'There will be no need for that.' Hugo's voice was firm, even as he wavered to find his balance on standing.

'I know, my love,' the nurse said, taking his arm and

282

giving his shoulder a pat. 'But sometimes it helps to get another view on things.'

Charlie began to move after them, then caught a glimpse of Hugo's expression. For a second, their gazes held and she read something in his eyes. He was asking her for something, no, almost pleading. Then he turned and she watched the back of his head as he moved away. She looked over to the nurse, who was waiting by the door for her to come through.

'He's right, you know. I've been away until just recently, and I'm really not sure I'd be able to add anything.' She took a step across. 'My sister would normally have been here, but she had an emergency at school.' How much of an emergency, though? Charlie was pretty sure she could have used the elderly father card to get out of PTA duty. 'I think he'd be happier without me there.'

He seemed to be in there for a long time. Charlie read through the leaflet on memory loss more than once, and then another one aimed at the sufferer's family, and what they might expect. None of it made for happy reading, even with the positive spin the writers had attempted. One thing was for sure: she'd better not leave it too long before trying to talk to Hugo about any of the past months' happenings. And another: she needed to have a proper conversation with Eleanor. It was her own fault she'd been left out of decisions up to now, but the sense was building that she couldn't just turn her back on what was coming. She thought about *Skíðblaðnir,* about the life she'd just begun to feel was possible. Her and Bella, peacefully working out how the

283

rest of her life was supposed to be. And that led to Britta, nearly making it to that same place. How different would the world now look if she, Charlie, had come back to find Britta there? Would any of them have been allowed to share it with her, or was her plan actually to drop off the map, go and find her first daughter, start over? And would that have worked? She stared at the door into the treatment room, where Hugo was answering questions, or not answering questions, or matching up cards or re-ordering pictures. It all led back to him, in a way. Getting away from him, being landed with him. Eleanor seeming to be making a choice between her father and her husband. But in the end he might forget who they all were, retreat into some shadowy world where nothing was real. She thought she'd feel angry about that, but instead she felt sad. They were all just trying to get to the best world they could manage, and it struck her that Hugo's might be the worst of the options.

Back at the house, Charlie followed Hugo up the stairs, moving a couple of steps behind with one hand ready to hold him up if necessary. At the top he came to a halt.

'I very much appreciate your taking me to the hospital,' he said, his tone formal, speaking ahead rather than turning towards her.

Charlie stopped where she was. 'That's OK.' She waited, wondering what he was trying to say, trying to decide what she should say. He shuffled forwards and put a hand on the door of his room, then paused again. Charlie could feel the tension building, all the words that needed to be said. Which, if he went through that

284

door, might never be said. 'Dad, did you actually stop Mum from seeing her daughter?'

Hugo froze. He still didn't look round, but after a stretch of time in which Charlie could hear the creaking of the house around them, he began to speak. His voice was uneven, some of the words too quiet for her to hear, others coming out with a surge of noise. 'She was so young and so pretty and I knew I was rescuing her from something, whatever that was. I was a foolish man.' Charlie saw a shudder run across his shoulders. 'But she didn't tell me. Who she was, what happened. And I didn't know how to ask what was wrong.' He was breathing heavily, a man unaccustomed to emotion. 'I took her for what she was, and I questioned the wisdom of bringing the child, the young woman, back into our lives.' He turned to meet Charlie's face now, and she saw that his cheeks were wet. 'It had already done so much damage. I was wrong, I can see that now, but I was trying to do the best I could, for you, for Eleanor.'

He turned back to the door and carried on through, closing it behind him. Charlie let him go. Now there was time to talk again.

She had tea ready for when Eleanor and the girls came back. The girls' chatter covered up Eleanor's silence, and Charlie kept them talking to her. Martha was bubbling over with everything they'd done at the museum, her earlier disdain forgotten. Poppy's class had been to an animal park, though she was more interested in what she'd bought with Charlie's money than in the lambs or pigs.

285

'It's a real dinosaur egg,' she informed them. 'I'm going to hatch the baby out and keep it for ever.'

Eleanor looked exhausted. When the girls had finished eating, Charlie settled them in the living room with a film, enlisting Martha's help to keep Poppy there with the promise she was sorting out the boat visit. Then she went to join her sister in the garden. She was sitting in the tiny paved area which caught the sun at the tail end of the day. Charlie sat on the other side of the wooden table, watching Bella nose her way around the flower borders. Something told her that she should leave it to her sister to start the conversation. As, eventually, she did.

'I found out how she bought the boat.' Charlie wasn't expecting that. Eleanor had been out all day, so when had she found the time to dig further into the depths of Britta's story? Eleanor must have caught her expression. 'Jon was up at the crack of dawn. I got up when he left, had another search through those boxes.' Charlie stopped herself from asking if Eleanor had spoken to Jon. One thing at a time. 'Did you know Mum had a brother?' Charlie shook her head. 'Well, she did.' Eleanor rummaged in the pink cardboard folder lying on the table in front of her. 'There's a hell of a letter somewhere, wait a minute.' A blue aerogramme emerged, the insubstantial paper letting the ink bleed through to show on the outside of its fold. 'He'd emigrated to Australia sometime before the scandal. One of those ten-pound tickets. Mum must have written to him asking for help, but he "couldn't see his way to enabling her misguided plans". Or something along those lines.' She held it out. 'Have a read. He sounds a right charmer.'

286

The ink had faded, making the words hard to read, but the sharpness of his abandonment was clear. Charlie felt the jab of every harsh word; how much more Sylvia must have felt, realizing she was on her own. 'And he's dead? Shame. I wouldn't mind writing to him.'

'I know. And yes, he died sometime last year. Never married, no children. Apparently, the propriety of leaving family money to immediate relatives trumped any earlier failures in behaviour.'

They sat in silence, Charlie wondering if he'd regretted his stance by the end of his life, this unknown uncle on the far side of the world. A bird sang out from the hedge, oblivious. Who was there to remember him now?

'So Mum inherited this money and bought the boat?' So many years of waiting, and when she finally made the move it ended too soon. 'It's a shame he didn't die a bit earlier, really.'

'I know. Though at least she had that. You know, she did it, or had it all planned, anyway. She was herself at the end.'

'Whoever that was.' Charlie paused, wondering if this was the time to bring up the question of Hugo and Jon and the whole house thing. She might as well. There'd been enough of not talking in their family. 'What's going on with you and Jon, then?'

Eleanor gazed out over the garden. 'I don't know, you tell me. You spent long enough talking to him last night.' There was a tense pause, and then she gave a sigh. 'Sorry, you don't deserve that. He just ... said some things before he left this morning.'

287

'Oh God, what?' Charlie reached out a hand and, after a pause, Eleanor took it.

'That he didn't want to have Dad living with us, so I had to choose between them. You know, tough decision.' Eleanor gave a crowing laugh. 'I don't want to live with either of them, as it happens, but where does that leave us? And I reckon Jon's having an affair. He thinks he's being so secret, but it sticks out a mile.'

'He's not, you know.' Charlie moved closer to her, still holding her hand tight. 'He's a bloody idiot, but he does love you guys. And last night I really thought it would be the best thing for Dad not to live with you.'

'I'm sensing a but.' Eleanor sounded close to tears, but whether that was relief or not, Charlie couldn't tell.

'I don't know. We talked after his appointment—' Charlie stopped herself. That could wait. 'Look, do you actually want to be with Jon? Because that's pretty fundamental, apart from anything else.'

'I think so.' Eleanor's voice ended up on a squeak, and now she did start crying. 'I know there are things we need to work on. Things haven't been right for a while, since before Poppy, really.' She kept her head down so it was hard to read her expression. 'But how do I know? I've never been in love with anyone else.' She laughed at herself, rubbing a sleeve across her eyes as if she was Poppy's age. 'Do you mean that, about the affair?'

'He was pretty insulted when I asked him last night.'

'You asked him?' Eleanor gave another sob-muffled laugh. 'I was so jealous when you took off, you know. And Mum. Both of us sitting there and wishing we had the balls to up and leave.'

288

'But it was easier for me.' Charlie felt herself shrink at the idea of being some trailblazing hero. 'I had so much less to leave than you, no kids to organize logistics for. Max and I weren't even married.'

'But you did it.' Eleanor gave her hand a shake and then let it go. 'You looked at the future and decided you didn't want what was coming, and you changed it. Good on you, little sis.'

The words brought a rush of emotion up into Charlie's throat. She'd never thought about it that way – had seen it as being weak, running away. But Eleanor was right. She'd taken back control of her life.

'You could do it too if you wanted.' Charlie shrugged, turning the corners of her mouth down in exaggerated suggestion. 'You can all come and live on the boat. We can squash in.' For a second, she pictured how it would have been had her mother not gone back to Hugo when they were young. She could see them, barefoot and suntanned on the towpath. A free-running childhood, not having to watch for every change of mood. And there was a third person in her mental image, a version of their mother, taller than the little Eleanor and Charlie, with her hair pulled up into a high ponytail. A big sister, with them.

'You make it sound so easy.' Eleanor's voice interrupted her daydream and Charlie turned, more shaken by the idea of that alternative life than she expected.

'It wasn't all it was knocked up to be, you know. I should have taken you all with me.' Charlie gave a sudden snort. 'All of us in a camper van following some hippy trail. That would have been pretty cool, actually.'

'And now you're a hippy on a boat.'

'I guess.' She took a deep breath. 'Listen, about the boat. And Dad.'

Eleanor laughed. She seemed happier than Charlie had seen her since she got back from Thailand, no, from way before that. 'You don't want Dad living on the boat? I guess that would sort things out.' She pulled a face to show she was joking, or at least that was what Charlie hoped.

'Not quite.' Charlie came up from her seat in her earnestness. 'Though we did talk today. It's not as cut and dried as it seems, you know. I don't think it was easy for either of them.'

Eleanor listened to her break-down of the morning and sighed. 'I know, I know. I was talking about it to one of the other mums this afternoon, and it made me think how Mum wasn't easy.'

'The thing is, I want you to have a choice about Dad, I want us to have a choice. I don't know, sheltered housing, taking turns being with him. I guess he needs to have a choice, right? And I'm going to need to work out what I'm going to do for the rest of my life, so let's build that into the plan, OK? Talk about it, come up with options.'

'Oh, bless you.' Eleanor closed her eyes with a sigh. 'I think it might be time to think about work for myself. At least work towards working towards it.'

'Shout if you need an au pair,' Charlie said. 'I could do that. Just as long as you remember I can only really cook one dish, and I'm no good at ironing.'

'Thank you for the offer.' Eleanor gave a snort at the

290

picture she'd conjured up. 'Maybe some respite every now and then. But no, you need to get back to your boat.'

'It's not really my boat,' Charlie said. The words spilled out before she could think, half regretted, half needing to be out there. 'I do know that. I'm going to sort things out with Max, just let him have what he wants and get going. Life's too short to be worrying about stuff like that.'

'Of course it's your boat.' Eleanor spoke with conviction. 'Mum wanted you to have it, for a start, and anyway it's the right place for you to be. But you know what else we need to do, right?'

'Find Elizabeth?'

'Yep.'

Charlie thought she could hear in Eleanor's voice some of the reservations she was feeling herself. There was no point to any of this if they didn't find their sister, Britta's baby. And she wanted to, she really did. It was easy to picture the positives, the blurry vision of reunion, of past wrongs being set right. But nothing was as straightforward as that. 'You won't be the big sister any more.' The words came out in a hurry, carrying a subtext of all the things that could go wrong.

'I'll always be your big sister,' Eleanor told her. 'So don't go imagining you can get away with anything.'

'You know what's funny?'

'Your face,' Eleanor shot back. 'I'm sorry, I've been with five-year-olds all day. Go on, what's funny?'

'You need a better comeback,' Charlie told her. 'But you're right, funny's not the word. It's just—' She hesitated, trying to work out how to say what she was

291

thinking. 'We don't know how much they talked, Mum and Elizabeth, or what Mum told her. She knows a completely different person, and I don't know who the real one is. Our mum or hers.'

'Let's not get ahead of ourselves.' Eleanor stood, looking back into the house. 'Especially as I haven't heard anything from those two for way too long. You need to come and practise those au pair skills.'

Thirty-two

She was on the train with just Martha. The two of them were heading down to the boat, Bella curled up at their feet. The rest of the family, including Hugo, were going to drive down to visit the following weekend, and take Martha back. *She's only got a week of school left,* Eleanor had declared, *so I'm going to go in and cry over the head until she agrees to let her out of school. And if she doesn't, I'm going to take her out anyway.* Martha's face had been worried on the first stage of the journey, which Charlie had put down to being away from her family. Then she'd cuddled in and whispered that she was scared Mummy would go to prison for letting her miss school. A little chat about the head agreeing that it might be a good thing for Martha to go with her aunty (*I tell you, I was in there for an hour, I swear, and by the end she'd have said yes to anything!*) put her mind to rest, and she'd chattered about school and boats and what they were going to do until they'd changed trains again. Then, suddenly, she'd run out of steam and gone to sleep across Charlie's lap. Moving slowly so as not to wake her, Charlie managed to work her phone out of her bag, wishing she'd taken some travel-sickness tablets before they'd left. She was usually fine on trains, but it was pretty warm. Probably looking at her phone wouldn't help, but there was something she wanted to get done before they arrived.

That was one thing about writing emails on a phone: she wasn't tempted to keep going back over it to refine or convince. This was intended as a statement of fact, a message to Max as a line drawn and finished. She was sorry about what had happened, she hadn't behaved well, but neither had he, or Zoe. She hoped they could put it behind them so, in this spirit, she was prepared to accept his offer without further delay. Without reading it back or letting herself think, she pressed send.

The first thing they saw as they walked down to the boat was a familiar face. Martha was running ahead of her down the towpath, Bella frisking at her feet. The air was warm, a sense of holidays in the air. Charlie was breathing in the space, anticipating the moment when *Skíðblaðnir* would come into view, holding down the little bubble of worry that she'd be underwater. A halloo came from a boat just pulling up alongside, and Charlie turned to see its familiar colours. There was Bob on the back, hat down over his eyes, and Libby leaning out of the side hatch, waving. There was a surge of noise as Bob went into reverse, and then they were bobbing in neutral, catching up on news.

'We saw your boat back down there,' Libby was saying, 'and we were wondering if we'd catch you coming along. And this is Britta's granddaughter, is it? Well, my lovely, you look just like your grandma!'

294

Martha, overtaken with shyness, had to be prompted into a reply, but Libby's warmth was all-encompassing. Soon, Martha was telling her about the train journey, and how she was missing school ('it is authoritied, so we won't get into trouble') to stay on the boat.

'And how are you getting on then?' That was Bob, cutting past the marginal stuff. 'Boat behaving?'

'It all seems to be OK.' Charlie grinned at him. 'I've got your number for when we start to sink.'

'Ah, that's not going to happen.' He was watching Bella twist herself round trying to catch a butterfly. 'Got yourself a dog, have you?' He didn't wait for an answer. 'I hear you've met Margareta?'

'Yes.' Charlie was taken aback. How fast did news travel here? Faster than the boats, by the sound of it.

'One of the first boats I ever went on, *Guillemot* was. Bit of a wild lad I was, you know.' For a second, their eyes locked, as if a message was being passed, and then he tipped his head up, glancing down the canal at an oncoming boat. 'We'd best be off,' he said, his words drowned in the forward churn of the engine.

Libby waved as they began to move away. 'See you back in Macc!' she called, and then she was gone. Charlie waved back automatically, but her mind was on Bob's last words. *Guillemot*, boating with Margareta. She tried to remember the face of the boy with the quiff, the one Sylvia had been gazing at so adoringly. Her mind was working overtime, sparking out ideas. Bob's face superimposed on the boy's, Bob being at the marina. Bob arranging for Britta to buy the boat. But was he enough of an actor to have kept it a secret? But then, he

295

didn't have to act. All he had to do was not talk about it, be his silent, reserved self. It wasn't until Martha came running back to ask how much further it was that she returned to the present. There was nothing she could do until she got back to Macclesfield, anyway.

They carried on, the handle of Charlie's bag of groceries beginning to cut into her fingers with its weight. She shifted it to the other hand, watching Martha and Bella race ahead again. They should be nearly there, just around the next corner. Martha spotted the name with a whoop, and cartwheeled along the path towards the far end. Then she stopped, turning uncertainly back towards her aunt. Before Charlie could respond, Bella had taken off at a dash, tail lashing. She was whining, in short excited squeals that rose in volume as a figure got up from his seat on the gunnels. Max.

Martha had been sent to explore the boat. Charlie and Max sat opposite each other in the living room, in an awkward near-silence. Bella weaved her way between them, curling herself first through Max's legs, then back to Charlie's, pushing her nose up and under her elbow to remind her she hadn't had a biscuit.

'She's really grown up,' Max said at last, nodding down the boat to where they could hear Martha murmuring to herself as she opened cupboards and turned on taps.

'Yeah, she has.' Charlie bent forwards so that she could call down through the galley to Martha in the bathroom. 'Don't be wasting all the water!'

'I won't!' Martha called back, and the sound of the pump cut out.

296

'You seem happy here,' he continued, taking in the cosy, homely space. There was a pause, awkward, but at least with no aggro. Charlie waited for him to say more, to explain why he was there. Eventually he spoke. 'I got your email.'

That was fast. It wasn't far to the boat in a car, but he'd have had to be making a guess at where she was, taking some time to walk along and find her. 'I meant it,' she said at last, as he didn't seem to be carrying on with his sentence. 'I just think it's time to draw a line, you know?'

'Look.' His hands twisted together between his knees. He always sat like that when he had something particularly serious to say. He'd been sitting like that the night he'd proposed. A sharp twist of regret for all that was lost shot through her belly, fading into a surge of nausea. What was coming next? 'I didn't send that email, the one about Bella or nothing.' He waited for her to respond, but she was having trouble processing the words. He bounced his hands up and down with even more earnestness. 'It was Zoe. I left my laptop at home that day, and she knew my password. I'd never have—' He stopped and took a deep breath. 'I'm sorry. About Bella, about everything. And if it means anything, Zoe's gone. I'm not quite sure . . .' Again his voice trailed off.

'It's me that should be sorry.' Charlie was thinking about Eleanor and Jon, how they both had that underlying need to be together. She looked Max straight in the eyes. 'Not for leaving. I had doubts, you know that, and there were too many gaps between what we wanted. I couldn't promise babies.' She thought about Max's

297

sister, taking her aside on that awful Easter to point out how much Max wanted children, how unfair it was of her, Charlie, to keep him waiting. 'Your sisters staged an intervention, you know.' She caught sight of the anger sweeping up his face and put a hand out, touching his knee. 'No, it's fine, honestly. They were right, I think, though I couldn't see it at the time. It made things clear, in one way.' Her hand was still on his knee, and she tightened her grip, feeling his muscle and bone under her fingers. 'But I should have talked to you about it properly, not just panicked and run away.'

His expression was still dark, but not directed at her. 'I wish you had,' he said at last. 'Did you think I wouldn't understand? I was never with you because you were some kind of—' He stopped to give an incredulous laugh. 'Some kind of breeding machine.'

'Max, I know.' Charlie could feel tears building, the pressure tight and hot behind her eye sockets. 'And it wasn't ever that. I don't think I really knew myself at the time. I had to leave so that I could understand.'

He put his hand over hers, the warm weight of it familiar and comforting. 'Friends?'

She smiled at him, her eyes still a bit blurry. They'd moved so far apart now, had become new people. He knew it as well, she could tell by the tiny hint of relief in his voice. 'Friends,' she agreed.

'So, what's the next plan?' he asked as she got up to put the kettle on.

'A week with Martha here, having some fun.' She smiled as Martha came up from behind to wrap herself into her back. 'Though also some homework, yes?'

298

Martha gave a groan and wriggled on past, to collapse cross-legged beside Bella. 'Then, I don't know. I might take the boat back up north for a bit, be within reach for Eleanor.' So many more things she could have said. *Decide on a new career, find my long-lost sister, get to know who my dad really is before it's too late.* So many things that would never be part of their shared experience. *Take the boat to London. Find out if Dave was more than a brief encounter. A life after Max.* Her life. 'Max, thank you.'

She'd arranged for Margareta to come and visit the next day. Everything was ready, the kettle just needing to boil, and fancy biscuits arranged by Martha on one of the pretty vintage plates. Charlie was searching in her bag for some tissues and touched a package she hadn't noticed before. It was small, flat, wrapped in brown paper. She pulled it out and saw Eleanor's handwriting on the outside. *A little something for the boat. Can't wait to see you there!* Inside was a picture frame, in plain brown wood, with a small snapshot inside. Eleanor had tucked another note in there. *Found this in one of the boxes, thought you'd like to have it x.*

In the picture, Britta was sitting on a bed, her blonde hair tucked up into a scarf. She was smiling, with a reckless, giddy happiness that made Charlie's heart contract. On either side of her, tucked under her arms like chicks in a nest, was a girl. Charlie on one side, Eleanor on the other. Charlie was grimacing, clowning for the camera. Eleanor was more subdued, her face turned towards her mother with a hint of a question.

'Is that you?' Martha had popped up at her shoulder.

299

'Yes, me,' she dabbed at the glass, touching the little bright face, 'your mum and Granny Britta.'

'Granny Britta who was really Sylvia?' They'd had a long conversation the night before, Martha soaking in the details with fascination. 'And the lady who's coming now is sort of like your granny?'

'Well, not really.' Charlie looked at the photo again, wondering who had taken it. Was it Hugo, in a rare happy family moment, or Margareta herself, when Britta had made her brief run for freedom? 'She was a special person to Granny Britta, though. I think you'll like her.'

They got on straight away, the old lady and the girl. Charlie sat and watched them, Martha chattering to Margareta, asking her to teach her more Norwegian words. 'I can say *Skíðblaðnir*,' she heard her announce. 'Aunty Charlie taught me that. And she told me about the story, that you could fold the boat up and take it with you in your pocket.'

'You must say it like this: *Skíðblaðnir*.' Margareta's pronunciation made the syllables skip across the surface, like a stone skimmed on water. 'A useful possession, I always thought, to be able to fold up your boat.'

'You'd need a big pocket for this one,' Martha said, and they put their heads together and laughed.

Margareta caught Charlie's eye with a smile. 'Now then,' she said to Martha. 'We'll learn some more in a while.' She picked up one of the old paperbacks that Martha had brought from the bookcase. 'Why don't you read this, and tell me which of the girls you like best?'

As Martha settled down in a corner, Bella settling onto her lap, Margareta patted the sofa next to her for Charlie to come and sit. 'So, this is Britta's boat?' she asked.

'Yes. Is it what you expected?' Charlie felt warm being next to her, their relationship subtly different from the last visit, in Margareta's home. Now it really did feel as though there was something familial between them.

'My dear, I could be back in the cabin of Guillemot,' she replied. 'Not exactly, you understand. It isn't a replica. But the feeling is the same.' She held Charlie's hand with a squeeze. 'I think your mother must have been happy here. And you will bring the next generation on board, yes?'

'Martha?' Charlie squeezed back and laughed. 'She loves it here. I might have a permanent house guest. Or boat guest.'

'But no one for yourself?'

'Bella is enough for me.' The dog heard her name, lifting her head with a sigh, as if to ask if she really had to get up. Seeing the two of them sitting there, she dropped back down. Charlie watched Martha's hand rub across her ears and felt a blast of contentment. 'Can I ask you something?' she said. 'But say if you'd rather not answer.'

'How mysterious.' Margareta turned to her, her eyes very blue and direct.

Charlie nearly changed her mind, but the question had been needling in her mind. She needed to ask someone. 'Do you ever regret it, not having children, I mean?' She kept her voice low enough that Martha wouldn't hear, not knowing what she hoped to hear, or if asking it would cause offence.

Margareta smiled at her. 'I think I can tell you that I have never once regretted it.' She picked up Charlie's hand, asking for all of her attention. 'I am a selfish old woman, and I am afraid that being a mother would not have suited me at all. But this is a question that is different for every person. You must make up your own mind, you know, and not listen to anyone telling you what you should think.' She smiled, following Charlie's gaze to where Martha was sitting. 'And enjoy being an aunt to your beautiful niece. Now, tell me what you will do next.'

'I don't know. Find out who I am, maybe?' She caught the sly glance Margareta was giving her and grinned. 'I know. But this is a bit more specific than it sounds.' She paused for a moment, her gaze back on Martha and Bella as she thought about it all. 'The thing is, I'm having a bit of a crisis over names.' It was a relief to say it all out loud, and a second relief that she didn't sound ridiculous. The boat being in the name of Charlotte Nilsson, the wider question of women changing their names, her own uncertainty about her allegiance being assumed through any one choice. She wound up. 'So, I have Britta wanting me to have a name that was never hers and, by extension, a nationality that wasn't hers either. And I feel a responsibility to keep my family name, to stay part of my family, except Eleanor's already changed *her* name. And there's this other sister, who might already be calling herself Nilsson.' She shook her head to clear it of all the words.

'Is it vital in any way to make a decision yet?' Margareta's voice was both calm and interested, as if this was a perfectly regular choice to be making.

302

'Not really, I suppose,' Charlie answered. 'Though it feels like . . .' She looked around, at the boat, at Britta's room gradually shifting to become her room. Was that all it took, to move some things, to add others? She'd already started thinking about which of her stored possessions she'd like to bring on board, and which things would never fit in. 'I don't know. Sometimes it feels like I can't move on until I decide. But there's a little bit of me that likes having no name. Because if I don't exist, I can't make any wrong decisions. Is that a cop out?'

' "What's in a name? That which we call a rose, by any other name would smell as sweet." ' Margareta's eyes were laughing. 'Sometimes the old ones are the best.' She reached for Charlie's hand. 'If you would like to be a Nilsson, my country would not mind. If you would not, we would not hold it against you. But why be held in by what other people hand to you?' She gave her hand a squeeze. 'Perhaps the name will find you.' They sat in silence, their hands still linked. Then Margareta spoke again. 'And your new sister? Will you find her?'

'I hope so.' Charlie turned to look at her. 'I think it's what Mum would have wanted. If we do, would you like to meet her?'

'That would be very nice.' Margareta sighed. 'It may not be easy, making this new family, you know. We imagine these alternative lives we might have had to be perfect, but that is only because we have never had to live them.'

'I know. What do they say? Expect the best and plan for the worst. That's me.' Charlie let go of Margareta's hand to flick at a hopeful fly. It flew off jerkily, and she

303

watched Bella snap as it went past her nose. 'Eleanor's here next week. I'd love to bring her round to say hello.'

Margareta nodded slowly in agreement. 'I will look forward to that, Charlotte.' She moved her hand back, this time to lay it on top of Charlie's. 'And I would like to say that I am grateful that you found me. It, what do you say, finishes a chapter for me.'

They sat together in silence now. Outside, a blackbird began to sing. Could it really be that easy, Charlie wondered, to just open your mouth and let all of the notes out in the right order? Bella's ear twitched as another dog ran past along the towpath, but she stayed where she was. *Skíðblaðnir* pulled gently against her rope before settling back to her state of temporary stillness. From somewhere in the boat, it was as if her mother was watching her. But not her mother. Someone very like her mother but with a new sense of identity. Britta. Standing by the cooker, sitting by the fire, but always answering with the same words. *Welcome, Charlotte. What took you so long?*

Acknowledgements

Thanks as always to my fab agent, Carrie Plitt – the voice of reason throughout. It's been a pleasure to go through the editing process with Natasha Barsby at Transworld (with thanks to Bella Bosworth for being there at the start of it all), and Claire Gatzen demonstrated copy-editing at its absolute best. More thanks to the whole Transworld team: Vivien Thompson, Josh Benn, Antonia Whitton, and all those I've not been in direct contact with, but who make it all happen.

The Prime Writers continues to be the best place for writerly support, so big thanks to all of you. The Ann Atkinson Writers saw this book through its early incarnations: hope you all approve of how it has ended up! Especial thanks to Jo Bell for the expeditions on board *Tinker* (Charlie's boat may bear some passing resemblance . . .), and Robbie Burton for the conversations about tunnels. The Northern Women

305

Writers' Network provided valuable writing time, and the Manchester meetings of the Savvy Writers' Snug are always great fun: big thanks to Caroline Hulse for organizing.

Coming back to the process of publication reminds me how awesome the blogging community is: special thanks to Anne Williams (beinganne.com) and Linda Hill (lindasbookbag.com) for remembering me between books and being excited that the new one was (finally) here! Your support is so appreciated. Susan Hampson (booksfromdusktildawn.blog) not only blogs, but provided the name for Libby Rae (courtesy of her grand-daughter, and THE Book Club on Facebook's charity auction).

Another FB group Women on Barges is a wonderful community, and always ready for queries and opinions about all things boat. The 'cill' is for you, ladies! Any boating fails are my own!

Thanks and love to Fuchsia and Hatty – my wonder-ful girls who believe in me however long it takes me to get there. (I highly recommend growing your own fan club!) And Gabe, who recently had to pull his first all-nighter to finish reading a book (not mine, but still . . .): love you too. Hatty also came up with the right name for Charlie and provides me with a wonderful network of extra daughters. Chloe, Emily, Eliza: ♡ ♡ ♡

I can't write without my dogs. Huge love and mem-ories of my Abby, who was there for most of this book but left us as the final draft came to an end. We miss you. Kizzy is a writer support dog extraordinaire, and

Dexter has come to fill a very necessary gap (and keeps my lap warm at all times).

Graeme, thanks for putting up with the Jasmons. We love you.

Great stories.
Vivid characters.
Unbeatable deals.

Page TURNERS

WELCOME TO PAGE TURNERS,
A PLACE FOR PEOPLE WHO JUST LOVE TO READ.

**In bed, in the bath, at the dinner table.
On your lunch break, at the gym, or while you wait for
your kids at the school gates. Wherever you are, you love nothing
more than losing yourself in a really great story.**

**And because we know exactly how that feels, every month we'll choose
a book we love, and offer you the ebook at an amazingly low price.**

**From emotional tear-jerkers to unforgettable love stories,
to family dramas and gripping crime,
we're here to help you find your next favourite read.**

**Join us on Facebook at
facebook.com/ThePageTurners**

**And sign up to our FREE newsletter for amazing monthly ebook deals at
penguin.co.uk/newsletters/pageturners**

DON'T MISS OUT. JOIN PAGE TURNERS TODAY.